When You Least Expect It

Finding the Right One Isn't as Hard as You Think

ANGELA CORRAO

Copyright © 2025 Angela Corrao.

All rights reserved. No part of this book may be reproduced, stored, or transmitted by any means—whether auditory, graphic, mechanical, or electronic—without written permission of both publisher and author, except in the case of brief excerpts used in critical articles and reviews. Unauthorized reproduction of any part of this work is illegal and is punishable by law.

ISBN: 979-8-88640-603-0 (sc)
ISBN: 979-8-88640-604-7 (hc)
ISBN: 979-8-88640-605-4 (e)

Because of the dynamic nature of the Internet, any web addresses or links contained in this book may have changed since publication and may no longer be valid. The views expressed in this work are solely those of the author and do not necessarily reflect the views of the publisher, and the publisher hereby disclaims any responsibility for them.

One Galleria Blvd., Suite 1900, Metairie, LA 70001
1-888-421-2397

Acknowledgements

I would like to thank my family and friends for their unwavering belief in me and constant encouragement. Your support made all the difference.

I also want to express my appreciation to my publishing company for their guidance and insights.

Prologue

He was the first volunteer fire fighter on the scene, arriving with the Seward Fire Department. He knew that even though he was there, he couldn't do anything but reassure Marie, she wasn't alone. The fear of losing Marie was suffocating him.

"Hang in there Marie, the paramedics are here and doing everything they can."

He glanced up and was faced with the array of rescue personnel, blinding red and blue strobe lights, ear-deafening sirens sounding, shattered glass, blood and pure chaos.

Hearing nothing except the sound of his heartbeat, he solely focused his attention on Marie and said, "It's going to be okay," soothing her as best he could. She started to fade in and out.

"Keep your eyes open and look at me," he smoothed back her hair with a gentle motion, "you're going to be okay. Don't close your eyes. Just hang on Marie—you're going to be fine."

Holding on to Marie's hand and comforting her to the best of his ability, sensing she may not survive, he silently started pleading to God in prayer.

"Please God . . . please let this woman live, please Lord!"

Marie was losing a tremendous amount of blood and fading fast. Everything was happening so rapidly that feelings of helplessness enveloped him like a dense fog in a deep valley.

Watching the E.M.T. start an IV for a saline drip and administering 4mg of Morphine for pain management, he was thinking, *even if they started a saline drip, with all the blood she's losing, it's not going to save her.*

"We need to get her to the hospital stat! Call in the airlift, now!"

He pleaded with another E.M.T., "She's not going to make it if we don't hurry!"

Marie remembered John, her husband, had been driving their car. She was frantically trying to locate him with the little bit of strength she had left and started calling out, "My husband—where is he? I want to see my husband! John! John! Where are you, John?"

Trying to call out for her husband with the little bit of strength she had left, she didn't hear a response. Marie didn't know what was going on and then suddenly visualized the car coming towards them and the crash. She had an intuition; she wasn't going to make it.

The thunderous thumping sound of the helicopter blades spinning was deafening and made it difficult to concentrate. It was chaos. The whirling winds were forceful, throwing dust, and trying to see was a challenge. The wind was beating against their bodies, making it hard to walk forward. Maneuvering Marie on the stretcher towards the opening of the helicopter was not easy, but successful. The paramedics lifted her into the helicopter and closed the cabin door. Marie stared into the eyes of the man who was with her the whole time and felt safe, but scared. The helicopter started to ascend.

In the helicopter, the volunteer fire fighter was still holding Marie's hand and noticed Marie trying to give him something.

"Here, take this. I trust you'll know what to do with it when the time is right."

He held out his hand, Marie dropped it and closed his hand around it. Seeing the fire fighter's sadness, Marie said, "It's dear to my heart and I know it will find its way into the proper hands. Please take this and keep it safe."

Not knowing what to do, his eyes started to tear, he shouted, "We're losing her! We're losing her! No, no, no! Marie, open your eyes . . . Marie!"

Marie's hand slowly relaxed and fell from his grip.

While on the helicopter transporting Marie to the hospital, the E.M.T. called it—"Last breath is 4:46 pm."

He stared at Marie's limp body with such anguish, wishing she could have held on a little longer. He then realized Marie's husband John didn't survive the accident. She would have experienced a lifetime of sadness if she recovered. Marie was with John, now and forever. Tears stained his cheeks—fully aware Marie wasn't coming back, and laid his head on her chest. He whispered, "I will keep it safe. I promise."

He watched the helicopter approach Anchorage Hospital's helicopter pad and knew this was his last day as a volunteer fire fighter.

Chapter 1

Four Years Later . . . .

Just twenty-nine, the younger of two, Marlo is sassy and ravishing with her long flowing, espresso brown hair covering her shoulders in free-flowing curls. She has seductive blue eyes, high reddish-pink cheek bones, pouty, full scarlet red lips, and a body that would stop an Amtrak in pursuit of taking ambitious travelers to their next destination. Her mother always told her how stunning she was and never to fret about the right man coming along—one day he would enter her life when she least expected it.

It was a brilliant August day around five in the evening. Marlo was relaxing and staring out over the ripples on the lake, sitting in her sister's Adirondack chair. She was wiggling her toes and watching how the polish glimmered in the sunlight. Marlo knew the littlest thing for her can be a total and utter distraction.

She stared out over the lake and began lazily pondering where the days had disappeared to, she thought, *there has to be something better out there for me. I just have to find it.* Trying to figure out who *she* is, now that her parents are gone and the idea of a fresh start, she thought, *I haven't been the same since my parents' accident. I need to get a hold of reality and move forward. I need to come to terms with my parents' death. I need to make a life for myself and begin my journey to a happy and healthy future.*

Marlo was slowly healing, but was irrevocably close to her parents, especially her mother. She drifted into a daze and started to remember how she and her Mom would go shopping in downtown Minneapolis, just the two of them, and select Gusto's for lunch. They would laugh to the point of not breathing and people would look at them like they just left the funny farm. Not being able to share those moments again really pulled at Marlo's heart strings. She missed her parents to the point of heartache and despondency, even though it has been four years; the loss weighs heavy on her heart.

In addition to losing her parents, she's had enough mediocre relationships that came and went from her life, like newspaper headlines for *The Chicago Tribune.*

Why is it, every time I find someone who I think 'might be the one,' he turns out to be a total thoughtless jackass? As soon as they find out my parents have passed away, they look like a cold fish from the freezer and have a loss for words. It's like I have the plague or something.

Marlo took her sweet precious time dragging her self-pity butt out of her favorite chair, the one place she felt she could think, and walked up to her sister's house like she had lead feet. Clare opened her ornate patio door with a crestfallen look on her face watching Marlo trudge her way up the hill in jeans rolled up unevenly, a canary yellow tank top, and bare feet.

Clare motioned to Marlo, "Come in and help me with dinner before Jack and the kids get home. We can discuss what you were thinking about so intensely down by the water."

Clare was always the solid one, who for sure, knew what she was doing. She never had to wrestle with the ins and outs of relationships because Jack was her high school sweetheart. He was there for her to confide in when she needed a shoulder to cry on or someone to talk to after their parents' demise; she had that support. Marlo, on the other hand, was completely overwhelmed and fragile when her parents passed.

Clare and Marlo have always had their differences, but the one thing they can always manage to agree on is having someone in their lives to love and be loved. She has had success; Jack is the perfect husband. Marlo has yet to find Mr. Right. Honestly, she could care less at this point. No men, no relationships, no mess to clean up.

Clare's husband Jack, an executive who works with Clark, Harris and Brillstein, an advertising company which aids in making American television commercials, walked in the house with the twins following behind him, toting backpacks and lunch boxes. Dilly and Bentley ran out the door to the lake after giving their Mama kisses and hugs.

Dilly and Bentley, seven year old twins, are complete opposites in every way. Dilly, a cartoon watching, pb and j munching little girl, always wanting Dad's attention and Bentley, a feisty *'have it my way or the highway,'* little boy, were always causing havoc for Clare.

When the excitement from Jack and the kids being home subsided, Clare and Marlo finally had some peace and quiet to discuss the inevitable.

"So, tell me why you were deep in thought down by the lake earlier," said Clare.

Marlo looked at Clare with disappointment, watching her cut up tomatoes for a salad.

"I need a new life, Clare. I'm through with feeling like I'm not going anywhere and just existing—not living. My thoughts often drift to not having someone in my life to share what you and Jack have. The children always running around, going to sleep at night, knowing the person next to you is the other half of your heart, the everyday conversation you have with the one you love, are all things I don't have. I always start something, but never finish, like knitting that blanket for Dilly . . . never finished. Or, starting college after high school . . . . never finished. Why am I such a scatterbrain? Also, when it comes to men I date and deflate. Seriously, Brad was three years older and biking to work everyday because he couldn't afford a car on his skimpy salary working at the local smoothie shop. See . . . dated and deflated. It's like that with all the men I date."

Marlo plunked herself down on the barstool by the kitchen island while Clare prepared her famous Italian dressing. Clare thought about what Marlo said, but before she answered, she had to compose herself to avoid a giggle from escaping.

"Okay, I see your point. It's all about doing something and sticking to it, no matter if you think you're going to succeed or fail. You can't just stop doing something when you don't know the outcome; give life a chance."

Marlo thought about it and agreed, but something else was on her mind. She lifted her eyes to Clare and said, "Clare, there's something else that is bothering me."

"What is it?" asked Clare.

Marlo inhaled a deep breath, "Now, no matter how this comes out, you are all I have to support me, so please listen carefully."

Completely unaware of what Marlo was going to say, Clare prepared herself for the worst.

"Alright, I'm listening."

"After Mom and Dad died, I felt like the world came crashing down around me and I haven't been the same since the accident. I've tried to compartmentalize my feelings of their death, but it's much more than that. I never felt like I was given enough time to grieve their passing . . . so, I was thinking . . . I want to go to Alaska, but . . ."

Cutting Marlo off before she finished, Clare shouted in surprise, "Alaska? Are you crazy? I was thinking a trip to the local resort for a spa treatment or a weekend of reading books and doing a 1,000 piece puzzle. Not get eaten by a fifteen foot Alaskan Grizzly Bear!"

With rolling eyes because she knew Clare couldn't listen without interrupting, Marlo said, "To be as close to Mom and Dad as I possibly can. Since Alaska is the last place they were—that's where I want to be. Something is pulling me to them—to Alaska. I have to do this, Clare!"

Stunned and in shock, Clare sat motionless listening to Marlo and when Marlo finished, nothing came from Clare's lips. Finally, when the words sunk in, Clare stood up and walked to Marlo. Clare reached for her, taking Marlo's hands in hers and softly said, "Marlo, if this is something you feel this strongly about, then you should take the chance. Jack, the kids and I will be here for you when you return and we can keep in touch, via phone and texts. I know you and I are all we have and I want you to know that I support you, and, I know Mom and Dad would have supported you, too."

"Thank you Clare. I am relieved you understand that I have to do this."

Marlo could use a breath of fresh air and decided to go outside. She walked along the flower garden in Clare's front yard, extending her arm and brushing her fingertips along each petal.

Even with Clare's support, I'm not sure about uprooting my life and possibly moving to Alaska . . . in exile. And, adventuring off into the wilderness is a little nerve-racking. I must say though, it does sound like a good plan. This would give me time to start on a new path to my new life. It would give me the chance to be close to what my parents experienced; the air they smelled, the roads they traveled, and the places they visited. Also, there wouldn't be any overbearing men dictating my daily events or commenting on my expensive new caramel colored leather Prada boots I recently purchased. Even though this is going to be scary, it will be worth it. I have to do this. I have to grab hold of the one thing that remains in my life, the missing piece . . . yet to unfold.

Later that day, Clare spoke to Marlo about spending the night at her place because she wanted to keep a close eye on her, thinking she was 'losing her mind.' But the more Marlo thought about this trip to Alaska, the better *she* felt. She felt brave, confident, and ready to take on whatever obstacles she had to overcome. She could feel the weight of feeling 'she wasn't going anywhere,' coming to an end. Marlo knew she had one last chance to make her own story, to feel she had purpose. No one was going to keep her from doing just that.

Quite early the next morning, Marlo woke up to two screaming twins, trying to evade the inevitable—brushing their teeth with every excuse under the sun. Marlo could only think *thank goodness I don't have to deal with the tooth paste ordeal, but I sure am going to miss my niece and nephew. I'll see them soon, though.* Marlo then was jerked back to reality; today was the day. She popped out of bed, jumped in the shower and sang, *get ready cause here I come. I'm on my way. Alaska, here I come.* After her refreshing and cool shower, she pulled on a green T-shirt and white jogging pants she cut into shorts three years ago. They were her favorite. She threw her dampened hair up in a messy bun and grabbed her Samsonite suitcase.

Trampling down the stairs, suitcase in tow, Marlo said, "Clare, I'm heading out. It's now or never."

Marlo saw Clare in the kitchen drinking coffee.

She looked at Clare smiling and said, "Thank you for understanding my reasoning to venture out on my own to see what's out there. Without your support, I don't think I would have been able to do this, so . . . thank you. Plus, I think having solitude will do me some good, I hope."

Lowering her cup onto the counter, Clare said, "Going to Alaska and risking your life, I have to say, frightens me. I wish I would have suggested Bunko with some girlfriends," said Clare jokingly, wishing she didn't give Marlo her blessing.

Marlo smiled, "Clare, you'll see, this will be perfect for me and you'll have a place to visit."

"Only the in-laws are supposed to say that."

With a loving smile, Marlo gave her one and only sister a genuine squeeze and headed out the door. Clare watched Marlo back out of the driveway thinking, *Please don't get eaten.*

With the exquisite view of the Kenai Mountains, Duncan moored his pathetic excuse for a fishing vessel to the boat slip inside Resurrection Bay, following a lengthy day of pulling in salmon for the local market in Seward. The bay was usually calm and the voyage peaceful, but the feeling of being spent was pronounced throughout his body. He was exhausted from his head to his untied boat shoes.

He packed up his much needed necessities he used for his trip in his backpack and reached for his good luck charm, whispering, "Thank you for my safe voyage and return."

Stepping off the boat onto the dock, Duncan felt the heat of the sun burning the back of his neck.

He heard a faint shout in the distance, "Hey Duncan, successful day?"

He saw Sandra walking towards him.

"Hi Sandra, it was a profitable day. However, I'm overly tired and in desperate need of a fully loaded burger with crispy curly fries and a large ice water. I'm slowly progressing in route to the pub to meet up with Brady. Why don't you and Clay meet us there?"

With daylight at its peak, she replied, "Sure, I have to make one more stop and then I'll head home and pick up Clay. We'll meet you there."

Duncan waved in agreement and with his sea-beaten body and snail-like motion, he followed behind Sandra, who was prompt in her exit, unlike Duncan, who was taking on the form of Play-Doh. When Duncan reached the truck he tossed his Kelty backpack into his 1972 Ford F-100 with a grunt, slowly climbed in the front seat, started the engine, and headed home.

Chapter 2

On Marlo's way to her apartment, which was all too expensive and not even in a great part of town, she started thinking. *I need to do this before I change my mind. I have to fly by the seat of my pants or I'll chicken out. Get in and get out, like a re-con mission.* So . . . she called her best friend, Mandi. Mandi has been her best friend since grade school. Before calling, Marlo thought, *Mandi knows who I am as a person and she knows I'm adventurous. In college, Mandi and I would hang our underwear to dry on the porch railing of the house we rented because we couldn't afford the dryer change. She'll think this new plan of mine, will be the ultimate plan.*

"Alaska! Marlo, what the hell has come over you? Alaska? What are you doing? You're nuts! And besides, you're being completely irrational and I suspect some crazy in there, too. I can't think this is what you've come up with from being with Clare. Clare has more sense than to just make you think Alaska is the answer!"

Mandi always flipped her lid and didn't even hear the part where Marlo mentioned wanting to be close to her parents.

Marlo sat on the phone waiting with patience before responding because Mandi was a total fruit loop.

"That wasn't the response I was looking for from my best friend—Mandi. I was hoping for a . . . 'woo-hoo, you go!' Or, 'that's exactly what you need,' a Marlo De-tox. Not—I'm being irrational and crazy.'"

After Mandi thought about what Marlo said, she changed her tune, "Well, okay. You are my best friend and best friends are always there for one another, so . . . no matter the decision you make, even if it's a 'Marlo De-tox' in Alaska, I'm fully on board with your decision. I know I'm going to regret this, but if this is what ignites you, then bombs away. Hey, maybe you'll meet a rugged, handsome wilderness man. You can always benefit from one of them," said Mandi with a sly tone in her voice.

"That's the last thing I want to find in Alaska, Mandi. I'm strictly going there to start a new life and possibly be close to the one thing I miss the most, and a man is not it. I will call you as soon as I arrive in Seward. Don't worry about me. I will keep in touch. I promise."

Marlo finally arrived at her apartment in record time. She had to take care of some last minute details before buying an airline ticket to Seward, Alaska, just south of Anchorage on the Kenai Peninsula. It's the perfect place to have a view of the mountains and the ocean all in one spot. And, it was her parents' number one place in the world to vacation. She ran upstairs, packed a small army truck of personal items and essentials, made a few phone calls, and loaded up her car. Just when Marlo was all set to go, she sat in her car, knowing she may or may not come back to Minnesota. She looked out the side window of her car and began thinking back to the day of the accident.

They passed away one year after Clare had Dilly and Bentley. It was an unexpected car accident outside Seward, Alaska. Our dad was driving and our mom was reading in the passenger seat. She always loved to read on trips. They were heading to the airport in Anchorage for their flight home. The car in the on-coming lane swerved into our parent's lane and they hit each other head on. Our parents were airlifted to the closest hospital, which was Anchorage. By the time Clare and I had reached the hospital, both our Mom and Dad had already passed away. We didn't make it in time to say our good byes. Clare and I took a long time grieving their death. Their death still fills my thoughts on a daily basis. How does one ever stop thinking about the death of their parents? How does one go on without having the chance to have said good-bye? I am going to find out and Alaska is the answer.

The airport was crazy busy with women wearing big flimsy wicker hats and brightly colored floral dresses, men sporting Hawaiian shirts, white shorts and sandals. *They must be heading some place warm, like the Caribbean or an island in the Keys. The number of military uniforms walking towards family members holding up white cardboard signs with the name of the person they were looking for in big black sharpie marker lettering was more than I could count.*

Marlo was in the airport only for herself and she was happy about that. She was proud, knowing she wasn't going to settle anymore—for zero. She was going to discover what being in Alaska and her parents have in common.

Marlo knew the ticket was going to be expensive because of her last minute decision, but she was on a mission. There was no retreating now. She's made all the arrangements with her sister, packed up her car and now was standing in the undeniably slow moving line waiting to purchase her ticket.

The ticket lady behind the counter with a hair style that resembled Jean Stapleton's in *'All in the Family',* and blue eye shadow that disappeared into her brow line was looking at Marlo suspiciously.

"How can I help you?"

"Yes, I'd like to buy a ticket to Seward, Alaska, please."

When the lady was printing out the ticket, Marlo couldn't help but detect . . . all airport employees had a badge hanging from their neck and this particular employee's badge said, Lucinda.

"Here's your ticket dear. Enjoy your flight."

"Thank you, Lucinda. I'm pursuing a new life without a man who thinks with the other head that gives him an ego boost."

Walking away heading to terminal C-5, Marlo left Lucinda with her mouth hanging open.

"Next please."

After several hours of traveling, Marlo arrived in one of the most eye-opening places on Earth. The tall, snow-covered mountains with avocado swatches of moss spreading across the bottom were breathtaking and humbling to her eyes. Marlo saw the natural phenomenon, and thought, *I have never seen anything of such jaw-dropping beauty. This is why Mom and Dad loved visiting Alaska so often. Now, I have a sense of what was going through their heads the first time they got off the ferry and saw what I'm seeing now.* Marlo scanned her surroundings and knew she had made the right decision to come to Alaska. The town of Seward is a quaint fishing town bordering Resurrection Bay; it's a welcoming place for tourists. However, since fishing is not Marlo's *forte*, she knew asking someone for directions to the nearest B & B, would be a better idea.

Walking down the boardwalk, trying to avoid tripping on the uneven planks, Marlo observed a man mooring his lines and securing his fishing boat. He seemed to be at ease working on his saltwater salmon fishing charter, totally oblivious to everything else around him. Approaching the boat and getting a closer inspection, Marlo couldn't help think, *holy mackerel! That is the most rugged man I've ever seen. This man was standing first in line when God was giving handouts. Broad shoulders that tapered to a trim waste, brown hair peeking out from under is hat with wispy curls toward the under part of his ears, green eyes the color of jade shadowed by long dark lashes, a three day scruffy beard and the healthiest full red lips. He was dressed in a white T-shirt that had seen better days, a pair of khaki cargo shorts that made you guess what was underneath and a pair of untied boat shoes; this man is a hottie!*

"Excuse me, do you know of a good place to stay here in Seward?" asked Marlo while checking him out, but trying to avoid him noticing her undercover scrutiny.

Duncan looked up from securing his boat, but the sun glared in his eyes. He stood to get a better look.

"Hello ma'am. You say you're looking for a place to stay?"

"Yes, I'm visiting Alaska for a while and I was hoping to find somewhere reasonable."

"Well, ma'am . . ."

"You can call me Marlo."

"Yes ma'am."

"It's Marlo, Marlo Hart." *Does this man not understand English?* Marlo waited for Mr. Hottie to respond.

"Sorry ma'am—I mean, Marlo. If you're looking for long-term, I suggest heading out of Seward a little ways north. Seward is not the cheapest place in Alaska, but it *is* the most beautiful."

He extended his arm and pointed north.

"Thirty minutes north of here, just off the Seward Highway, you'll find cabins that you can rent out for a reasonable price. I haven't stayed there before, but I've heard people have been satisfied with the accommodations."

"Thank you . . . . Mr.—," looking up at him, "I didn't get your name."

"It's Duncan, Duncan James, ma'am."

"Seriously Duncan, are you originally from the South?"

"No ma'am, my Mother just raised me right," said Duncan, thinking, *why would she ask that? Do I have a southern drawl or something?*

"Thanks for the directions, Duncan. I appreciate it."

"Good luck Marlo Hart, and enjoy your stay, however long it may be."

Marlo turned on her heels and headed down the boardwalk. Looking back, she took one last glimpse of Duncan before putting all her faith in his directions. Something sparkly caught her attention from inside the boat. Wondering what it could be, but dismissing the thought, Marlo turned and kept walking.

When Marlo headed down the boardwalk, Duncan viewed the beautiful sight with curiosity, *that's a force to be reckoned with,* he thought. *A woman on a mission with her tight denim blue jeans, knee high brown leather heeled boots, a white tank top and a belt to accentuate her God given curves. I think that swagger was for . . . someone else, 'not for me.' She's high-maintenance,* thought Duncan. Shaking his head, he went back to mooring his lines.

Heading down the pine tree lined highway, Marlo realized she was in a bit of a pickle. She couldn't find the cabins Duncan mentioned and was trying to read a map during rush hour traffic. The map was strewn out, filling the entire front of the car, disrupting her vision. She was swerving all over the highway. Vehicles were speeding past her and whaling on their horns. "Oh yeah, well honk all you want, you crazy Alaskans!" yelled Marlo, from her smaller than small rental. She felt like Inspector Clouseau from 'The Pink Panther.' *Humph, I need to pull over and look at this map.* Marlo slowed down and pulled off onto the shoulder of the road. *I'm completely lost,* shaking her head, she thought, *Duncan told me these cabins were thirty minutes up the highway. I can't find this place and I'm in the middle of nowhere! So much for hot men giving directions!*

Parked on the side of the road, Marlo amused herself by clicking her pen against her teeth while looking over the map and thinking, *go figure; I'm in Alaska, the place of grizzlies, men with guns and the disabled idea of starting over.* She lifted her head and noticed a dirt road that veered off the highway, *maybe that's the road I need to take.* Starting her Inspector Clouseau car, she drove ahead and merged off onto the dirt road that wound back into the woods. *I hope this is it.*

Tall pines and thick patches of ferns lined the well-beaten, rutted drive, but looked newly constructed. The road kept going and Marlo was thinking, *how long is this drive?* Bumping along the ruts and accruing a stomach ache, she finally reached her destination. *These must be the cabins Duncan was talking about. It would have helped if he said to look for a DIRT ROAD, ugh!* Frustrated with Duncan, she was happy to have found the cabins. Marlo took a deep breath to calm her anger and looked around. She saw eight Alaskan style cabins and all were tucked in the woods. The cabins had the same rustic appeal to them . . . small and cozy, but would accommodate Marlo, just fine. The roof was covered with a galvanized tin. There were cut stones placed in the ground for a path which led up to the steps. At the top of the steps was a handcrafted wrap-around porch. There were azaleas that adorned either side of the porch steps leading up to the front door, which was constructed of wood. To accent the door was a door knocker and off to the side, an old fashioned ship's lantern. *This could be the perfect place. It isn't big, but it would fit me perfectly and it has a lot of charm,* thought Marlo as she got out of the car.

Walking up to the main cabin where she would check in, she opened the door and saw a middle aged woman in her late thirties. She had perfectly straight blonde hair that framed her face, hazel eyes, and a nose that looked like a tulip. Marlo was observing the woman standing behind the front desk looking down at some papers, hoping she was finishing up the previous guests' departure. *I need a place to stay,* thought Marlo.

The woman looked up and said, "Hello Miss, welcome to Birch Cabins. My name is Sandra Birch. How can I help you?"

"Hello, my name is Marlo Hart and I'm looking for a place to stay awhile. I'm not sure how long, but I know it could be up to a few months. Would you be able to accommodate me that long?"

"We should be able to. I don't see a problem with that." As soon as we book your stay, I'll show you to your cabin. You'll be in Cabin D. It's the last cabin on the end and, right now it's the only one vacant."

Marlo stood there, thinking *thank goodness . . . I'm in!*

"Don't worry, you'll love it. It's on the river. You're lucky. That's the cabin that always gets rented first, but since the last guest just left, it became available."

This is going to be just what I need, Marlo thought while Sandra was penciling her in.

"Where are you coming from, Marlo?"

"Minnesota."

"Are you staying for business or is this a needed get-a-way?" Sandra asked.

"It's a needed get-a-way. I want to see what else life has to offer."

"I think that's a great idea. I wish I was that brave when I was younger."

While Sandra was getting Marlo's reservation in order, Marlo couldn't help but think back to the dock and that *'sexy as hell dingbat of a man'* on the boat. But, just as she started to drift further, Sandra said, "Okay, honey, let's take you to your home away from home."

The girls started down the dirt path to Marlo's temporary new home and the one thing Sandra noticed right away was Marlo wasn't accompanied by a man; she was alone. Marlo noticed herself shivering from her head to her toes.

Opening the door to her new *home away from home,* she took in a breath of astonishment and said to Sandra, "Its charm flows from the outside to the inside. I love it!"

"I'm so glad. We try to make it comfortable and cozy for our guests. Alaska is a long way from home for most, so Clay and I try to make it feel warm and welcoming."

"Well, it sure is warm, welcoming and cute. It's perfect for me. Thank you Sandra."

"Oh, honey, you're most welcome."

Before leaving Marlo to get settled into her new place, Sandra left the cabin keys on the kitchen table, "If you need anything, I'll be in the office until nine tonight."

Before Marlo could answer, Sandra slipped out and walked back to the office. Marlo was amazed by the character her cabin displayed. She couldn't have picked a quainter place to stay. *Thaaank you, Duncan.*

The floor was covered in wide pine planks with dark weathered knots scattered throughout. Cotton white curtains with scalloped edges covered the windows, but were currently pushed aside, allowing light to shine through. A handmade barn-wood bookshelf full of books stood behind the wooden pine-plank table with four mismatched colored chairs in the petite living room. A worn camel colored leather chair was in the corner and a free standing antique brass lamp with a milk glass shade set on low, next to it. There was a tiny bathroom off to the side that housed a white pedestal sink and an old white framed oval mirror that hung above it. Also, in the bathroom, was a rag rug on the floor to keep warm feet from touching the chilly floor in the morning. And, to Marlo's surprise, was an enamel woodstove in the corner of the living room for chilly Alaskan nights. *Hello . . . where am I going to get wood for that?* Marlo thought and then continued to survey her new home. There was a rug in the middle of the room that was welcomed by many visitors, amazingly, still vibrant with colors, considering how worn the rug appeared. There was a small kitchen that was combined with the living room. In the kitchen was an old country white porcelain farm sink and curtains that replaced the cupboard doors below. Open shelving above the sink was lined with dishes and silverware for easy reach. Also, in the cabin there was a loft which seemed quite spacious. There was an oak bed covered in a white chenille spread and at the foot of the bed, a wooden chest that housed more blankets for cold winter nights. In addition to the oak bed and cedar chest was a four drawer dresser accented with a mirror, most likely purchased at an auction.

Thinking out loud and observing her new place, Marlo said, "I can't believe that I found a place so quickly and where I feel comfortable and welcomed."

Beginning to unpack and recognizing the feeling of home, Marlo turned to see the door to her cabin was open a crack. She opened the door and looked outside, but no one was there. *Sandra probably didn't shut it all the way when she stepped out*, thought Marlo while shutting the door. Feeling the breeze, she realized, even at the end of summer, Alaska was a little on the cool side. Marlo experienced an involuntary shiver and knew firewood was a must. She started up to the main cabin and was surveying her surroundings. The wilderness made her feel humble. She couldn't stray from the thoughts of the grizzly bear that was going to eat her or the mountain lion that was stalking her, waiting to pounce. Marlo quickened her pace.

Finally reaching the main office, she opened and shut the door quickly.

She heard, "Well honey, how do you like the cabin?"

"Oh, it's perfect. I love it. I couldn't have found a better place to stay."

"Well wonderful. I'm happy to hear that. Is there something you need, Marlo?" asked Sandra.

"Yes, actually I do have a question. Do you know where I could get some firewood? It's cool out and I'm not used to it being colder at night in the summer," Marlo said, as she looked at Sandra, waiting for a response.

"Summer here isn't like summer in Minnesota. It gets cold around now, so I hope you have the proper clothing. My Husband, Clay, has cut and split all the wood needed for the cabins, so whenever you need any, either you can take some to your cabin or Clay can pile you some up for a few days at a time."

"That would be great, Sandra."

Before heading back out into the quiet scary wilderness, she turned and said, "Before I go, I was wondering, what is there to do around here? I know Seward is about thirty minutes south, but is there anything closer?"

"There's a book store up the road called Alaskan Books and Company and there's also The James Bros. Pub. That's where most of the night life goes when it gets too cold to venture out of doors."

"Great, thank you Sandra. And, thank you for having Clay deliver wood to my cabin, I really appreciate it."

"No problem, Marlo."

Seeing Marlo out of the office, Sandra was happy that someone like Marlo was taking on a new direction and searching out something of worth. *Life goes by too fast to become stagnant. Take that leap of faith and see what's out there,* Sandra thought while opening the door to the office and quickly closing it to omit the heat from warming all of Alaska. *I really like that Marlo, she's all—woman. Strong-willed, beautiful, obviously smart and well-versed. I think Duncan is going to have to meet this vixen.* With a match-making mission ahead of her and distracted by her new guest, she tried to continue with her work.

Marlo finished unloading her rental car and brought her small army truck of belongings into the cabin. It was starting to feel like home by the second. Within a couple of hours, Marlo was unpacked and parked her car next to the cabin. Heading over to her little abode was Clay, Sandra's husband, with a wheel barrow full of chopped wood. Marlo was eager to thank him in person. She slipped her leather loafers on and went out to meet him,

"You must be Clay. I'm Marlo Hart," said Marlo shaking Clay's hand. "Thank you for bringing me some wood. I didn't think it was going to be *this* cold in August," Marlo said with a smile.

"Yeah, cold is an understatement around these parts. Where are you from, Marlo?"

"Minnesota."

Clay looked to be in his late thirties, handsome and polite. He had sandy blonde hair and a boyish smile, accented with dimples that could hold quarters. He was tall and from what she could see and muscular. Sandra and Clay made a nice couple and seemed more than hospitable.

Wishing she had that special someone in her life, she heard Clay say, "I've never been to Minnesota, but I'm sure it's a friendly place to live."

"It is a wonderful place. It's busy though. Have you lived here all your life?" asked Marlo.

"Sandra and I built Birch Cabins ten years ago and we've been here ever since. We originated from Anchorage and decided to move to the Seward area because of its vast beauty, wide open landscape, and it's a wonderful tourist area. People are always looking for a place to stay outside of Seward; staying in town can be costly. Birch Cabins has done well in the past ten years and I suspect we'll be here until we can't run the cabins anymore."

"Well Mr. Birch, it's a beautiful place and it's perfect for what I'm looking for."

"You can call me Clay, Marlo. What *are* you looking for . . . if you don't mind me asking?"

"I'm looking to start over and figure out what life has for me outside of Minnesota."

"And, you picked *Alaska* to rediscover yourself? That's a pretty risky move, but you look like you can handle it. If you need anything, just let me or Sandra know and we'll help you out the best we can . . . . Oh and welcome to Birch Cabins."

Clay gave a welcoming smile as he headed up to the main cabin to see what Sandra was up to.

"Thank you, Clay," Marlo said, walking to her cabin, hearing leaves and sticks crunch and carry on beneath her feet.

Standing in the doorway, gazing at her new rustic Alaskan cabin, Marlo felt an accomplishment for making it this far on her journey to self-discovery. She walked over to the windows with her hair up in a tortoise shell clip, which she retrieved from her bathroom drawer. Tucking the loose ends behind her ears, she drew back the white streamlined curtains, accented with charming scalloped edges, and was in awe. Marlo couldn't believe her eyes. She stood by the window like a statue, taking in the view. She let out a sigh. *Those are the most beautiful mountains I've ever seen. They are the back drop for the free-flowing river that runs at the base of the mountain. Now, that's something you don't see in Minnesota,* Marlo said, when she realized she needed to contact her sister, Clare. *I better call Clare before she thinks someone took me out salmon fishing and I fell overboard.* Her best friend, Mandi, was also in need of a call. She needed to let them both know she made it to Alaska, safely. Marlo decided to call Clare first.

Chapter 3

Clare was in the kitchen listening to music and making a cake while the twins played in the living room.

The phone rang and she picked it up, "Omigod, I was so worried about you. It's been two days since you called and Jack and I were wondering if you were okay. How is it over there?" asked Clare, watching Dilly and Bentley whip legos at each other; one flew into the kitchen. Swatting at it with a spatula, Clare heard Duncan come from the ear piece.

"Who's Duncan, again? I couldn't hear you. The kids were throwing legos at each other."

Frustrated, Marlo repeated herself, again.

"Duncan is this guy who was working on his fishing boat by the dock and I asked him where I could stay. He suggested Birch Cabins up the road. Clare, they're perfect. I love it here. It's stunning and you should see the mountains and river behind the cabin—it's *so* picturesque."

"Who's Duncan, again?" Clare asked.

"He's just a guy I talked to . . . focus Clare," Marlo replied with a definite annoyance.

"Well, he sure sounds good looking and polite, from what you've described. Maybe, he will become your new adventure," Clare replied with a giggle behind her tone.

"Yeah right, I don't think so, Clare. I am not interested in any man at this junction in time. You know I'm discarding all men right now. I know you find this amusing, but I have been down the broken road before and I can honestly say it sucks!"

"Alright, well, what are you going to do now that you're all unpacked and taking up residence at Birch Cabins hiding?"

Clare spoke the second Jack walked in and he raised his brow with curiosity.

"I'm not hiding out, Clare. And as far as Duncan goes, I'll probably never see him again. He's over in Seward filleting fish or something."

"Call me in a couple of days and make sure you have bear repellent, spray or whatever they call it there. I love you, sis. Be careful."

"I love you too, Clare. Give Dilly and Bentley hugs and kisses for me."

She hung up the phone and decided to call Mandi later. She was hungry.

Instead of staying in for dinner even though she had all the equipment to make a meal, minus the one vital necessity food, she decided to head over to James Bros. Pub, hoping she could get a meal there instead of back tracking to Seward.

She jumped in the shower and dolled herself up for a dinner for one. She wore a dark blue denim pair of skinny jeans, her favorite knee high brown leather heeled boots, a white button down shirt, unbuttoning it a few buttons to make life interesting and the sleeves rolled up to her elbows, silver hoop earrings and a bracelet to match. Her dark hair fell on her shoulders like one of Charlie's Angels. She looked amazing, and more importantly, she felt amazing, even after two days of traveling and feeling jet-legged. Marlo locked the cabin on her way out and got in her Inspector Clouseau rental car. She drove off down the nauseating drive, hoping she didn't get lost trying to find the pub.

Marlo pulled into the parking lot of James Bros. Pub and realized it was Saturday night because the lot was packed. *I'm just going in for dinner and a beer and then I'll head back to the cabin*, Marlo thought, a little nervously. This was all new to her. She was in a place she's never been. *What if the men in Alaska are as scary as the grizzlies here? I don't have any bear spray on me either.*

"Crap," mumbled Marlo before opening the door to the pub and seeing a dance floor with several couples dancing the two-step.

The last bit of Travis Tritt blared from the jukebox and the bar was full of people; she could barely squeeze through. Guys were occupying the pool tables. Couples were dancing on the dance floor. People were standing around and talking above the other to hear themselves over the loud music. The bar was packed with people drinking and wanting more drinks.

When Marlo finally made her way to the bar, she looked up and said, louder than normal, "I'll take a Bud Light, please and if the kitchen is open, I'd love a cheeseburger and fries."

To her surprise, she found Duncan smirking at her in his flannel shirt, white Stetson and tight fitting jeans. *Great, of course I would run into Mr. Southern Hospitality and y'all, ma'am.*

"Hey you, what are you doing here?" asked Marlo, a little annoyed, thinking, *great . . . just perfect.*

"What does it look like? I'm tending bar. My brother Brady and I own this place."

Duncan fixed a drink order for a pretty blonde and then asked Marlo, "How's it going over at the cabins?"

"Good, after I found it," said Marlo, irritated with Duncan's cocky tone. It was quite loud with the jukebox going and everyone hootin' and hollerin' over Brooks and Dunn.

"I told you where to go."

"You failed to mention the *dirt road*. That would have been helpful. I had crazy Alaskans yelling at me to get off the road."

"That doesn't surprise me . . . you're a woman."

Duncan looked at Marlo and had a smile curve up, seeing he was getting under her skin.

"Right, it's my fault that sexy fisherman give lousy directions."

Duncan smiled at Marlo's feistiness and thought she looked cute getting all riled up. *Did she just call me a sexy fisherman?*

Marlo leaned over the bar and said, "Let me guess, you're a fisherman by day and a bartender/pub-owner by night?"

"That about sums it up. You're a quick one. I better be careful around you."

Evading his comment quickly because she wasn't in the mood to continue their wonderful pleasantries, she said, "The cabin is great, thanks for sending me there; it's perfect. Sandra and Clay Birch, the people who own the cabins, are really great, too," Marlo shouted back wondering . . . *what are the odds of seeing him, again?*

"Speaking of Sandra and Clay, they're sitting at the end of the bar; you should go say hi to them."

"Good idea, I will. Thanks Duncan."

"Thanks for what?" Duncan shouted.

"Thanks for the Bud Light!" Marlo said, holding up her beer and walking to the end of the bar.

Duncan watched Marlo walk over to Sandra and Clay thinking, *holy hell, I'm in deep water. That girl has trouble written all over her.*

Marlo sauntered over to her two new friends.

"Hey, Sandra, Clay. Wow, this place is packed for a Saturday night."

"It's always packed on the weekends. Duncan and Brady really know how to run a pub. We didn't expect to see you here tonight, Marlo. We're glad you came down. How's the cabin treating you?" Sandra asked, looking at Duncan looking at Marlo.

"It's awesome. I figured I would celebrate my first night eating out since I made it the whole day without getting eaten by a grizzly. I'm all unpacked and even though I have pots and pans, I forgot one necessity . . . food. I'll have to go shopping tomorrow."

"You'll have to go into Seward for that. The other grocery store is forty-five minutes north of here, yet."

"That sounds fine to me. I don't mind traveling a little further to get staples and what not. The cabin is so much more than I expected. I am really pleased with the location, the cabin itself and the scenery; it's just amazing," said Marlo.

"It is a pretty special place. Clay and I really enjoy it. We've put a lot of time and elbow grease into Birch Cabins. It's our lively-hood."

Marlo looked at Sandra and thought, *I want to have something special one day to be proud of, too.*

"Have you met Duncan, yet?" asked Sandra with her match-making mission underway.

"Yeah, I saw him at the bar and I met him down by the docks in Seward, earlier today. He actually told me about your cabins for rent when I got off the ferry. I didn't know what to do, so . . . I asked him where I could stay and he mentioned your cabins. He was very informative and polite. He kept addressing me as 'ma'am' until I convinced him to call me Marlo. Does he own a fishing boat as well? He was working on a boat when I bumped into him down at the docks."

"Duncan owns a charter fishing boat. He takes people out and they pay a pretty penny, too. All the tourists like to go on Resurrection Bay or out to the gulf and fish. They can see whales playing and seals on the banks. It's a tourist's dream come true."

"That sounds amazing. I bet Duncan enjoys watching them catch, *The Big One.*"

Surveying the bar and realizing how everyone seemed to be having a great time, Sandra chimed in, "You should have Duncan take you fishing one day while you're here visiting."

Holding their tongues, Duncan walked over and handed Marlo her cheeseburger and fries.

"Here you go darlin', enjoy your dinner."

Turning away from Marlo, he winked at Sandra. Sandra knew what that wink meant, *that's my boy.*

Marlo looked at Sandra suspiciously and asked, "Sandra, what was that smile all about and why was Duncan winking? I'm just curious, are you trying to set Duncan? Just to let you know, I'm not here looking for a relationship, much less, a one night stand.

Thinking, if that door slammed hard, but not if she could help it, Sandra replied, "Nope. I was just thinking it might be fun to do some deep sea fishing."

Marlo gave Sandra a skeptical look, "I've had many relationships I've botched up and I can't emotionally afford another one," Marlo said, hoping to put Sandra's match-making schemes at bay.

Sandra noticed Marlo was out of beer and gave Duncan a shout, "Hey Duncan, how 'bout another beer for my new friend, Marlo?"

"Coming right up, Marlo . . . a Bud Light, right?"

"That'd be great, thanks!"

She looked at her much needed beer and took a long pull thinking, *after all that traveling and unpacking, this hits the spot.*

She looked around the room examining the pub. It was well built, had a woodsy feel and wood flooring; which seemed to be the choice of floor covering around these parts. The lights were set on low and there was back lighting by the bar. The walls were decorated with a selection of stuffed fish and mounted heads shot and killed from the vast wilderness of Alaska, Marlo assumed. Typical neon signs and an assortment of alcohol and beer posters also adorned the walls. There were three pool tables off to the side and a foosball table and dart board in back. Marlo was getting tired and started to yawn. She was ready to go back to the cabin.

"Well, Sandra, Clay, I'll be heading home. I'm beyond tired and I need to get up early in the morning to start the first day of my new life in Alaska."

"What do you plan on doing tomorrow?" asked Sandra just when Marlo started to put her coat on.

"I'm not sure. I think I'll get those groceries and I also need to purchase cold weather attire. I didn't bring warm clothing because I thought August would still be warm here. I'm not sure what the day has in store for me after that," Marlo said, itching to get out of the bar.

She could barely keep her eyes open. She wanted to get back to her cozy cabin, have a cup of hot cocoa and snuggle in for the night with a good book.

"Tomorrow Clay and I are heading to Seward to pick up some fish from the market, it's a fun place. The market is located on the boardwalk and you'll find anything and everything you could possibly need or want. They have vendors that come from all over semi-locally and set up booths. You are more than welcome to come with us. I mean you were going there anyway, right? We could drive there together to save on gas. What do you think?"

"Sure Sandra, that sounds like fun. I should take an inventory of what I might need. I don't care to drive into Seward every time I need something, thinking I have it and I don't. I'll pop over after a quick shower and a cup of coffee in the morning."

"That sounds perfect. We'll take my truck since your rental car might not hold everything we need to bring back." Marlo thought, *that's an understatement.*

"Awesome! Okay, I'll see you tomorrow then."

Heading over to the bar, Marlo gave a quick shout out to Duncan, "Bye Duncan, good seeing you again and tell your cook he makes a mean burger."

"Will do. See ya, Marlo and thanks for stopping by. Be careful heading home, grizzlies cross the main highway," Duncan said, wishing he was the one driving her home.

Marlo looked back at Duncan as the door slowly closed in front of a surprised look on her face. *Um, thanks for the heads up, I think. Bears? Great, now I have to deal with bears, again?! I don't want to see any bears and definitely not up close and personal,* thought Marlo, nervously walking to her car faster than a one legged man in an ass-kicking contest.

Chapter 4

Heading back to the cabin and keeping an eye out for the local bear waiting to eat her and her, Inspector Clouseau rental car for its next meal, Marlo was thinking how thrilled she was with the people she's met so far and couldn't wait to meet more Alaskans. They were down to Earth, genuine, hospitable people. She started down the bumpy road and thought, *I need to get rid of this rental and buy a real vehicle. But, not a car since there's heavy snow up here; I'd probably need four-wheel drive. Humph, that's going to be fun to drive. Well, I'll just have to get used to it. At least it will absorb some of the heavy grooved ruts in this awful drive.* Marlo parked her car next to the cabin and went inside.

She stood with her back against the door and said, "I'm passing on the hot cocoa and book. I hear the bed calling my name."

Marlo crawled up the ladder to her loft and dug in her dresser for something to wear to bed. She pulled out a short sleeve shirt and called it good. She slithered into bed and was fast asleep when her head hit the pillow.

The next morning, Marlo woke to the tall pines whistling in the wind and the rapid water flowing over the rocks in the river. She made herself a cup of coffee and drank it while she took inventory of what she brought with her to Alaska. She was in need of some thermal underwear, wool socks, sweaters, jeans, snow pants, a jacket to match, hat, mittens and boots. She wondered if they sold fleece underwear. Shaking the ridiculous thought from her mind, but hopeful, she opened the door to get an armful of wood and a sharp wind blew the door shut. *It's windy as a bugger out here. Thank goodness I'm getting prepared for winter today because it isn't going to be long before the first snowfall.*

Marlo threw a couple of logs on the fire that was down to smoldering coals. She closed the damper a little more so the wood would last longer. Marlo figured she was going to be gone at least half the day and wanted it warm and toasty when she returned home. She took a quick, but hot and steamy shower, got dressed in the warmest clothes she had, threw on some makeup and put on her leather world travelers. She closed the door and started up towards Sandra and Clay's place.

"Are you ready to go?" Marlo asked Sandra.

"I am, just let me get my purse and we'll be on our way. I can't wait to take you down there. You're going to love it."

"It sounds great. I'm excited to see what treasures I can find."

Downtown Seward was more striking than Marlo remembered it the first day she arrived. Native Alaskans were sauntering down the streets, visiting all the local shops and waving hello to other people, like they've been here forever. Sail boats, fishing charters, personal fishing boats, and speed boats all lined the docks in the marina. Seagulls were congregating over the boardwalk, singing to the locals in hopes of snatching flying leftovers from lunch in mid-air. Fudge shops and souvenir shops lined the streets along with the local yarn, book, and hardware store.

"Sandra, this place is more beautiful than when I first saw it."

"That's because you weren't really looking, Marlo."

"I guess you're right. I was so busy trying to find a place to stay. That's when I found Duncan and he gave me directions to you."

"Speaking of Duncan," Sandra motioned, "he's right down there by his fishing boat; let's go pay him a visit. He loves to have company after a morning of fishing alone."

"Ah . . . okay, but I really want to get my shopping done," Marlo stressed.

"We'll be quick. Clay wants me to get home as soon as possible because we need to clean out a couple of cabins for guests who will be checking in the day after tomorrow."

"Okay, let's go," Marlo said, wanting to finish her shopping, not *'window-shopping'* the goods of Duncan James, local fisherman and pub owner.

"I take it, you don't like Duncan?" asked Sandra while they were walking.

"No, that's not it. I just don't want to deal with any men right now," Marlo exhaled with a sigh, putting her hands in her pockets.

"I'm trying to stay away from that part of life until I know what I'm doing with myself."

Sandra couldn't help seeing through Marlo's cursed feelings for Duncan. She noticed it right away when she saw Marlo's undercover flirting last night at the pub.

Hesitantly, putting one foot in front of the other down the pier to Duncan's boat slip, Marlo could see how sexy he was with the sun making his skin glow and his eyes sparkle. He had on the same shorts and another white T-shirt with 'Duncan Charters' on the front and boat shoes that weren't tied again.

"What is with that man not tying his shoes?" Marlo asked under her breath. Duncan eyed Sandra and Marlo making their way down to him. He was emptying the holds, stowing his gear, loading his backpack with his personal belongings and thanking the one thing he holds dear for his safe voyage and return.

"Hey girls, what are you up to this fine Seward day?"

Classic is the only word I can think of, Marlo thought.

"Oh, we were out and about and thought we'd stop by and say, hello," Sandra said.

"Hello Duncan, taking anyone out today or are you just working on your boat?" asked Marlo, making polite conversation and desperately wanting to flee from Duncan's breathing space.

While Marlo was standing there, Duncan could clearly see she was uncomfortable with him. She looked like she couldn't wait to leave. *What is that girl up to and why is she so uptight?* Duncan was mesmerized by how she was oblivious to the ache that presided deep within his stomach. *How can this woman show a total lack of interest in me, yet I'm saluting her with my manhood and the only thing missing is the 'Fuck Me' flag that hangs in the wind?*

"I just came in from a morning of fishing. I've got some people that want to go fishing tomorrow at dusk, so . . . I'm unloading today's catch and gearing up for tomorrow's trip. Maybe, one day when you're more settled, I could take you out on the boat. The whales meander into the bay and play around. It's a sight to see—you'd love it."

"Sure, that sounds great."

Turning to Sandra, Marlo said, "Hey, I'll be back, I have to run to the rest room. Give me five minutes?"

"Alright, hurry up, though!" Sandra called out wondering if Marlo heard her.

Duncan looked to Sandra and asked, "What is up with that girl? She seems uptight around me all the time," said Duncan with amusement and the impulse to wrap his arms around her.

"She doesn't want to be in any relationships while being in Alaska. She came to Alaska to find a way of life she's happy with. She wants to start a new life with no road blocks. From what I know, Marlo has had a lot of failed relationships. I feel bad because I did kind of push her your way last night at the bar."

"Sandra, I'm not looking for a relationship either. I've been single a long time and I like it. I'm set in my ways and I'm happy with the status quo. Quit with the match-making schemes, it's not your calling. Marlo probably senses it, too and gets weird around me no thanks to you."

"Duncan, you can't stay single forever. Hell, the reason I thought you were single was because you already dated every girl in Seward," Sandra said, with a playful smile on her face.

"Sandra, did anyone tell you how *'not funny'* you are?"

"Well, there's another woman in town now, so try not to scare her back to Minnesota. I like her," Sandra said, with triumph.

"I have no intentions of *scaring* anyone, so if you don't mind, I'll handle this *my way*. Not, Sandra Birch's match-making way." Duncan chuckled looking at Sandra and thinking, *we go way back, don't we?*

"Just having met Marlo, she seems great and would make an awesome buddy to hang out with. Let's just leave it at that for now, okay?"

Duncan was hoping Sandra would be on board with that.

"Sounds good, Duncan. However, maybe Brady would like to take her out on the boat someday?"

"What? Are you a few degrees shy of north? You're hitting below the belt, now," offered Duncan with a smirk.

"My brother wouldn't know a treasure like Marlo if she smacked him in the face with a salmon."

Sandra laughed, "Oh, Duncan, what am I going to do with you?"

Before Sandra started to leave, Duncan reached for her and spoke quietly, "Hey, I've been thinking of this ever since the first day I saw Marlo, but she looks awfully familiar. Does she look familiar to you at all?" Duncan inquired.

"No, I don't think so. I don't think she's been up this way before. I would know; I know everyone in this town. I'm sure she just looks like someone you've met before. You do take a lot of people out on the boat. Maybe it's just one of those things. I need to find Marlo. I'll see you later, Duncan."

Sandra didn't know why Duncan would think she looked familiar, but he did for some reason.

Heading down the pier to meet up with Marlo, Sandra caught her on the phone talking to someone.

"He's the perfect guy you could ever meet. He's tall, sexy and has the most beautiful green eyes you could possibly imagine. He's sarcastic and playful and has a way about him you just simply can't ignore. I just don't want to get into another atrocious relationship. You know? I'm just going to keep my distance from Duncan. I'm keeping him at bay—literally. He can stay on his fishing boat for all I care. Too bad, if I was actually looking for a relationship, he would fit me perfectly."

"Hey, Marlo, are you ready to go?" Sandra called out. Whispering, Marlo said, "I have to go, Mandi. I'll call again, soon."

Marlo hung up quickly as possible and looked at Sandra.

"Yep, I'm ready. Let's head out. Hey, I'm sorry I didn't come back down by you. I got hung up on a phone call to Minnesota."

"Don't worry about it, it happens. I was just finishing up talking to Duncan and he had to finish what he was doing, so . . . we're good."

Sandra and Marlo started walking and Sandra drifted in thought, *that's interesting, Marlo does like Duncan, but doesn't want anyone here to know. I wonder why. Maybe she wants to keep this impenetrable façade going because she wants to figure things out first, like she said. I'll keep that bit of four-one-one to myself. Duncan and Marlo would make a great pair. I wonder how long she's going to stay in Alaska.* All excited to learn that Marlo *does* like Duncan, she continued to walk along side Marlo; not giving any hints that she over heard her conversation. When they reached the truck, they loaded their things and headed off to Birch Cabins.

Watching out for the crazy Alaskan drivers, Sandra happened to mention to Marlo, "I uh . . . happened to talk with Duncan about the possibility of dating you while you went to the bathroom. Duncan didn't see eye to eye with me on that one. Actually, he didn't want anything to do with you romantically and just thinks friends would be the more operative way to go."

Marlo could not believe what she was hearing. *Maybe I should just throw myself out of the truck now. I mean really, there's no reason to go on.*

"What? Omigod, first, why would you talk to him about that and second, why wouldn't he want to be with me romantically?" asked Marlo.

"I admit, I probably shouldn't have mentioned it, but I just wanted to see what he would say. To answer your second question, he just has a lot on his plate and probably is content with his life right now," replied Sandra.

"What's wrong with me that he doesn't approve of? You know what . . . don't answer that, its better this way. Actually, it couldn't be better," Marlo said with great satisfaction . . . she thinks. "Oh, and for future inquiries, just don't ask," said Marlo peeking over at Sandra and thought, *I have another Mandi sitting next to me.*

"If you don't want me to, I won't . . . deal?"

"Deal."

Back at the cabin, Marlo unloaded her groceries and the winter attire she purchased at Seward's local market. She put all the cold groceries in the refrigerator and stocked the open shelves with dry goods; cans on one side and boxes on the other. She put away all her winter gear and was happy with the selection of clothing and outdoor wear she purchased. *Perfect,* she thought. *I feel more and more at home as the days go by. Tomorrow I am going to look for a vehicle that can handle the cold Alaskan winters and if I plan on staying here for awhile, I should find some work.* Marlo started making a list.

- ✓ Warm clothes
- ✓ Vehicle
- ✓ Job

Duncan . . . . no scratch that . . .

"Not a very big list, but big necessities," she said as she wrote, "Not including Duncan."

Later that night, Marlo heard someone or something on foot outside her door. She carefully opened it thinking, *I hope this isn't the Grizzly Bear everyone keeps talking about.* She carefully peeked out, afraid she was going to be face to face with the well-known picnic basket thief, Yogi Bear, but saw Clay.

"Hi Clay, what are you doing out this way?"

"I wanted to load you up with at least three days worth of wood. You go through it faster than I thought you would."

Feeling like she never lived in the north before, she was embarrassed when she said, "I'm sorry, Clay. I'm not used to the cold nights, yet. It doesn't get cold until early October in Minnesota."

"I figured. No worries. Is the cabin retaining heat?"

"Oh yes, it's quite warm and comfortable."

Clay thought Marlo was a nice young girl.

"Alright, well, you have a good night, Marlo and I'll see you soon. Oh, I wanted to tell you that Sandra told me she had a wonderful time with you today at the market. It's nice that she has someone here for a longer stay. She really likes talking to people, but their visit is usually brief."

"I had a lot of fun with her, too. I can see us becoming great friends."

Smiling and nodding in approval, Clay closed the door and finished unloading the wood next to her cabin. Listening to the split wood logs hitting the side of her little house, Marlo figured she'd get the fire stoked up, get cozy under the covers with a good book she found on her bookshelf and read herself to sleep.

Chapter 5

She made her way into her welcoming warm bed piled with blankets after a long day of shopping. Just as she was starting to relax and sink into the mattress, she heard a knock at the door. *Now what? Who could that be?* Marlo complained while climbing down the ladder in her fuzzy purple slippers and flannel pajamas. She walked over to the door, unlocked it, turned the knob, and opened the door a crack, not wanting to expose her tired self, and peeked out. She saw Duncan standing there in jeans that had frays hanging off the bottom of his pant legs, a University of Alaska sweatshirt, and ball cap with his hair peeking out from under it and a pair of Asics, holding a bottle of wine and a pizza.

Come in so I can rip your clothes off and make hot passionate love to you before I go crazy trying to avoid you at all cost. Don't even go there, thought Marlo before speaking.

"What are you doing here, Duncan?" Marlo asked with a sigh and slight irritation in her tone, hoping to hide her redness radiating off her face when she saw Duncan.

"I was heading home from the docks and I locked myself out of the house. Brady has another key, but he won't be home until tomorrow. He had to go to Anchorage to purchase inventory for the pub. Do you mind if I bunk here for the night? I brought wine and pizza," said Duncan with a pouty look on his face, but then smiling.

"Um . . . hold on. Let me get dressed," said Marlo in a panic. Duncan thought her modesty was adorable.

"It's okay; you don't have anything I haven't seen before." On that note, Marlo shut the door. *I'm going to choke him!* Quickly rustling around looking for clothes, Marlo was making a lot of noise and Duncan was left outside wondering, *what is that woman doing in there, rearranging furniture?* Marlo found a purple shirt with bleach spots on it and a pair of faded jeans with frayed holes in the knees. She approached the door, put her head down and reached for the knob. When Marlo opened the door, Duncan put his unanswered thought aside.

"Come on in, Duncan," Marlo said, panting.

"Phew, for a minute there I thought I was going to spend a night in the cold, Alaskan air," Duncan said trying to lighten the mood, thinking, *this woman is crazy.*

"Why didn't you ask Sandra and Clay if you could stay with them for the night? I'm sure they would have said yes. I mean, I've basically just met you."

"I know and I really appreciate it. Sandra and Clay aren't home or they're already in bed. All their lights are off," said Duncan with a little confusion, as if Marlo knew something he didn't.

Marlo gave a sneering look, and replied, "They were just on a few minutes ago. Ugh, never mind, not a big deal."

Marlo, completely frustrated and wanting to pull her hair out, didn't know what to think about this arrangement, but she knew she didn't want Duncan to be there because of the feelings he was stirring up inside her. While Marlo was pacing the living room, which was inadequate for them to be in because of the close proximity, Duncan was unsure of what to say.

"I have a question to ask you, Marlo."

Worried what he was going to ask, Marlo gave it a go. "Shoot."

"Are you uncomfortable around me?"

If that doesn't put a damper on this already awkward situation I don't know what would, Marlo thought before answering.

"Well, for the simple fact that I just met you a couple days ago and you're spending the night with me in my cabin, what would make you think that?"

Duncan had a smile brewing, but didn't know how to hide it. "Okay, you may have a point. What do you want to know about me to make you feel you know me?"

Watching Marlo squirm and reluctant in answering, Duncan sat back in her leather chair and bit into a slice of pizza.

Stammering her words, Marlo said, "I . . . I had a lot of things end badly in my life and something else, might just break me."

Woe, come out with the big guns why don't ya, thought Duncan before asking with curiosity.

"What do you mean . . . things end badly?"

Duncan couldn't help notice that Marlo was retreating to a place in her mind and he didn't want to press her. He could tell she was evading something, something that caused her a lot of pain and she didn't want to share it with him. Searching for something to say and coming up with nothing, he took another bite of pizza. He looked over at Marlo sitting on the floor up against the wall with her knees pulled into her chest and her arms wrapped around her legs.

She looked up at Duncan and smiled, "Hey Duncan . . ."

"Hey Marlo, what do you say to a game of Yahtzee? I know Sandra and Clay have these cabins stocked with games."

"Duncan, that's the best idea I've heard yet."

After a few rolls of the dice and a few games of Yahtzee, Marlo and Duncan went through their bottle of wine and were feeling a little tipsy—laughing up a storm. Marlo got up and Duncan soon followed, to help her stoke the fire. It was getting colder out the closer fall approached.

"Ouch," Marlo said looking down and seeing a splinter in her finger.

"Let me see it. I'm good at getting slivers out of fingers," offered Duncan reaching for her hand and inspecting her finger.

Marlo laughed at Duncan's quirkiness and thought, *do not let Duncan's charm get to you, Marlo.*

Glancing up at him and seeing how careful he was being, she saw how sensitive he was and felt what she knew was her breaking-point.

"Okay, but don't hurt me. I'm kind of a baby when it comes to pain."

Duncan looked at her with his talented smirk, "Really? I wouldn't have guessed. A tough cookie like you hauling your cute little tush all the way to Alaska, renting a cabin from the advice of a guy you happened to see working on a fishing charter . . . it can't be true."

Marlo couldn't hide the laughter that was bottled up inside and she let out a belly laugh making Duncan blush.

"Well, you know, girls from Minnesota are independent and are always ready to take on the world."

"Uh-huh."

Marlo looked at Duncan and he could see her eyes were hungry, but she was hesitating.

"I like hanging out with you, Duncan. I had a lot of fun tonight, but I think I'm going to head to bed. I'm really tired and it's been a long day."

"That sounds like a perfect ending to a perfect night," replied Duncan trying to stifle a yawn.

When Marlo was heading up to her loft she realized there wasn't a place for Duncan to sleep. She started wobbling back down the ladder because of too much wine and turned to find her face in Duncan's chest. The only thought flooding Marlo's mind was, *god; he smells good, like fresh soap and a hint of fish.*

She looked up at him and said, "We have a problem . . . there's no where for you to sleep."

Already having observed that, Duncan managed to say, "The leather chair will suit me just fine, Marlo."

Even though she had her answer, she couldn't start back up the ladder. She felt her feet glued to the pine planks of the cabin floor and couldn't stray from his striking green eyes. She kept saying in her head, *turn around and go up to bed. You can do it Marlo . . . turn around. Move your feet and haul your ass up to bed, NOW!"* She snapped out of her trance and quickly turned to move up the ladder, but Duncan stretched his arm out and rested his hand on her shoulder, softly turning her to him.

Before she could resist, Duncan slowly leaned down and looked at Marlo's parted lips. He placed his finger under her chin and raised it, lowering his lips to hers. She could feel his warmth and smell the sweet wine on his breath. She licked her lips just before he was about to brush his lips against hers. Awaiting his kiss, her heart was beating a mile a minute. She felt like her heart was going to jump out of her chest.

He looked into her eyes and said, "Marlo, I've wanted to do this since the first moment I saw you on the dock."

Leaning in, he lowered his lips to hers and kissed her softly. Pulling her into him, he deepened the kiss and opened her up to him. He softly massaged her tongue and felt her give into his kiss, tasting him and trembling under his touch. She let out a little moan of pleasure and stopped him.

Backing away from him, Marlo said, "Duncan, I can't do this. This is not why I'm here. I'm here to start a life for myself and if I get mixed up in a relationship I'll be everything you want me to be, *for you* and not what I need to be, *for me*."

Holy crow, what just happened, was Duncan's immediate thought. "Its okay Marlo, it was just a kiss, nothing else. If I crossed the line with you, I . . . I'm . . ."

Before Duncan could finish, Marlo muttered an expletive, reached for Duncan's shirt and pulled him to her. She stood on her tip toes, wrapped her arms around his neck and pulled him down to her, kissing him with intent, but drawing back slowly. She outlined his lips with her tongue giving a little tug on his lower lip with her teeth and kissed him again. When they broke from the kiss he stood there, satisfied, but confused.

"Duncan, I couldn't help myself. I was trying to be strong for the reason I came to Alaska, but my desire for you took over. I hope you can forgive me when I say, that can't happen again."

Duncan looked at Marlo and said, "That was hot! Are you sure we can't do that again?"

Marlo looked into his piercing green eyes and answered, "I'm not saying no to you forever, but I need to make sure what I'm doing in Alaska is the right thing for me."

Duncan smiled, "You should clarify what you mean when you say, 'you need to make sure what I'm *doing* in Alaska is the right thing for me' because when you said that, I started feeling things in places I shouldn't be feeling; like in the tightness of my jeans."

Marlo was grinning from ear to ear. "You know what I mean, Duncan."

"It's kind of hard to avoid thinking that way when you just kissed me like I was the last man on Earth."

Marlo didn't even give a second thought when she said, "Duncan, why don't you sleep with me tonight, as long as you stay on your side of the bed."

"No offense Marlo, but I think I should sleep in the chair tonight."

When Marlo looked back from heading up to the loft, Duncan gave her a smack on the bottom and she smiled.

Chapter 6

When morning arrived, the sunlight filled Marlo's cabin. She awoke with tired eyes and stretched, letting out a welcoming yawn and squeak. Sitting up in bed, forgetting Duncan had spent the night, she rubbed her eyes and it dawned on her he had. She peaked over the railing and didn't see him in the chair. She heard the shower running and grinned, *stay focused, Marlo. You can not get in the shower with Duncan James, it's forbidden. You have to buy an SUV and get rid of the Inspector Clouseau rental car. That's your goal today, buying an SUV.*

Duncan came out of the bathroom with his hair towel dried, sticking up in every direction. His face was damp and flushed, looking so inviting with a towel around his waste.

"What are we doing today?" asked Duncan thinking, *you don't even know how cute you look when I have you all frazzled.*

"Buying an SUV?" said Marlo with a sheepish grin.

Of course, no dealerships were in Seward, so without a moment to ponder they trekked up to Anchorage and went SUV hunting. They went to Mountain Ridge Auto, the dealership that Duncan knew and trusted. Walking around the lot and looking at the array of vehicles which would suit Marlo in Minnesota wouldn't be practical for Alaska.

She looked across the lot; *here comes my pushy car salesman, right now.* He was balding on top with fuzzy red curls in the back and on the sides. His skin was pale with freckles and had blonde curly hair on his arms—a stench was coming from his direction. Possibly . . . yep, a serious case of putrid body odor.

"Well now, this here beauty is the perfect car for a woman your petite size. You'd look real good driving this here vehicle," Burt said, approaching Marlo.

"Ah hey Burt, how are you doing?" asked Duncan, walking out from behind a vehicle he was looking at.

"Oh, hello Duncan, what are you doing up here?"

Burt thought he was going to try to swoon Marlo into this handy dandy car made for a woman, then quickly changed his mind.

"My friend, Marlo, needs an SUV. She's going to be staying in Alaska for a while and needs something reliable."

Marlo gave Duncan a quick glance and thought he sounded sexy, so sure and confident.

Burt is an honest car dealer, but Duncan could see he was trying to make a quick sale. *Money short this month, Burt,* was all Duncan could conjure up. Burt looked over at Marlo, feeling like a donkey's behind,

"Well Marlo, what are you thinking about buying?"

Marlo stood there with her finger on her chin and said, "See, it's just me and I want to be able to handle it, so nothing too big. I need four-wheel drive because of the snow and terrain. I'm thinking about a Jeep Wrangler. Do you have any of them?"

"I do have three Jeeps left; those are hot sellers. All are four-wheel drive. Two are automatic and one is standard. The standard has 500 miles on it because we use it sometimes, so if you choose that one, we'll give you a discount."

Discount, did I hear discount? Lead the way, Marlo thought, knowing she could benefit from the discount.

After a test drive and some paperwork Marlo was following Duncan back to Seward in her Midnight Blue 2011 Jeep Wrangler. *This is* the perfect size for me. I love it! Now, how am I going to get this back to Minnesota? I'll have to take it on the Ferry and then drive the rest of the way. That's a long way. I don't think I want to drive all that way. That's like an eight day trip. Crap!*

Back at the cabin while Duncan was building Marlo a fire, she was fixated on Duncan's body. He was a hard working man—Marlo could see that by staring at his muscles. They were pronounced in his back. She could see them moving under his shirt. He had strapping arms. His forearms flexed when he picked up each piece of wood. She saw how physically powerful his legs were. His thighs were hard and she could see the outline of his muscles through his jeans. She was distracted by his tight butt when he squatted to throw the wood into the woodstove. *How am I ever going to stay sane and keep from jumping him when he builds me fires? Get control Marlo, jeez.*

Trying to keep herself from falling over and drooling, she said, "Thank you for taking me to Anchorage today, Duncan. I'm glad you were with me or *Burt* would have tried to pull one over on me. Why do car dealers think they can pull the wool over women's eyes? I guess when it comes to the *Auto Industry* women are at a disadvantage, or I should say *some women*."

Duncan looked over his shoulder at Marlo strumming her fingers on the table, "You're welcome. Yeah, some people do try to take advantage where they shouldn't. I don't think Burt is that way, usually. I assume he just needed a sale because his cash flow is non-existent right now with the crashing economy," Duncan answered, looking up at her when he closed the door on the woodstove and adjusted the damper just right.

"Listen, I have to go into the pub tonight to do some stocking and inventory; not my favorite thing to do. I was wondering if I could come by tonight after work and climb into bed with you."

Shocked and flattered, Marlo jokingly couldn't help herself, but made Duncan feel ashamed.

"Duncan James! What do you think this is, *Goldie Locks and the Three Bears?*"

Smiling, Duncan stood there with this *pretty please* look on his face.

"Alright, if you don't want me to, I won't."

"It's not that. I just . . ." stammering, Marlo tried explaining to Duncan a piece of her rocky past, but couldn't.

"Marlo, you sure look cute when you don't know what to say. I'm starting to wonder if that's how you're luring me in."

"You think so, huh?"

"I do."

Marlo stared into his eyes and then quickly retreated to the bathroom.

But Duncan thwarted her, and with his hands on her shoulders, feeling her tremble, he asked, "Then when can I see you again?"

Even though the desire for Duncan spending the night with her at the cabin was inevitable, she felt it was too soon.

"Soon, I promise."

Marlo needed some time alone to think about her life and her happiness. She desperately sought after that connection with her parents and since she's been in Seward, she hasn't really had time to reflect.

"I'll see you soon then, Marlo Hart."

Duncan gave her a soft kiss on her plush lips and walked out of the cabin.

When Marlo heard Duncan drive off down the road she put her long North Face coat on and headed down to the river. She hasn't seen it yet and knew the sounds of Mother Nature would soothe her while trying to bring her past to the present. By revisiting her past, she knew she would feel closer to her parents and not feel as though she was forgetting them. She parked herself on the side of the bank and observed the beauty that was right outside her cabin. The river looked frigid, but beautiful. The rocks on the bottom loomed in earthy reds, blues, speckled browns and greens. She could see them through the clear, rippling water. Tall looming Cattails and grass blades were in a grouping across the river, down a little ways. Further yet, she could see the starting of a beaver dam. Marlo sat in Alaska's beauty and began thinking about her life. She asked herself, *why is being in Alaska so important? I could have come to terms with my parents' death back home. I could have had happiness with a man in Minnesota. It's almost like my Mother told me to come here, but why? Maybe she knew something I didn't or I have this feeling of her knowing something I don't. I want to be in Alaska. I want to figure out why all my relationships fail. Mom said not to worry. Maybe I should just run with that and take it one day at a time. Yep, that's what I'm going to do. Stressing over this can't be healthy.*

Heading up from the river to her cabin, Marlo surprisingly missed being in Duncan's space. Considering the idea for a moment, she decided to take a hot shower. She went inside and picked out something conservative. She turned the radio on and was singing in the shower, taking her time. Marlo dried off and leisurely brushed her hair and put her make up on. She looked in the mirror and thought, *what are you doing, Marlo? You basically just told him you weren't ready to move forward and didn't want him to spend the night. Yet, you're compelled to see him and look good for him. What is wrong with you? You're tangled in self-doubt, that's what's wrong with you. Whatever, I'm standing here naked in my bathroom having a conversation with myself. Okay . . . enough!*

Throwing on a long sleeve thermal, her favorite wool sweater, tight dark blue jeans and boots, Marlo shut the lights off, locked the door and headed to James Bros. Pub. Not wanting to give into her desires, she had to . . . *play it cool*. Marlo knew she wanted Duncan, but she didn't want the aftermath. It would start off blissfully and end tragically; that was the Marlo way.

Marlo tossed her purse on the seat and drove down the bumpy drive. When she arrived at the pub she walked in and immediately saw Duncan and a guy next to him, obviously his brother, Brady, having an intense conversation at the end of the bar. She decided to take a seat at the opposite end and patiently wait for Duncan to come to her. Duncan knew she was there and wanted to go to her, but couldn't break away from Brady. *They must be discussing bar inventory or something Brady forgot when he went to Anchorage.* She dismissed the thought when she saw Sandra and Clay over by the pool tables and proceeded to make her way over there just as a man with a purpose came walking up to her.

"Can I take this seat next to you?"

Not thinking anything of it, Marlo said, "Sure, go ahead, it's a free country."

"I haven't seen you around these parts before. Are you new in town?"

Seeing where this conversation was going, Marlo answered annoyingly, "I'm visiting for a while and I'm not sure how long I'm staying."

"Well, if you want, we could get out of here and go back to my place," putting an arm around Marlo.

"Not if you want to live to see tomorrow," Marlo said taking his arm off of her and twisting it.

Hearing a tinge of pain exhaling from the creep, Duncan thought, *what the heck is that guy doing? Obviously she's not interested, buddy.* Excusing himself from Brady, he came over to Marlo.

"Hey Marlo, anything interesting happening tonight?" he asked, handing Marlo a longneck Bud Light.

He looked at the creep with an ultimatum. The guy mumbled, "I'm outta here."

Trying to relieve Marlo of the frustration she illustrated, Duncan said with a joking smirk resting his forearms on the bar leaning into her, "Going for the older clingy men now? What, am I not good enough for you?"

Marlo was just thankful that creep took a hike.

Marlo smiled and said, "Nothing I can't handle, Duncan."

"I can see that. You handled yourself pretty damn well. I mean heck, if you twisted me up like a pretzel I would definitely be afraid," said Duncan with one eyebrow raised and a scuff.

"Uh-huh."

Quickly switching subjects, Marlo said, "Duncan, I know you don't have time right now, but maybe tomorrow morning you could stop by. I want to talk to you about a couple of things . . . if that's okay with you."

Sorting through their previous conversations, he was momentarily defeated. Maybe she wanted to talk about what she couldn't talk about earlier.

"Sure, that shouldn't be a problem. Coffee and banana nut muffins sound good to you?"

"Banana nut muffins sound delicious, Duncan. I'm going to go over and talk to Sandra quickly."

Getting off the bar stool, Marlo could see Duncan watching her as she strutted over to Sandra, giving him just enough tease to make her chuckle.

"Hey Sandra," said Marlo sitting in the chair next to her.

"I saw you talking to Duncan, how's that going?" asked Sandra with an elbow nudge.

Sandra is relentless, thought Marlo.

"Good. He drove me to Anchorage this morning to help me get my Jeep. I needed something for the winter and the rough roads."

Thank goodness Duncan was there or I would have had to endear Burt's poor selling escapades all by myself.

"I happened to see you driving the Jeep today and when I saw you get out I thought . . . no more rental car."

"Yeah, that needed to be turned in. Even though I was getting used to it, I couldn't keep it forever and besides, I was getting awkward looks from people. They were probably wondering what the heck I was doing driving that kind of car in Alaska."

"It was funny, watching you drive that little thing," said Sandra lifting her beer to take a drink.

"Sandra, can I ask you a question?"

"Sure, honey. Ask away."

"What do you think about Duncan? I know I shied away from your sad attempts to set us up," winking at Sandra, "but I'm interested now and kind of wanted to know what you think of him."

It's about time this girl got on the band wagon, Sandra thought before she answered Marlo, nonchalantly.

"Duncan? Oh, he's a diamond in the rough. You couldn't meet someone with more heart. Duncan is one of those men where women seem to take advantage of because he wears his emotions on his sleeve. He would go to the ends of the Earth to help someone out, given the chance. Duncan has had a few bumpy roads in his lifetime, but he manages to pull out of hard times with triumph. Not saying they don't try to get the best of him, but he does okay. Once you get to know him, you might see you two have more in common than you think."

Absorbing Sandra's insight, Marlo replied, "Thank you Sandra, for being honest. It's hard being in a new place and not knowing who to trust. I can see you have a good heart and are an honest person. I'm glad we met; I really am," said Marlo.

"Well Marlo, as long as you stay, we'll have you. Clay and I enjoy you as a neighbor and a friend, and I know Duncan has taken to you as well."

"How can you tell that?"

"Honey, you don't have to be a wizard to see that you and Duncan have some serious chemistry. When you walk in the room, the bar gets twenty degrees hotter from all the heat that radiates off Duncan."

Blushing with a smile, Marlo answered, "I can see Duncan has a big heart and he sure does kiss . . ."

"Wait, you guys kissed?!? How did that little unknown turn out?"

"A woman never reveals her secrets; you know that Sandra."

"I know, but come on girl. Spill the dirt! Nothing interesting ever happens around here."

"I would love to kiss and tell," Marlo said, "but I have to get back home."

Marlo was getting ready to leave and was saying good bye to Sandra. She started for the exit.

Right before Marlo reached the door to leave, Duncan caught her arm and when she turned to see who it was, looking in his eyes, she knew there was something profound. She was hooked. Hooked like a big bellied blue gill waiting to be eaten.

"Will you have this dance with me?"

On the jukebox was, 'Feels so Right' by Alabama. Looking into Duncan's eyes she didn't have to say a word. He slid his hand down her arm intertwining his fingers in between hers and walked her to the dance floor. Reaching behind her and placing his hand on the small of her back, he pulled her in close, really close. He took her other hand and put it up to his heart and held it in place while she reached up behind his neck and rested her fingertips under his button down shirt collar. With no breathing space in between, he leaned down and put his head next to hers while closing his eyes and taking in her scent; a collage of shampoo, body wash, perfume and a scent she had all of her own. It was all he could do not to take her right there on the dance floor. Marlo looked at Duncan with seriousness in her eyes.

"Duncan, why aren't you with anyone, a girlfriend or married?"

"Well, I like being single and I'm happy that way. I can do what I want and I don't have to worry about some woman trying to control me."

"Has there ever been a serious woman in your life, I mean before you decided to be single?"

Knowing he wasn't prepared to answer that, without saying a word, the song ended and Duncan thought this was the perfect time to softly kiss Marlo's lips, just a soft sweet gentle kiss.

"Thank you for the dance, Marlo."

Guiding her off the dance floor he said, "I have to get back to the bar. I'll see you tomorrow then?"

Speculating Duncan's girlfriend dodging, Marlo came up with nothing, except, maybe he had a past that he didn't want to share with her.

"Thanks for the dance. I'll see you tomorrow, good night Duncan."

Chapter 7

After the pub closed and all the people were gone, Duncan and Brady cleaned up, cashed out, locked the doors and headed home.

"I'll see you tomorrow Duncan," said Brady walking across the parking lot with his hands in his pockets and his hood up over his head.

"Yep, see you tomorrow." With a quick wave and jumping into the truck cab, Duncan was mischievously thinking, *technically, it is tomorrow*. He made a U-turn and headed over to Marlo's cabin.

Hearing a knock at the door, Marlo rolled over and with squinting eyes, tried to see the time on the clock. It was late and wondering who it could be, she murmured an expletive and descended her loft to open the door.

"Duncan? What are you doing? It's late and I was sleeping." Stepping forward and leaning in holding her face in his hands,

he kissed her fully on the mouth, embracing her with all his desire. Marlo gave into his passion and moaned a sound of pleasure that made Duncan move up on Marlo sharing with her the feeling of him hard against her.

He pulled back, and looking into her eyes with hunger, said, "Sleep sweetly, Marlo."

Before Marlo knew what happened he was driving down the road back home. Marlo, who was stationary in the wide-open doorway shocked and in disbelief, was heating all of Alaska. When she came back to reality she shivered and shut the door. *It's freezing out there.* Marlo crawled back into bed and thought, *if Duncan keeps kissing me like that, who knows what will happen.*

The next morning, with the sun shining and feeling the warmth on her face, Marlo sat on her porch steps. She was wrapped in a fleece blanket with a cup of coffee warming her hands and watching the river. It was peaceful and quiet out. The sound of the river was relaxing and comforting. She didn't want to go in and take a shower, but remembered Duncan was going to be coming over soon, bringing muffins. Just as Marlo was getting up to go in, she saw Duncan coming down the drive. *Great, my hair looks like I got into a fight with an electric fence and if I turn and run, Duncan will know I didn't want him to see me like this. Stay calm, Marlo.*

Duncan parked his truck and sauntered up to Marlo with a white pastry bag from the bakery.

"That's an interesting take on a new hairdo," Duncan said, not knowing what the heck happened.

Maybe she went crazy in the night.

"Why, thank you. I was going for the spastic rocker look. I haven't perfected it yet."

Snickering, thinking how cute she looked, he said, "It's perfect. It suits you just fine."

Trailing behind Marlo and her fuzzy purple slippers, he heard her say, "Come on in. I was hoping to have been showered before you arrived, but as you can see, I didn't get that far. Would you like a hot cup of coffee to go with a—," peeking in the bag, "Banana Nut muffin?"

"I would love a cup, thanks."

Reaching for a cup from one of the shelves above Marlo's kitchen sink and taking it to her, he noticed how beautiful she looked in her blanket and slippers. He wondered how a woman like Marlo could manage to omit all ideas of having a relationship.

"Mmm, the coffee tastes wonderful. I thrive on a good cup of Joe in the morning."

Watching Duncan drink his coffee, she was wondering about last night.

"I have a question."

"Shoot!"

Duncan said while trying to chew his muffin and not spit crumbs while answering.

"What was that kiss all about last night and stopping by so late; or should I say, early?"

She watched Duncan take a sip of his coffee and look at her over the rim with what she knew was the same feeling she was having . . . a craving to see what was under those clothes.

"I just wanted to give you a good night kiss before heading home."

Raising her eyebrows and nodding, Marlo said, "It was nice, thank you."

Duncan was in a little bit of a rush and told Marlo, "Get showered and dressed. I want to take you somewhere you haven't been."

"Should I be worried?"

"No, not at all; now, hurry up."

"I'm going. I'm going."

With a sigh, Marlo put her cup in the sink, turned off the coffee pot, went up and got a change of clothes and headed to the shower.

"Would you mind if you had company, Marlo?"

"You said I should hurry. How can I hurry if you accompany me in the shower? We'll never leave then."

"Just checking, thought I could help you wash your back or clean between your toes."

Facing away from him with a big bright smile, she headed into the bathroom, looked back at Duncan and shut the door. *Man, she's a tough nut to crack.*

Since Marlo was in the shower, Duncan went outside and lowered himself onto the steps out front while he carefully sipped his steaming cup of coffee. He looked out over the river, his eyes seeing through it where everything else around him was a blur; except for the impenetrable vision he was having. He was thriving on the Alaskan morning air. It was refreshing and revitalizing to Duncan. *I've lived here my whole life. I know this place like I know my childhood nursery rhymes. Think Duncan, think dammit! Where have you seen her before? Why can't you put thoughts of her familiarity at bay?* Tapping his foot and losing himself within his mind, going somewhere other than where he was, he couldn't hear a sound. Not a bird chirping, not a breeze wafting through the pines, not the river's natural flow. He was centered and focused, thinking of Marlo. Seeing her in Alaska stirred up bewildered thoughts, thoughts that he couldn't place. The more he saw Marlo, the more he felt the answer on the tip of his tongue. Something was trying to come forth in his mind, but Duncan couldn't get a hold of it. He couldn't figure out why he was having these unexplained feelings and thoughts; ones that pertained to Marlo and him.

Marlo opened the door and looked out. She saw Duncan sitting on the porch steps.

"There you are. I was wondering where you had gone. I knew you couldn't be too far; this place isn't that big."

Coming out of his state-of-mind, he was spooked, but refrained from reacting when he heard Marlo approach him. He didn't want to frighten her. He helped himself off the porch by placing his hand on the weathered deck and pushing himself up.

Still holding his empty cup of coffee, he said, "Hey beautiful. Wow, you look great."

Tossing her hair back with sarcasm and a little sway in her step, Marlo said, "I try."

Duncan thought, *I like my woman with a little fire and this woman is burning hot!*

"Yeah, I uh . . . was out here finishing my coffee, captivated by the flourishing view."

Looking at Marlo in her pure splendor, he thought, *how did I ever meet someone sensationally beautiful, witty and desirable?*

"Are you ready to go?" Duncan asked, signaling to his truck.

"I am. Wow, it's bright out today. I'm excited to see where you're taking me. Can you tell me or do I have to wait to find out?"

Marlo had wanted to talk to him earlier today and they didn't get a chance.

Duncan had this awe-inspiring special place that presented itself with self-belief. He had to take Marlo to his favorite spot, Kenai Fjords National Park, where the glaciers were true and confident—inspiring. And, he wanted to give Marlo the confidence to share with him what weighed down her heart.

"You have to wait, it's a surprise. Don't worry, you'll like this surprise. I promise."

It wasn't too far of a drive, but the journey made Marlo anxious and curious as to where he was taking her. The drive was breathtaking. Trees that were soaring into the sky, under them, the tops weren't visible they were so tall. There were snow covered mountains as far as the eye could see and the wildlife was a bit humbling up close. Marlo drifted with the quietness of the drive and thought, *look what I would have been missing if I never took that leap of faith and traveled to Alaska. What a shame that would have been.*

Up ahead was a dad, mom and baby moose on the side of the road in the lengthy grass, shadowed by vast mountains. Pulling on Duncan's sleeve and glowering out the window of his truck, Marlo said quickly, "Are those . . . what I think they are? Pull over, quick!" Pointing at the window, Marlo was showing him where they were.

"Do you see them . . . over there . . . by the mountain ridge?"

Marlo was staring out the window and listening to Duncan's response.

"They are one of Mother Natures' most endearing creatures. They come into Seward sometimes, walking right through town like they've always belonged there; and they do. We have to learn to co-exist with them. It's their home, too."

Marlo was fascinated.

"They are so prodigious, even the baby is colossal. How does one not feel daunt when they lay eyes on something of such stature?" Marlo asked in bewilderment. "Duncan, I've never seen anything like this in my life. I mean in real life, up close. I've never seen a moose, it's amazing. I can't even describe to you what is going through me right now."

Completely baffled, Marlo just stared as Duncan drove away and continued on with their journey to his surprise spot. He loved how excited she was.

Pressing ahead through Alaska's lands and innocent allure, Marlo was, for the first time, taking in all of Alaska's natural gifts she had to offer. Duncan peered over at Marlo from time to time and couldn't help but fall in love with the way she viewed Alaska, like it was a precious gem-stone. She presented a childlike quality and charm, promoting her excitement without a second thought as to what she looked like or how she sounded.

Approaching Kenai Fjords National Park, Duncan asked, "Are you ready to see the reason I wanted to bring you here?"

In all her excitement she exhausted, "Yes."

Marlo drifted for a moment in thought, *I wonder what I did to deserve the selfless genuine man Duncan truly is. I've never been treated like this from any man, until now. It truly is, wonderful.*

"This is Kenai Fjords National Park; because of the coastal Fjords, is how it got its name. The main reason people come here is to see the natural glaciers and the wildlife that reside here. Dolphins, humpback and orca whales, puffins, sea otters and sea lions live in the park. It's an amazing sight to see and humbling when you see a whale up close. Most of the park has to be accessed by boat. They give tours starting from Seward's boat sanctuary, but we don't need to be on a boat to see what I'm going to show you."

Spinning in a slow circle, Marlo was taking mental pictures of the panoramic view of the park, which was phenomenal.

"Come on, let's get our things. I want to take a walk with you. This is only the beginning," said Duncan.

Unpacking the truck and getting their gear, Duncan heaved a backpack over his shoulder, carrying a picnic lunch, a couple of water bottles and a blanket. He held Marlo's hand, escorting her to the path that led them where he wanted to show her some of the most magnificent glaciers Alaska exhibits.

Smelling the moss on the rock and feeling the coolness coming from the glaciers, Duncan knew Marlo was going to remember this day forever. Advancing the bend in the trail, Duncan glanced over at Marlo, taking in her amazement while they came upon one of Alaska's own natural marvels.

When they were approaching the glaciers, Marlo said to Duncan, "I'm speechless Duncan. I . . . I can't even begin to depict into words how in awe I am."

"Isn't it breathtaking? This is my favorite place in Alaska. I wanted to share it with you."

Duncan felt a warming sensation throughout his body standing next to Marlo.

"Thank you Duncan. I don't know what to say, except, thank you."

"You don't have to say anything."

They were studying each other for a moment and then Marlo broke the stare and walked over to the glacier, admiring its beauty. The face of the glacier was smooth and jagged at the same time. It looked like deep vertical ripples with crevices and had a bluish tint to it. The glacier had a shape like a Popsicle that was sucked on for a long time and never bitten into, smoothed over on top. There were several of those in a row, tapering down.

Marlo, in amazement, was gaping up at Mother Natures' wonder. With her mouth open she moved towards the glacier not paying attention to the warning signs. She was unaware of the dangers associated with them. Duncan thought, *this doesn't look good. She needs to stay back.* Duncan came up behind Marlo and grabbed her arm when she was getting dangerously close, and said,

"Marlo, be careful. You can't get too close to the glacier's face. Ice drops from them all the time. Stay back here with me and admire them from a safe distance. Besides, I want to enjoy them with you by my side."

Marlo felt like a child, naïve and innocent, but stupid because she should have thought of the dangers. She stood there with her hands in her pocket.

Duncan could see the embarrassment in her eyes and said, "I'm sorry, I should have told you that before we arrived here."

"No, I'm sorry. I . . . I didn't realize . . . of course I will stay back here with you. I had a pre-lapse in judgment. I obviously wasn't thinking."

"It's okay. We just need to be careful."

Holding her around her waist and taking in her scent, he looked around and said,

"There are but a few people here. Usually it's not too busy during the week. Most of the tourists visit the park on the weekends. What do you say we go set up the blanket and eat lunch over there?"

Pointing to a lush grassy spot on a raised hill, Duncan said, "We'll have a full view of the glaciers."

"Sounds wonderful, Duncan. Thank you for bringing me here. It's just beautiful. I'm blown away by how epic Alaska is—it's phenomenal."

Duncan and Marlo picked a special spot and laid their blanket down on the grass. He opened his backpack and took out their picnic lunch.

"What did you bring us?" asked Marlo, peeking into the backpack.

Duncan laughed at her curiosity.

"I packed us two turkey and roast beef sandwiches with Amish Swiss cheese and mustard, cut up fruit and pretzels. I hope you like turkey and roast beast."

Marlo started laughing at his 'roast beast' comment and Duncan said, "What, what are you laughing at?"

"You're just funny. You said roast beast like it was a natural thing to say."

He smiled at her and loved how she was responsive to his sense of humor.

"Yeah, I guess it did just come out."

While they were eating and appreciating how powerful and humbling the glaciers were, Duncan said,

"Glaciers are a true work of nature's art."

"They sure are and we get to enjoy it," said Marlo. They watched how the sunlight was blanketing them.

"Do you see how the glaciers hang in the balance? Well, they release massive ice shards and snow at a moments notice. That's why I was nervous when you were closing in on them earlier."

She smiled up at him. *He worries for my safety and packs picnic lunches, hmm, I could get used to this.* Tear drop shaped water droplets were dripping from the base of the glaciers high above. Marlo and Duncan sat close to each other and enjoyed their romantic lunch while appreciating each others' company in one of Alaska's most sought out places.

A little later when it was cooling down Marlo looked into Duncan's beautiful greens and asked, "Duncan, how long have you had this planned?"

He looked at her, taking a sip of his water.

"Yesterday when we were heading up to Anchorage to buy your Jeep, I was watching you take in the landscape. It was like watching a sixteen year old stare at their first car. I thought you would appreciate this little trip to the park."

Studying him, thinking how grateful she was, she couldn't help but think what an amazing man Duncan was. He was above anyone she's ever met and knew he was being his true self and not trying to make her think he was someone he wasn't.

"I don't know what to say. I don't think I've ever appreciated anything more. Seeing this is magical to me, knowing this is nature at its finest. I'm astonished by this magnificent sight. Thank you Duncan, thank you so much!"

She glowed with gratitude. All Duncan could see in Marlo was an incredible woman. During their time together picking at their lunch, Duncan was reluctant to mention that she wanted to talk to him this morning about something, but he did anyways.

"Marlo, can I ask you something?"

"Sure Duncan, what is it?"

"Last night at the pub, you wanted me to come over because of something, what was it?"

Marlo realized she did do that and said, "Right, I did say that. Um, well, there are some things I would like you to know because I feel we are becoming good friends."

She looked down at the blanket while her fingers manipulated the softness. *She's nervous about what she's going to say,* thought Duncan.

"I want to be straight forward and honest with you about my past."

Staring at Marlo with a serious expression, he said, "I'm listening, Marlo, but I want you to know, if there's something you don't want to tell me, that's okay."

"Thank you Duncan, I understand and I appreciate that." Knowing Duncan was giving her an opportunity to not be forthright, if there was something she didn't want to mention, like her parents, then she wouldn't. However, Marlo wanted to be honest with him.

She breathed in heavily and said, "I've had some unfortunate events happen to me in the past that may have altered my ability to have a healthy relationship." Duncan was looking at Marlo with concern; she continued.

"Four years ago my parents died in a car accident and I never really grasped what losing my parents had done to me, if anything at all. I'm not quite sure. My sister Clare and I went to therapy for a year following their death and she has fully recovered with the help of her husband, Jack, and their two children, Dilly and Bentley. I, however, seem to be sabotaging my own path to happiness."

Patiently listening to Marlo explain her past, he couldn't help but feel overwhelmed with sadness. He felt for her on a deeper level than he expected.

"Every relationship I've had since the accident has been destroyed by me because of my prolonged anger due to my parents' death. The men I have dated did not understand why I took my anger out on them, and neither did I; I still don't. It was never my intention, but I always felt they never understood me fully because they didn't look deep enough."

Duncan looked at Marlo, listening to her.

"They never cared to talk to me about how I might have been feeling a certain day, brought on by thoughts I was having about my parents. They just wanted to put my loss aside and focus on the present. However, when a person hasn't dealt with the trauma they've experienced, there's no way that person can move on." Marlo breathed a sigh. "There is something that hits my heart like a wrecking ball, though. My Mom used to always tell me, "Marlo, the right man for you will come along when you least expect it." Well . . . every time I met someone after the accident, I always assumed, *maybe this man is the man for me*. Then, two three four weeks into the relationship, sometimes a month or two, it would start. They didn't understand me. They didn't know how to talk to me. They didn't try to figure me out. They just said, "Forget this, it's too complicated," and that's it relationship over. I've basically given up dating because I know it's not who I date, it's me."

Soaking up everything Marlo said, Duncan pulled Marlo into his arms and held her with more authentic affection than she's had in a long time and with that tears began to fall.

Marlo gave into Duncan's affection and whispered with a raspy voice, "I'm sorry for getting upset. I haven't had a *real* man in my life since my Father and I was unaware of how this conversation was going to affect me."

Feeling completely helpless and unsure of what to say, Duncan quickly gathered his emotions and words.

Holding her hands in his, he said, "Marlo, your feelings mean everything to me. I understand how a man could be without words for something so powerful. I understand how a man would be without comfort. It's a tragedy some can't wrap their heads around, but I can tell you one thing for sure. I will bear your loss with you and together we will overcome the feeling of the impossible. You will feel free to love again, I promise."

Holding Marlo in his embrace and feeling the tension and sadness leave her body; Duncan felt her suffering go into him. He wanted to take away her pain. Together, they would understand Marlo's ache and rebuild her strength. In tears, Marlo knew the man who was holding her was the man her mother was hoping she would one day find and forever love and be loved.

After a few moments, Marlo gained her composure and together they packed up their picnic lunch, empty water bottles, and blanket. Duncan was looking at Marlo with a devilish smile,

"What do you say we head home and get naked under the covers and wrestle? I'll pin you down so you can't move and then tickle you until you can't breathe."

Duncan started twitching his eyebrows and laughing wholeheartedly.

"Duncan, you're a freak! You better not or you're not coming over!"

Laughing at her and falling over himself, he started chasing her, tripping over his feet trying to get to her. He loved watching her laugh and smile and knew they were going to get beyond this.

Chapter 8

On the way home from Kenai Fjords National Park, Marlo fell asleep in the truck, resting her head on Duncan's lap. Driving into the setting sun, Duncan noticed her hand was tucked under his thigh. He loved feeling like he was a part of something that holds promise. He knew he was the man she's been searching for, but never found, until now.

Sharing something as intimate as Marlo's loss brought forth thoughts of his own life. Knowing he had a past that weighed heavy on *his* heart, he wasn't ready to share his sadness with Marlo, not just yet. So, he thought about his past relationships instead. They weren't all fireworks and the tightrope of happiness. He had some trying times. But Duncan, unlike Marlo, repressed his emotions and didn't want to fault himself for failing. He never liked to lose and because he never found the right person, he felt defeated. He dismissed dating for several years. He was content with where he was in his life, but since meeting Marlo, he's hoping for a second chance.

Marlo started to wake up with a sense they were close to home. She sleepily sat up and glanced over at Duncan. She had a wave of calmness come over her. The feelings she shared with Duncan at the park would only bring them closer. Although, she felt uneasy, thinking this could result in another failed relationship, she still kept an open mind while staying optimistic, and was well aware of Duncan's genuineness. She pushed the uneasy feeling aside.

Pulling up to Marlo's cabin, Duncan left the engine idling.

"I have to go to the pub tonight. Brady is expecting me. What are your plans for later this afternoon and tonight?" inquired Duncan.

"I have to get in touch with Clare and my best friend, Mandi. I haven't talked to them in a few days and promised them I would give them a call. Then, I might see if Sandra wants to go to the pub and have a beer or eat dinner. I've really grown to like her, Duncan. We get along really well and she speaks her mind. I like that about her."

"You haven't been around Sandra long enough to like how her mind *says whatever it wants* and her mouth doesn't hold back, either."

Marlo thought Duncan was just adorable in every sense of the word.

"Well, it sounds like you've conjured up a healthy plan, little miss."

Getting ready to leave for work, Duncan couldn't resist feeling the softness of Marlo's lips against his. Without saying a word, he pressed his lips against hers, savoring the flavor of her mouth. Duncan could feel Marlo melt with every touch and every caress of his tongue. Releasing her and feeling her warmth beneath his touch, he figured he better get out of there before taking Marlo into her cabin and undressing her while kissing every inch of her body.

"Baby, I have . . ."

"Baby? Aren't pet names a little pre-mature?"

"No. Do you not want me to call you baby?"

"You can, I just—that's fine. I like it."

"You sure?"

"Yup."

"Positive?"

"Yup."

"Okay then . . . *baby*. I have to go, but I'll see you when you stop by the pub," Duncan said while winking.

Marlo leaned over and gave Duncan a soft kiss before jumping out of the truck. She looked back watching him drive off. *How did this all happen again? How did I go against my own plan of avoiding men at all costs?* Marlo let out a soft laugh and went inside.

Before heading to Sandra and Clay's place, Marlo thought, *I need to call Mandi. She's going to wonder why I haven't talked to her lately.* Marlo poured herself a cup of coffee that was still in the pot from earlier that morning and heated it up. She nestled herself in her worn leather chair and covered her feet up with a handmade blanket that lay over the back of the chair. She dialed Mandi's number.

"Hey Mandi, its Marlo, how's it going?"

"Great! I have been looking forward to your phone call. I have so much to tell you. Are you sitting down?"

"I am actually, what's up? Why do you sound so energized?" Curious to what Mandi was going to say, she sat there hanging on to every word and to her surprise, was exuding happiness,

"Are you kidding, seriously?" asked Marlo.

"I'm totally serious. My plane leaves tomorrow and I'll be there in a couple of days. I was so excited, I wanted to wait for your call to tell you, but I thought I was going to have to take matters into my own hands and call you if you didn't call me before I departed."

"You're serious; you're actually coming to visit me? This is beyond anything I expected to hear from you today. I can introduce you to everyone I've met. You'll love where I'm staying."

"I know. It's a well-deserved break from all the work I've been doing at the firm. I'm so tired. I can't wait to just relax," Mandi said, while neatly folding her sweater and laying it in her suitcase.

"I'm so excited for you to meet Duncan. I never finished explaining to you how we met because Sandra came up to me and I had to go, but he's the guy I met in Seward. When I got off the ferry I approached him, asking him if he knew of a relatively cheap place to stay. He sent me where I'm staying now. It's called Birch Cabins. It's a quiet place just outside of Seward. The people that own Birch Cabins, Sandra and Clay, are the friendliest people you could ever meet. I'm going over there to invite Sandra to the pub down the street, after we're done talking. We have dinner there some nights and its fun to socialize with the locals." *And, admire the sexy and amazing owner,* Marlo thought to herself.

"Okay, this is what we'll do. Since you have plans and I have to finish packing, I'll let you go and then we can pick up where we left off when you pick me up from the airport, deal?" Mandi asked Marlo, wanting to get the heck out of Dodge.

"It's a plan. See you soon, Mandi."

"Ditto."

After Mandi hung up the phone, Marlo was completely stunned. She sat in the chair with the phone still pressed to her ear and the dial tone was deafening. She was thrilled that her best friend was traveling all the way from the Twin Cities to see her. *I can't even fathom that Mandi is going to be arriving in Alaska in a couple of days. This is wild, but exciting at the same time. I can't wait!* Leaping from the chair, she put her empty enamel coffee cup in the sink and went up to the loft to change into her comfy clothes. She wanted to get to Sandra's before she made plans for dinner. Marlo quickly fixed her hair, looked in the mirror, and shut the door.

Trying to hide her enthusiasm, Marlo knocked on Sandra's cabin door with a sense of urgency because of her newly found excitement. She stood, waiting impatiently for Sandra to answer the door. She was tapping her foot and looking around patting her thighs with her hands. Marlo thought, *so much for trying to hide my excitement, I'm doing a terrible job.*

Opening the door, Sandra said with surprise, "Hey Marlo, I've been wondering where you've been. What have you been up to? Come on in. I was just making myself a cup of tea. Would you like a cup?"

"No, thank you," Marlo said scoping out Sandra and Clay's cabin. She noticed how beautifully decorated it was. There was dark, smooth, leather furniture in the living room and pictures on the wall. Above the large rectangular oak farm table was a deer antler chandelier casting a soft glow that filled the kitchen. She also noticed marbled granite counter tops and knotty pine ceilings that made her feel she was in the woods. Marlo couldn't help but wish she lived here, instead. "You and Clay have a beautiful home. I love how you decorated it."

"Thank you. It's larger than the other cabins, but we live here all year round. We like it because it's cozy and quiet. How's your cabin, do you like it?"

"I do . . . I love it. I'm adapting to the space. It's reduced in size compared to my apartment, but it works for me."

Sandra sat at the kitchen table and waved Marlo over, sipping her tea. Marlo took a seat across from Sandra and struggled to withhold her excitement, knowing of Mandi's arrival. Also, she wanted to see Duncan and she was famished. She had a lot on her mind.

"Sandra, I was wondering, I'm heading up to James' Bros. Pub. Do you want to join me for dinner and a beer? I would really enjoy your company right now."

"That's exactly what I want to do, how did you know?"

With a wink and a wave of her hand, she said, "Just one second, I'll get my shoes and we can go."

The pub wasn't all that busy like it was Saturday night. There were a few younger guys playing pool at one table and a handful up at the bar with their girlfriends or wives. Duncan, not surprisingly at all, looked sexy as ever behind the bar. He was dressed in a long sleeve dark blue button down rolled at the wrists, faded jeans and his cream colored Stetson. Taking a quick glance at Marlo, he smiled. She returned the smile and thought, *that smile could bring a crowd to its knees*. He strayed from her and continued wiping down the bar with a white wash rag dipped in bleach, vaguely permeating the air and washing bar glasses for the night crowd. Brady was busy bringing up cases of beer from the basement to restock the coolers under the bar.

Looking over, he shouted to Sandra and Marlo, "Hey pretty ladies, come on up to the bar and let me pour you a cold one."

Taking his advice, they slowly swayed to the bar with the intention of turning heads.

Marlo was observing who was in the pub and Sandra shouted over the jukebox, "You read our minds."

"What'll you have Marlo?" Duncan asked, leaning on the bar with his mouth peaked the corners and staring into Marlo's eyes.

"Hey *baby*," Marlo said with a seductive stare and a moonlight tone coming from her parted lips. "I'll have a Bud Light in a bottle, please," she said glancing up through her dark lashes at Duncan.

He was highly aware of the teenage twinge that was taking over his body and a rush of blood flow in the one place he needed relief every time Marlo occupied his space. He thought to himself, *if I don't get control of this situation and my tight jeans, I'm not going to make it until closing.*

Using a bottle opener, Duncan popped the top off of Marlo's Bud Light with a swift motion.

He looked at Marlo and said, "Nice."

"Now, why does she get asked what she wants, first?"

Sandra pointed at Marlo with a thumb jester and a smile, laughing at Duncan.

"Of course you ask Marlo first."

Smiling deviously, Sandra mumbled, "Love birds."

"Hey now . . . I was just waiting for you to get situated, *Sandra*."

Feeling proud, Sandra accomplished her mission to get a rise out of Duncan.

Raising her eyebrow, Sandra replied with sarcasm in her voice, "Sure you were, Duncan." Then, she turned to Marlo, and said, "I'm going to head over to talk to Brady and give you and this gorgeous man some time alone."

Sandra grabbed her beer and walked to the other end of the bar. "How are you Brady? You and Duncan seem to have some down time. It's not busy by the looks of it."

Brady was stocking the coolers with beer glancing at Marlo and Duncan, admiring the newly found relationship between them.

"It's one of those slower nights; gives us time to restock and socialize. Hey Sandra, I have a question for you," glancing back at Duncan and Marlo.

"I'm listening," Sandra told him leaning her elbows on the bar and moving in to get a closer listen.

"How does a beautiful woman like Marlo just appear out of nowhere and of all people, Duncan, my horse's ass of a brother, get the girl? Life just doesn't play fair."

"True. How did that happen?"

Mocking Brady and enjoying his envy for wanting something much the same, Sandra knew Brady would find *his* true love one day; it was just a matter of time.

She couldn't help saying, "Well Brady, eventually you'll find someone who will put up with you and your stubbornness."

Brady displayed his annoying boyish expression. Sandra laughed so hard because she knew Brady was ready to jump over the bar and take her down.

"What do you know?" Brady responded with a little feistiness and smirk.

"Brady, you'll find someone. It just hasn't happened yet, but it will. The right woman will come and you'll know it as soon as you see her."

"I hope you're right because I'm about to burst."

Sandra and Brady sat there talking and laughing for the next half hour or so while Marlo and Duncan were curious to what was making them laugh.

Finally, Duncan shouted down to them, "The peanut gallery is being kind of loud down at the end of the bar! This place isn't that big."

Throwing a balled up bar napkin at Duncan, Brady shouted back, "Whatever, slacker! Look at me slaving over here while you flirt with that cute little thing."

Marlo smiled at Brady trying to mask the feeling of embarrassment and her face glowing scarlet red.

Marlo walked over to Sandra and Brady and said, "You mind if I steel Sandra from you?"

"Not at all, she's all yours."

"Thanks Brady."

Marlo turned to Sandra and asked, "Do you want to get a seat before they're all taken?"

"That's a good idea. Let's go."

Sandra and Marlo found a seat in the corner by the front window and were thinking about what to order for dinner. They both opened their menus to see what was appetizing. Sandra knew it was taco night. Two for a dollar and all the fixings you wanted.

"Can't pass up taco night . . . they're cheap and tasty," Sandra said with her mind set on eating four of them.

Marlo didn't know what she wanted to have for dinner, but she was thinking tacos seemed pretty good at this point and didn't want Sandra to wait for her while she tried to decide what she was in the mood for.

She figured, *what the hell,* "Tacos for me tonight, as well."

"You won't regret it. Trust me."

Sandra looked up at Marlo and reached out for her arm.

"Since you asked me to be your dinner date, I want you to know you appear to have this, *'I'm going to run down the street in my panties, screaming if I don't get out what I want to say,* expression on your face."

"What?" asked Marlo, thinking, *is it that obvious?*

"Seriously, you look like you're going to turn inside out. What is on your mind?"

"Well, since you asked, I am pretty stoked. My best friend Mandi, from Minnesota, is coming to Alaska to visit me. I just found out tonight before I came over to get you."

"That's why you had the bug-eyed look. Just so you know . . . it doesn't suit you, but it is kind of funny. It was hard to ignore."

"Shut up! I did not. Did I?"

"You did."

"I'm sorry if you had to endure that. I will try to relax. I have to say Sandra, that I was really fortunate to find a place to stay and to meet you and Clay. You guys have been really great and I just want to say, thank you."

"Well, Clay and I are happy to have met you. If it wasn't for you asking Duncan directions, we would never have been introduced. How are you and Duncan doing? From the looks of it, it seems like you guys have become close friends." Seeing Marlo's eyes light up like Yankee Stadium at the sound of his name, and her face turning the color of the Sierra Desert at sunset, she could guess . . . pretty good. Sandra wanted all the details of this brewing romance. "Would you like to share some of the juicy details? I can see you are overjoyed being here in the presence of Duncan. You can't stop smiling when I mention his name."

Marlo knew that was true even though she didn't want to admit it. "Well, I'm not sure how this *thing* is going to pan out because I didn't have any expectations of pursuing a relationship when I arrived in Alaska. I mean, the whole reason for coming here was to re-evaluate my life, and most importantly, reconnect with something that I have yet to come to terms with from my past."

"I understand. You'll do what's best for you, but I have to say . . . Duncan is a serious catch, if you know what I mean. I'm going to flag Duncan down. It's time to order our tacos."

Duncan was *trying* to stay busy and replace the anxiousness he was feeling with Marlo in the bar. He kept fleeting a look here and there, trying to avoid being seen. He was desperately in love with this woman. Nothing was stopping him and he was going to look like a total idiot if he didn't get his emotions under wraps.

"Duncan, Marlo and I would like an order of six tacos. We're starving."

"I'll let Brady know. They'll be out in a few minutes."

"Thanks Duncan."

When Sandra was walking back to the table she noticed Marlo in a daze.

"What are you thinking about, Marlo?"

Marlo came back to reality when she heard Sandra speak. "Truthfully Sandra, I'm head over heels for Duncan. I'm trying to keep in mind the reason I'm here and not throw myself at him, but it's difficult. Every guy I've dated jumped ship for reasons I don't dare mention at this point. However, Duncan and I did have a thorough conversation about it and he only expressed empathy and assurance."

Listening to Marlo explain her situation, Sandra couldn't help but wonder why Marlo was holding back, but knew one day when she was ready, would share with her what she couldn't now.

"I'm sure you've already observed this from Duncan, but he's far from the other men you've dated. From what I can see, he's completely nuts for you. You should really liberate yourself and just allow Duncan into your life." Sandra was reading Marlo's curious expression and then asked, "What would be the worst thing that could happen if you let Duncan into your life, exclusively?" Sandra asked.

Marlo knew she had a good point.

Thinking about that, she didn't have an answer for Sandra. She could feel her life crumbling at the thought of another relationship fed into the grinder because of her inability to deal with the loss of her parents.

Marlo tossed her hand in the air suggesting 'I don't know.' "I feel cursed," she said quietly to herself.

Sandra knew Marlo was in a tough place right now. *If I could talk to Marlo about what's interfering with her relationships, maybe we could come up with a solution together and understand what's preventing her from giving her and Duncan a shot.*

"Marlo, I think for the short time you've been here, we've become good friends. I want to be able to help you understand what you're going through. Maybe, you would benefit from an older . . . not much older, woman's wisdom. I'm here for you if you want to trust me with your uncertainty."

Marlo took a brief moment to contemplate what Sandra said.

"I do. It's a long story, though, and I don't want to bother you with my unresolved issues."

"Talk to me Marlo. We've got all night."

Marlo began to fill Sandra in with the details of her past. After hearing Marlo's story, Sandra had a heart sinking feeling in her stomach for Marlo. *I can't imagine what this poor girl has been through and no one, but her sister to share it with. Even though her sister has moved on and accepted the way things are, Marlo hasn't.*

"Marlo, I'm so sorry to hear about your parents, but would they want you feeling this way? Walking around unfulfilled because you haven't found the one you should spend the rest of your life with? Maybe you have. Duncan is a wonderful man and if your mother were here, I think she would welcome him with open arms."

Sandra made another good point. My parents wouldn't want me dragging my feet and avoiding happiness.

"I have something I have to do, Sandra. Hang on one second . . . I'll be back."

Marlo stood up, pushed in her chair, and confidently walked up to Duncan by the bar. She stood on the bars' foot rest, hopped up and slid her butt on the bar top and swiveled her hips so her legs were dangling in front of Duncan. Marlo wrapped her legs around Duncan's thighs and pulled him into her. Sliding her hands up behind his neck and into the thickness of his hair, she looked at him and whispered, "This is long overdue." She looked into his eyes and saw how hungry he was to have her sweet tasting mouth on his. She went in and devoured him, tasting his sweetness and absorbing the passion that was flooding his veins. Feeling the heat between them, she knew his response was complimenting her yearning. Slowly departing lips and giving a little tug on his bottom lip, Duncan looked at her with wonder and wanting more.

"What was that all about? I mean . . . I liked it, but it was unexpected."

"Life is full of the unexpected, embrace it. I'll see you later," Marlo said as she swirled around, hopped off the bar and started walking back towards Sandra, smiling. Marlo whipped out her lip gloss and started to smooth a shiny soft pink layer onto her lips since Duncan kissed her lips clean.

"Maybe sooner than later," Duncan shouted to her quickly.

Turning her head around while walking away, she mouthed, "Maybe."

All Duncan could think was, *holy hell, I want that woman.*

Going back to the table where Sandra was, she took a seat, and thought, *that was nice. I need to take control more often.* Sandra leaned into the table, scooting forward with her mouth still open.

What she thought was going to be a brief pub porn flick, she said, "Now that's what I'm talking about, taking matters into your own hands."

"I know. I couldn't help myself."

Brady stood at the bar thinking, *where the hell is my kiss? I want that, too.* Scanning the bar, he didn't see any women that matched up to Marlo. *Nope. Not that one. Uh-uh. Hell no! Oh, cripes, I'll never find someone.* Duncan noticed his brothers' anguish and put a hand on his shoulder. He beamed, "Soon Brady, soon." Patting his arm, Duncan walked away, laughing under his breath.

Coming home from a long, but stimulating night at the pub, Marlo hunkered down for the evening in her charming and cozy cabin. She put the outside light on. The soft brightness cast a glow onto the house, making for a storybook feel. Warmth filled her cabin in the pines with the sweet scent of an oak and northern pine mixture coming from the wood stove, along with the aroma of the cabin itself. Marlo climbed the ladder to her loft and retrieved what her nightly attire would consist of . . . light blue sweats, fuzzy wool socks and her fuzzy, purple slippers. Then, she headed to the bathroom for a warm, relaxing shower. She set her clothes on the top of the toilet seat and turned the shower on to warm the water. Waiting for the water to heat up, she looked into the mirror, running her hands down her face. She watched her eyes deform into what some people would refer to as a funny face, and sighed. Marlo pulled the shower curtain back and stepped in, letting the water droplets cascade down her soft, supple skin. She turned and felt the water fill her hair while it smoothed over and lying in a 'V' shape against her back, she relaxed into herself.

After a long, well-deserved shower, she walked into the kitchen and made herself a cup of Earl Grey Tea. Marlo added a little sugar and milk and called it good. Sinking into her favorite and only leather chair, she took a sip of her hot tea and laid her head back, staring at the ceiling. Finally, she had a moment to reflect.

Chapter 9

Drifting into the past and remembering the day like it was yesterday, both Clare and Marlo were anticipating their parents return and then the phone rang. They received a phone call from a Dr. Scott Linster. Clare spoke to the doctor and he briefly informed her of what happened, but wouldn't provide them with any more information over the phone. He told them to fly to Anchorage immediately. It was a long flight to Alaska. Marlo and Clare were unsure of what happened exactly, but instinct told them otherwise. They knew their parents were in a car wreck leaving Seward, heading to Anchorage for their flight home.

    Tears slowly filled Marlo's eyes, reliving the moment four years ago. She thought back to when she and Clare arrived at the hospital in Anchorage. She remembered them urgently trying to find the information desk to locate what floor their parents were on; both of them were crying and out of sorts. A staff member from the information desk informed them to head up to the third floor and go to the nurse's station. Heading to the elevator, Marlo looked at Clare with a, *'I can't believe this is happening'* expression, and pushed the round plastic circle No. 3 button. Both were apprehensive about what news they were going to receive involving the accident and their parents, but wanted answers. Upon exiting the elevator, they walked down the hall and approached the nurse's station. They identified who they were and why they were at the hospital. The nurse told them to have a seat in the waiting room and the doctor would speak to them in a few minutes. Trying to get comfortable in the most uncomfortable chairs, listening to the endless turning of magazine pages crinkling as they were flipped, and Barry Manilow over the sound system, Marlo had to get up and pace. Tears and blotches of red stained her face.

She went to the window and leaned her head against it, and said, "I can't believe this is happening to us. Why, why is this happening to us, Clare?"

"I don't know, Marlo. Come sit down with me."

Marlo walked over to Clare and sat in the chair next to her.

"I know this is the most difficult thing we've ever had to face, but we can't let this separate us. We have to do this together," said Clare worried about Marlo.

"I know, Clare. We will."

Marlo leaned over and rested her head on Clare's shoulder.

Waiting for only a few minutes which felt like hours, the doctor approached them calmly and soft spoken. He told them to follow him to his office, where they could have some privacy. Marlo remembered asking repeatedly, "I want to see my parents. Where are they? I want to see them, now!"

Clare, trying to soothe Marlo, held her hand, and said, "Let's hear what the doctor has to say."

Marlo took a sip of her tea and wiped at her salty tears. Wandering into her thoughts again and dismissing the tears, she remembered it . . . clear as a bell.

Marlo heard the doctor's words, "I'm sorry to have to tell you this," looking down and hating this part of his job, "but both of your parents didn't make it. Your father died instantly at the scene and your mother died in the helicopter being airlifted here. I'm so, so sorry. We tried everything we could."

Clare stared into the doctor's eyes, unable to speak, and Marlo, unable to move, cried, as if she were a small child.

The doctor felt their sadness envelope him, and said, "I know this is going to be difficult, but both of you need to start making arrangements for your parents' funeral. We will arrange for them to fly home with you to Minnesota. I'm so sorry for your loss."

Leaving the doctor's office, they cradled each other and comforted one another until they could compose themselves. They spoke with the proper staff members and made arrangements for their flight home. On their way out of the hospital, after a grueling conversation with a few staff members, she remembered a man walking past them in the hallway with a distressed look on his face. She remembered looking at him and thinking, *he must have lost someone, too.* He briefly glanced up at Marlo to show his condolences, and kept walking.

Coming back to the present, Marlo sat in contentment for a couple of hours remembering that day and how it affected her; endless jobs, countless relationships, mistakes upon mistakes. She felt completely alienated. Thinking how different her life would have been if her parents were still living, she knew they would not want her feeling sorry for herself. They would want her to be strong, build a life worth living, and not give up. She misses her parents deeply, and the advice and comfort they would give when she was in need of their help and guidance. But, just as if they were here, she remembered the one thing her mother always reminded her of, and that was Duncan.

"He's the one Mama. He's the one."

Sensing her mother's love fulfilling her, Marlo fell asleep feeling the warmth of the fire on her feet in her warm leather chair.

Waking to the sounds of squirrels barking and wrestling in the leaves, playing and the river flowing over mossy rocks, Marlo felt alive and rejuvenated. She was ready to conquer the world. She was ready to see Duncan.

Marlo was sitting on her porch, wrapped in a wool striped blanket with a steaming cup of coffee in her hand. While making a plan in her head, she didn't notice Duncan driving up the road. He parked his truck beside the house and Marlo looked up, startled.

"The shear presence of me got you all jittery?" Duncan asked, with a skip in his step, crunching sticks beneath his shoes when he walked.

"Duncan, it's you. Thank goodness, I've . . . I've . . ."

"I know . . . you missed my devilish look and my hint of fish scent, right?"

"Yes." Marlo smiled, "I . . . I missed you. I know we haven't known each other long, but I do. And, I'm so happy you're here."

Hugging him with passion and knowing she felt safe in his arms, she just couldn't let him go.

"What has gotten into you, girl? You act like you haven't seen me in two weeks."

Wondering what has happened between last night and this morning, Duncan was clueless. She was acting like he was going to disappear or something.

"Well, it feels like two weeks, Duncan."

She wanted to tell him everything she thought about last night and decided against it. She didn't want to push her feelings onto him and she didn't want to scare him. This was something she needed to keep to herself.

"Come in, I made some coffee. Would you like some? It's still hot."

Seeing Duncan made her feel whole. She felt alive and ready for anything.

"I would love some with sugar, but not from the bowl . . . from your lips."

Standing behind Marlo with his arms around her, she poured him a cup of coffee. She added a sprinkle of sugar and few dribbles of cream and turned towards him. Giving him the cup, she was holding back tears and kissed him.

"Here Duncan, be careful, the cup is hot."

"Are you okay, Marlo?" Duncan asked with concern. "Oh sure . . . of course I am. Why do you ask?"

Trying to disguise what she was really feeling, she turned to give herself a second to compose and not show any signs of vulnerability and weakness.

"Well, you looked like you were going to cry."

"Nope, I'm fine. Let's go outside and enjoy the crisp freshness of the morning air."

Opening the door and walking outside on the porch, Marlo stood up against the railing and Duncan stood behind her.

"I would love to stay here if I were to visit Alaska. I sent you to the perfect spot."

Duncan smiled from behind Marlo because of his knack for sarcasm.

Marlo could sense his sarcasm and loved that about him, but instead of joking back she said, "You did well, Duncan. I don't think I would have found a better place on my own."

He gently soothed her shoulder with his left hand while holding his coffee cup in his right.

After taking a sip he said, "Wow, the river is beautiful. You have a wonderful view from your cabin and the mountain behind it just makes it all the better."

"I know . . . it is beautiful, isn't it?"

Both of them stood for a moment, pleased with the view. Then slowly turning Marlo around to face him, Duncan held her chin and tilted it up to him, and said, "Not as beautiful as you, love." Lowering his lips to hers, he softly kissed Marlo, attentively. He moved his mouth over hers with purpose and truth. Duncan wrapped his arms around her shoulders and waist pulling her into him. She was ready and willing to take this leap of faith and she gave into his kiss.

Guiding Marlo backwards to the front door, still holding onto her, he turned the knob and led her into the cabin. Shutting the door behind him, he continued to claim her mouth, exploring her with his tongue, making her moan in her throat. They could feel the warmth of each other's breath, playing with each other's lips and teasing each other with their tongues.

Duncan whispered, "I need you and I want you. You drive me crazy. I can't take it anymore," on Marlo's parted lips waiting for an answer. Staring into his hungry dark luring eyes, Marlo responded to him without words. He slowly reached around the back of her neck and intertwined his fingers in her full head of luscious flowing hair. Pulling her head back gently exposing her neck, he began kissing her with intent. Working his way down, he softly filled his hands with her breasts. He was moving over the buttons on her shirt, opening them as if they weren't even there. Pleasantly pleased, seeing her through her peach colored lace, he wanted to ravish her. She looked amazing.

Undoing her lace bra, he lowered it off her shoulders. Duncan gently caressed his thumb over the hardness of her nipple, kissing her deep and long. She was tingling everywhere. They started up the ladder towards the loft undressing each other. Duncan picked Marlo up and wrapped her legs around him. Holding onto her, he lowered her onto the bed and remained on top of her, moving her espresso colored hair with a delicate touch from her face and lips. Tantalizing her with his tongue, he moved over one breast then the other.

He saw how beautiful and radiant her body was. He slowly moved down her soft sensuous skin, past her belly button and to the inside of her thigh, working his way over to the one place he was dying to taste. When he hit the right spot she arched her back and pushed into him, feeling incredible. She started rocking and a few seconds later she moaned, while grabbing the sheets. He knew she was ready. She was sweet and totally decadent. Kissing his way up to her lips, he heard her panting and her labored breaths, waiting to be kissed. Running her hands up his muscular arms and shoulders, around his neck, down his back where the muscles rippled and over his taunt butt, she opened herself up to Duncan and guided him in.

Instantly emotions were running high. Duncan kissed Marlo with passion she never even knew existed, until now. He wanted to love her the way she should have been loved a long time ago. He moved over her, kissing her lips, playing with her tongue, and tasting her neck. Together, they moved in rhythm with one another, paying attention to each other's bodies. They fit perfectly. Feeling Marlo ready to orgasm again, he waited and solely focused on her. After hearing an intense moan escape her, he kissed her and watched her feel incredible then focused on himself. She was moving her hips, listening to him climbing. She was manipulating her hips under him so he didn't have to work as hard. Reaching climax he let out a moan and a sigh. He smiled down on her and kissed her sweetly.

He held her in his arms, their legs intertwined, embracing each other and then said, "I know this might sound *pre-mature*, but I'm in love with you, Marlo."

She looked at him and said, "And, I am in love with you, Duncan."

Marlo froze in place.

"What's the matter, Marlo? You look like you just got caught by Brady in your lace panties, which I think are the sexiest panties I've ever seen."

"Duncan!"

"What, what's wrong?"

Marlo was thinking she missed Mandi at the airport.

"Oh, no! What time is it? I have to go to the airport and pick up Mandi. She should be there soon!"

Jumping out of bed, Marlo frantically grabbed some clothes and headed to the shower. Quickly washing then drying and trying to whip clothes on as fast as she could, she threw on some make up. She wasn't pleased, but didn't care.

"What are you doing today Duncan? I wanted you to meet Mandi," asked Marlo running around the cabin like her hair was on fire.

Sitting up and watching Marlo run around in a total panic, not wanting to get up, he said lazily as he stretched his arms over his head, "I have to take a couple of guys on the boat. They're coming down from Anchorage to do some fishing. No worries . . . by the time you get back from the Airport, have dinner and get Mandi settled; I'll be heading home."

While Marlo grabbed an apple and a water bottle, Duncan was descending the loft ladder.

"You weren't going to leave without giving me a kiss, were you?" Duncan asked. Smiling at Marlo, he wrapped her in his arms and gave her a warm and soft kiss.

Not wanting to part his lips, Marlo said, "Mmm, that was nice, but I have to go. I'll see you later, right?"

"Yes love, you will most definitely see me later. I'm ready for round two already."

Feeling the pressure of arriving at the airport on time, she gave Duncan one last loving kiss before heading out the door.

She smiled and said, "See you soon!"

Weaving in and out of the airport parking lot, Marlo chose to park in the daytime parking and ran to the entrance. The first thing she did was read the Monitors. She was searching for the Alaska flight from Minnesota connecting in Washington. *Gate B2 . . . that's where I need to be.* After going through the security check point and putting her purse, her coat and her shoes on the conveyer belt, she was thinking, *I hate this part. It takes so damn long.* She went to the other side to retrieve them. Quickly grabbing her purse, throwing her coat over her arm and putting her shoes on, hopping away with one foot off the ground. Trying to avoid pure embarrassment of falling over, she finally inserted her foot in her shoe and started running to gate B2. She began running down the fast moving rubber strips that take on the resemblance of long flat treadmills, dodging everyone in her path.

Finally, seeing gate B2, Marlo was praying the passengers weren't unloading the plane. Frantically looking around and not seeing her, she thought, *thank goodness my treadmill exercise and looking like a fool, wasn't a waste after all.* Soon enough, the passengers started trickling through the corridor, looking for people they were meeting. *I don't see her yet. Nope, that's not her . . . still no Mandi.*

Startled, she heard someone scream out, "Ahhh, Marlo!"

Mandi bolted towards Marlo and embracing her in what felt like a bear hug, Marlo held on. They both were excited to see each other and were relieved they were finally together; like two peas in a pod. They were friends for life.

"How was your flight?" Marlo asked when they were heading down the ramp towards baggage claim.

"It was alright. I mean, at one point I thought the plane was going to give out and plummet to the earth because the turbulence was so awful, but for the most part, it was pretty good. Where's Duncan? I thought he would have been with you?"

"I was hoping he was going to come, but he had to take some guys fishing today. They're coming from Anchorage. Actually, he's already out on the water with them, I'm sure."

Completely unaware of their surroundings in the airport, they were mindlessly walking in the right direction.

"I have to say, Marlo, Alaska is magnificent. I couldn't believe the view of the mountains from the air. It was the most humbling sight, ever."

"Yeah, it is a beautiful place . . . that's for sure. I was thinking . . . tonight, since Duncan has to work at James' Bros. Pub, maybe we should grab a bite there and you could meet him and his brother, Brady. They both own the pub."

"Duncan has a brother? Hmm, yes . . . let's go to James' Bros. Pub and meet this Brady."

Sensing a little deviousness from Mandi, Marlo said with a shake of her head and smile, "and, Duncan too."

"Of course, I have to meet him, but he's yours. I want to meet this Brady. If he's anything like your description of Duncan, I might just have to miss my plane ride home."

They collected Mandi's luggage from baggage claim and started to walk towards the exit.

"You're a freak, Mandi! You would totally miss your flight for a hunky pub owner?"

Shaking her head, she said, "Let's get out of here and I'll show you my place."

Laughing, the girls loaded the Wrangler with the luggage, jumped in the Jeep and headed home.

Turning off onto the dirt road, bouncing and moving over the ruts that have been engraved due to heavy travel, Mandi didn't know if she was up for what Alaska had to offer.

"We're here . . . what do you think?" Marlo asked parking the Jeep beside her cabin.

"This is where you're staying?"

Not sure what that meant, Marlo was a tad worried Mandi didn't like it.

"I love it!" said Mandi with joy.

"Scratch that worry," Marlo said to herself.

"It's small but has a lot of charm. You're an Alaskan Native now, aren't you, Marlo?"

"I guess," laughing in disbelief, "for as long as I'm here."

Mandi opened the Jeep door and stepped out. She was taking in the landscape and the arrangement of the land and the cabins.

"I know I'm only going to be staying for a few days, but it would be an adventure to stay here and take up a permanent residence."

Marlo in agreement, "It would. I don't know what I'm doing yet, but sometimes I think I just might make ago of Alaska. I mean, Clare, Jack, Dilly and Bentley are all back in Minnesota, but what says I can't go back and visit or they visit me? I've kind of become attached to the town and this cabin. Of course, if I stayed, I'd have to find my own place or build, but I haven't put any thought into it so . . . I don't know."

"Does Duncan know you're thinking about staying here?"

Marlo knew she didn't mention her taking up a permanent residence to Duncan, but she would bring it up in time. Regardless of his opinion, she had every intention of making roots in Alaska. She loved it here and knew Duncan wouldn't have anything negative to contribute to the idea.

"Not yet, but I'm indecisive about my decision, so bringing it up would be jumping the gun. Come on, let's get you unpacked."

Unwinding after the flight and unpacking Mandi's things, they took a walk down by the river. The sun was shining and it was breezy, but the view was great. Dusk was nearing and Marlo was aware of Duncan coming home soon.

"Let's get ready for a night out and we'll head over to James' Bros. Pub. I know Brady is already there and Duncan will be there shortly. I've been talking about you since I've met them and they know you're arriving today; they're anticipating your arrival."

"Sounds awesome, let's go!"

Chapter 10

Vehicles were starting to fill up the parking lot and people were filtering into the pub. You could here the jukebox playing when the door swung open and then closed as customers went inside. The hearty aroma of steaks and hamburgers encircled the outside air. Nearing the entrance, the music on the jukebox had intensified. The door opened with a sweeping motion and a couple who was leaving held the door for Marlo and Mandi to enter.

"Thank you," they said, crossing the threshold, interested in finding *their* men. Behind the bar stood Duncan and Brady, attempting to serve everyone at the bar calling out drink names, "One Screwdriver, a Dirty Martini—extra dirty and two Miller Genuine Drafts!"

"Coming right up!" shouted Brady over the counter to drown out the jukebox.

Mandi leaned into Marlo with eyes of excitement, loving the nightlife in Seward.

"This place appears to have hijacked everyone in town," said Mandi. "There's not even a place to park our happy butts."

"This place is busy, but tonight's the busiest I've seen it, yet," Marlo hollered back.

Brady looked up from the bar and noticed Marlo.

Nudging Duncan he said, "Hey Duncan, there's your girl and . . ."

Who is that with her, Brady wondered.

"Who's that dynamite stick next to Marlo?"

"Oh yeah, that must be Mandi, Marlo's best friend. She went to the airport earlier today to pick her up. She's staying for a few days." *Or maybe a few years,* thought Brady.

"Hey man, you need to introduce us. I think this could be my chance," as he stared at Mandi with his mouth open.

"Maybe bro, but can you keep your mouth shut? We don't need any drool in the customer's drinks."

Making a scuffing noise, Duncan said to himself, "Oh boy."

"That shouldn't be a problem, Duncan, as long as you keep my mouth filled with cotton," said Brady while fumbling with the glasses in his hand; staring at Mandi. *That's one beautiful woman standing there.*

Mandi was a stunning woman with long luminous red hair and green eyes so brilliant they shone brighter than fireworks on the fourth of July. She has an amazing body with a full front and a healthy backside, which would fit perfectly in Brady's hands. She was letting her eyes drift throughout the room following behind Marlo, "This place looks like a lot of fun!" said Mandi, noticing a welcomed kiss behind the bar staring right at Marlo. "That must be Duncan," said Mandi, leaning into Marlo's ear.

Approaching Duncan, Marlo offered, "Mandi, I'd like you to meet Duncan James, co-owner of James' Bros. Pub and Duncan Charters out of Seward. Duncan, I'd like you to meet Mandi Crandell, my best friend since grade school and miraculously, still by my side."

Sticking his hand out, he graciously welcomed Mandi to Seward, Alaska.

"It's a pleasure to meet you, Mandi. Welcome to Seward. Marlo has told me all about you. I'm glad you arrived safely."

Looking at Duncan, Mandi thought to herself, *you are everything Marlo said you would be.*

Brady sauntered over, feeling the need to introduce himself, "Hi Marlo, who's your friend?"

"Hi Brady, this is my longtime friend, Mandi Crandell. Mandi, this is Brady James, the other owner of this fine pub, and Duncan's brother."

Reaching out to Mandi, Brady offered greetings with a handshake, but wanting to meet her with a taste of her lips.

He quickly thought . . . *that's pushing it*, "It's a pleasure, Mandi."

Mandi couldn't help notice his dark brown hair cut short and tapered to his neck. He had eyes the color of emeralds, a strong jaw line, and a clean shaven face with a muscular body that would welcome any woman.

"It's nice to meet you, Brady. I'm happy to finally be here in Alaska. It's been a long and tiring trip."

They locked eyes and the chemistry between the two was not going away anytime soon.

"What can I get you two beautiful women to drink?" asked Brady, not taking his eyes off of Mandi.

"I'll take a rum and Diet Coke, please Brady James."

"I like how you said my name."

"Maybe I'll say it like that every time I see you," said Mandi winking at him.

Interrupting the love in the room, Marlo made a sound of jester within her throat, "And I'll have a Bud Light, please, Brady."

Handing Mandi her Diet Coke and rum, he grabbed Marlo's Bud Light and removed the metal cap with a quick motion, and threw it in the trash.

"Two points! Here you go my future sister-in-law."

With a wink and a whisper, Brady said, "I guess I shouldn't have said that, huh?"

Spinning from side to side on her bar stool, she put her hand up to her forehead and covered her eyes in embarrassment.

Having a thought of smacking Brady upside the head, she said, "Brady, I can't believe you just said that. Duncan and I just met."

"I know Marlo, but I know my brother and he has never and I mean *never* felt about anyone, the way he feels about you."

"Really, are you sure?"

"As sure as I'll ever be." *Hmm,* thought Marlo. *I figured that out this morning.*

"Brady, do you think you can order Mandi and me a plate of enchiladas? We're going to eat here tonight," said Marlo, thinking, *I just want to be with Duncan.*

"Sure, Marlo, I'll tell the cook to whip that right up."

"Thank you, Brady."

"No problem, sis." Marlo looked at Brady with daggers in her eyes and he smiled.

For the rest of the evening, Marlo and Mandi sat at the bar enjoying their drinks and picking at what was left of their enchiladas. They were catching up from the past week and enjoying the atmosphere, including their two hotties behind the bar.

While Duncan was serving two women drinks, Brady came over to him and mentioned . . . "Ah, did you see Mandi?"

"I did."

"Don't you think she's smokin'?"

"Smokin' for you bro, I've fallen for Marlo and hard; it's embarrassing."

"How long do you think she'll be in town? Did Marlo tell you?" asked Brady.

"I think just a few days, maybe a week. I know she took some time off of work, but I don't know how much."

Duncan was wiping down the counter and looking over at Marlo. "Well, I'm definitely going to ask that woman out. She's just my kind of woman."

Brady threw an empty beer bottle in the trash and it made a loud clanking sound.

Marlo and Mandi went out to the dance floor when they heard 'Sweet Home Alabama' play on the jukebox. They were tearing up the dance floor like they owned the place. Duncan and Brady couldn't help notice all the men in the place watching their women rock out to Alabama. They knew the boys in the bar didn't stand a chance picking up the two most ravishing women in the pub.

Later that night, Marlo and Mandi decided to head out because Mandi was tired from her trip. The bar didn't close for another two hours and Duncan and Brady had to still clean and restock the bar. Marlo walked up to Duncan and told him they were leaving and she would see him tomorrow.

He walked around the bar and gave her a much needed kiss and held her, whispering in her ear, "I can't wait to see you, soon."

He looked at her again and gave her another kiss. Marlo opened her eyes slowly, taking in his softness.

"I'll be waiting."

She turned and met Mandi at the door.

Just as they were about to leave, Brady came up to Mandi and asked, "Hey Mandi, I know we just met, but I was wondering if you would like to go out with me, tomorrow?"

"I would love to Brady. Thank you for asking me."

They stared at each other for a second and then Mandi turned to leave the pub.

When Mandi left the pub she let out a silent, "Yes!" and thought, *Halleluiah . . . finally, a man worth my time. I had to come all the way to Alaska to find someone worth dating? Wait! Before I get ahead of myself, I'll wait to see how the date goes first.*

In a state of bliss, Mandi walked with Marlo to the Jeep and said, "Marlo, did you happen to hear what Brady just asked me?"

"I did. I think you and Brady will have a good time together. He couldn't take his eyes off of you. I couldn't help but notice how he was *eyeing you up,* all night."

Nudging Mandi's shoulder with her shoulder, Marlo asked, "What happens if you end up falling in love with him?"

"Please get real, I'm only here for a few days. I'm intending to have a night out on the town with him, or whatever he decides would be fun, and that's it."

"You never know, Mandi . . . he might just sweep you off your feet."

Mandi narrowed her expression with winced eyes and said, "Not a chance, I'm too wrapped up in my career."

"We'll just see about that. You know, Duncan and Brady are brothers and if Brady is anything like Duncan, you might just be in trouble . . . miss."

Mandi thought about that one, but only for a quick millisecond.

In the pub, Duncan and Brady were doing their usual tedious nightly routine cleaning, sweeping, mopping, washing tables, restocking and welcoming a new mutual addition discussing their women.

"I can't believe it. We have lived here our entire lives and never found anyone to fill our expectations of the perfect woman. Then two amazingly beautiful women arrive from the lower forty-eight and . . . . Bingo, we're in love."

"Brady, you just met her. You're in love with her appearance. It's a Heavenly sight, but"

"She's a knockout! And, you know it."

"She is, I'm definitely not disagreeing with you there, but just don't frighten her away like you did the last one," Duncan said with a momentary lapse in judgment, thinking, *I'm in for it now.*

"What does that mean? When have I ever *frightened* a woman?"

Brady was contemplating his last few relationships and failed to come up with anything.

"Jamie, that girl from the University, telling her she wasn't *Alaska Material* even though she went to college in Alaska dim-wit."

"Oh yeah," remembering Jamie. "Well she wasn't. She was just going to school there and then heading back to the lower forty-eight. So, technically she wasn't fit for Alaska," said Brady, annoyed.

"But, your relationship had vitality. She was perfect for you, I liked her," replied Duncan.

Brady felt defeated on Duncan's point and moved forward with, "I admit it, you're right. Now, let's focus on where I should take this arrestingly beautiful woman, who is also going back to the lower forty-eight and probably isn't *Alaska Material*."

Duncan looked at his brother putting down the wash rag and said, "Oh Brady, you're a mess."

"This is true, but you love me anyways."

Pulling into the cabins, Marlo and Mandi looked unruly with eyeliner seeping down their rosy cheeks and hair that has seen better days. They initially were going to crash for the night, but they were mutually inept to do that since both of them were floating on pure sense of lust and attraction towards the James Brothers.

"I'm not ready for bed. I just got my second wind. Let's make some coffee," offered Mandi.

"Are you sure? Aren't you exhausted from traveling and going out tonight?"

"A little, but I want to talk and hang out a little first."

"Alright, sounds good to me," said Marlo thinking, *if I just traveled all that way, I would be crashed out by now.*

After warming up with their cups of Columbian Blend French Roast dark coffee, Mandi had to do something to escape her every day boring routine.

"I have an impulsive idea that sounds preposterous, but in retrospection, is a marvelous idea." Being rebellious was one of Marlo's favorite past times.

So, she eagerly asked, "What? I'm totally in the mood to do something wild and foolish. What do ya got?"

"Throw your swimsuit on, were going to go take a dip in the river."

"Mandi, that doesn't sound impulsive, that sounds numbing. If you want to do something impulsive, then I suggest we go skinny-dipping and still be numb at the same time."

"YES! Let's do it. Ahhh, we're going skinny-dipping!" Mandi did a little victory dance and then stopped.

"Wait, what about the neighbors? Are they going to be coming down to the river?"

"Mandi, it's freezing out. What makes you think they're going to come down to the river? Unless they plan on spearing fish, I doubt they'll come down. Now, are you in or are you in?"

"I'm in, let's do this. I can't believe we're doing this. Okay, we're doing this."

"Mandi, did I ever tell you you're a total disaster?"

"Yes, but, I love you."

"I know, now come on before I change my mind."

They got undressed and wrapped themselves in towels and went out on the porch. They stared at the river for a moment feeling the cold air hit their skin.

Marlo looked at Mandi, "You ready?"

"I am, let's go. This is crazy, but it doesn't surprise me that you're my partner in crime," said Mandi.

Leaving their towels slung over the porch railing and moving like spies through the grass, they both felt completely ridiculous. No one was going to hear them anyways. The moon was high lighting up the landscape and the stars speckled the sky like lightning bugs.

When they reached the river bank Marlo jumped in and let out a soft scream, "Burr, this is really cold." Mandi tested the cold river water with her big toe and pulled it out quickly,

"Are you crazy? Bad idea . . . it's, too cold. I'm not doing this, nope, can't do it."

In a whispered tone, Marlo shouted, "Mandi, this was your crazy idea, not mine. Now quit being a chicken and get in here!"

Marlo looked away and was laughing inside knowing Mandi was going to hate this. She wasn't the adventurous type like Marlo was.

"It was your idea to go naked!" said Mandi.

"Right, like a swimsuit would have been warmer," replied Marlo. Mandi started mumbling, "Fine, but this is a bad idea."

"Just remember, it was your idea, not mine," said Marlo. Without another second to think about it, Mandi took the plunge. "Oh, oooh, oh, it's cold, really cold."

Mandi was flailing her arms and trying to crawl up the bank because the water was ice cold. Mandi tried climbing the muddy bank, but she kept slipping back into the water. Her hair was covering her face, looking like 'Cousin It.' She couldn't see anything. She tried moving her hair, but then only made it worse when mud smeared across her face and in her hair. Marlo was dying inside. With her teeth chattering Marlo couldn't compose herself enough to keep from laughing hysterically. Mandi finally gave up when she realized the river bank has defeated her and the water has frozen her hands and feet.

"What is so damn funny, Marlo?" asked Mandi with a frustrated tone to her voice. Words could barely escape her because she was laughing and talking at the same time.

"I . . . I can't breathe. You look hilarious . . . . you should see yourself. I can't breathe, my stomach is cramping."

Marlo was hovered over laughing without any intention of stopping soon.

"Hilarious. Just, hilarious. I'm glad I can amuse you," Mandi said rolling her eyes.

"I . . . I'm sorry, Mandi. Hang on, let me calm down."

A few moments later . . . "Okay, I'm good. You panicked when you hit the water and started spastically trying to get out, and then the slipping down the bank and the mud and you couldn't see. I just couldn't help myself."

Trying not to burst out in another laughing episode, Marlo started up the bank and Mandi briskly followed. Once at the top of the bank they forgot they left their towels on the porch.

"Crap, we left our towels hanging over the railing," Mandi said, wishing she brought her towel with.

"Ooooh . . . shit," Marlo said, wide-eyed and nervous. "What? What's the matter, what?"

"Duncan's truck is parked by the cabin," said Marlo, contemplating how they were going to handle this one.

"Why would he be here this late?" asked Marlo out loud. "Shit!" said Mandi.

"What? What are *you* saying shit for?" asked Marlo. "What if Brady came with him?"

"Double shit! Okay, let's not panic. Maybe they're just . . . crap! I never gave Duncan a key! That means they're in the truck. Oh, oh. They just got out of the truck," said Marlo.

"What are we going to do, Marlo? We can't just walk up there."

"Mandi, that's a brilliant idea."

"What the hell are you talking about, are you mad? Yep, I think you just earned yourself a stay in the nearest nut house."

Rolling her eyes, like Marlo always does and looking at Mandi, she said, "It's a perfect idea because we're women and we're not afraid of anything, even if we are totally exposed, vulnerable and crazy. We can do this."

"I can't do this," Mandi said hiding behind Marlo.

"Yes, you can. We'll just walk up there like we own the place. We'll calmly retrieve our towels from the railing and tell them we'll be out in a sec."

"Are you sure? We're really going to do this?" asked Mandi, totally embarrassed.

"Yes."

Duncan and Brady were wondering where Marlo and Mandi could be since the Jeep was parked for the night and the lights were on in the cabin. No one was answering and they couldn't see the girls inside. Squinting down the path to the river because it was dark, Brady happened to see two people walking up the path. *Who is that?* Then he realized . . . it's the girls . . . with no clothes on.

"No way, holy shit Duncan. Look whose coming up from the river. And, uh, they don't seem to be wearing any clothes."

Brady couldn't take his eyes off of Mandi and snuck a peek at Marlo, both stunningly breathtaking. Just standing there by the cabin with his hands in his pockets, Duncan didn't know what to do. *Do we retreat? Do we just stand here and take in the pleasant sight with smirks on our face we can't hide?*

"Yep, I see them. Wow! I don't know. I guess we should just act like nothing is awkward."

"Right, this should go over well," Brady answered.

Coming up to them, confident and knowingly beautiful, Marlo looked right at Duncan and asked, "What? Haven't you ever seen two naked women before?"

Duncan, trying to hide his grin and keeping his head down, said, "Well yes, but not when it's forty-degrees outside."

Duncan wanted to take her into the cabin and warm her with his naked body, and make passionate love to her. Seeing her front him, aware of her vulnerability, made him hungry for her and loving the way she was mentally strong. Mandi on the other hand, didn't handle it all that well. She hid behind Marlo until she could reach for a towel and quickly covered herself, hoping Brady or Duncan didn't see her in the nude.

Mandi headed inside, embarrassed and beside herself and Marlo, wrapping herself in her towel, told Brady and Duncan to give them five minutes to get dressed and they'd come out.

Opening the door to the cabin, Marlo glanced back at Duncan and they both eyed each other smiling. She slowly closed it, watching Duncan stare at her.

"I'm completely in a daze right now. I don't know what to say, except, Hot Damn!" said Brady. "I knew she was beautiful, but now I know she's gorgeous."

"Brady, I'm not surprised. What the hell were they thinking going skinny-dipping in forty degree weather? They're going to get sick with pneumonia."

"Listen to you, mother hen. They are not going to get sick with pneumonia. They were just experiencing the great outdoors of Alaska. Lighten up, Duncan. We've done many stupid things. That's the fun of it. If I didn't know better, I would say you're in love with her."

"Whatever, Brady. Just zip it."

"Yup, you're in love with her."

Chapter 11

Frantically sorting through the heaps of clothes they threw on the floor, trying to find whose is whose, they swiftly got dressed, accessorizing with towel wrapped heads. They put on their coats, shoved their bare feet in boots and went outside.

"Hey guys, sorry about that," Marlo said confidently, like nothing was wrong. "So . . . what are you two doing here? I thought you were heading home after work?"

"Yeah, we were, but we decided to come over here instead," Brady said with his jacket zipped up to his neck, his chin tucked in, and his hands in his pockets.

Mandi smiled at Brady and wanted to scoop him up and snuggle him.

"Can I talk to you for a minute, Marlo . . . in private?" asked Duncan.

"Sure, why don't we sit in the truck and Mandi and Brady can go in the cabin."

Taking their cues, Brady followed Mandi into the cabin and Marlo and Duncan got in the truck.

Marlo looked over at Duncan and asked, "What's wrong, Duncan? Is everything okay? Did something happen tonight at the pub after Mandi and I left?" Studying Marlo's features and seeing how she expressed concern for him, made him feel warm and loved; he thought,

I'm definitely in love with this woman. I know I've only known her for a little while, but she is everything I've been looking for in a wife.

"No, nothing happened. I have to tell you something that's bothering me."

"What is it, Duncan?"

"The other day when you were telling me about your parents, I felt this strong connection and I've been wrestling with it. I've been struggling with the reasons why I would feel this strong pull, but I am absent ideas."

Listening to Duncan's unusual and unrelated concern, Marlo couldn't think of a single reason he would have these thoughts or feelings. Duncan didn't have anything to do with her family or parents.

All she could summon was, "Duncan, you shouldn't burden yourself with my unfortunate loss and distressing past. It's going to be okay, Duncan. My life is full of questions that need to be answered, but they will be, in time. Please don't concern your thoughts with my past. I don't want you worrying."

Duncan was disturbed by his feelings like a magnetic pull to the Earth's core. Staring out the window and biting his lip he thought, *I know she doesn't want me to agonize over this association of belief, but this is too powerful to pay no heed to. I have to surmount to the idea that the feeling I am enduring is a possible reaction to Marlo's past, but why?*

Looking over at Marlo and laying a hand gently on her arm he suggested, "Maybe you and I can move forward with a manner to decipher your feelings for the loss of your parents together and how it ties to your relationships. And, in return, I can dismiss these thoughts I'm having associated with your parents' death. Then, together, we can overcome what's bothering you and what you feel you are missing. You should be happy in your life. You only get one, right?" Duncan asked looking at Marlo.

"We can try. I don't know if you're going to get the results you're hoping for, but I'll definitely try," said Marlo, showing him she was letting him in.

"I know you. I've seen how it weighs heavy on your mind." Hearing Duncan's last comment, Marlo didn't know what to do, except become defensive.

"What do you mean, you know me? You haven't known me long. You can't know what I'm feeling. You haven't experienced anything of this magnitude!"

Marlo looked at Duncan with anger in her eyes. She was ready to pummel him.

"Marlo, wait, listen."

Turning towards Marlo and facing her in the truck, he focused on her eyes.

"I do know what it feels like. I do know the hurt and the anger and the loss."

Duncan cleared his throat and began explaining.

"When Brady and I were kids, we were swimming in the pond by our house. Our father was outside in the garage working on his truck. It was just a regular Saturday in the middle of summer, nothing was different. We heard a car coming down the dirt road. Brady and I started towards the garage. The sheriff's cruiser pulled up to the house and my dad walked over to the sheriff and asked what was going on. We were all standing there and the sheriff told us, with a grief stricken expression, our mother had a heart attack at work. She was a welder for the steel company in our town. She was a hard worker and she loved her family. Our father was beside himself and after that day, he was never the same. He would go to the bar night after night and drink. Then when I was eighteen, I got home one night from hanging out with friends, and Brady was holding our father in his arms. Our father drank himself to death."

Duncan sat there in his tear soaked shirt and shaken hands, and said, "Marlo . . . I do know your pain. I do. I lost both of my parents."

Staring at Duncan through her tears, Marlo sidled over to him. She put her arm around his shoulder and he leaned into her, crying. Marlo held him close, comforting him and knew Duncan had kept his feelings locked up for a long time.

"Duncan, I'm so sorry," Marlo said, with tears on her rosy cheeks. "I didn't mean to snap at you. I'm truly sorry."

Duncan just cried in her arms, ignoring her apology, because she didn't need to apologize.

Marlo sat in the truck with Duncan and stared into the dark void of night, thinking about what Duncan had said. She has never been approached in a way of concern and love by a man. She's never had a man confide in her and expose his heart. When Duncan shared with her the story of his parents, she felt honored. He trusted Marlo to share that part of his life with her.

Then Duncan shifted in his seat and looked up at her, "We are going to work through this, Marlo. We are . . . together."

Glancing down at Duncan's touch, she moved her hand over his. She slowly lifted her eyes up his body and focused on his purity, when she said, "Thank you Duncan. Thank you for understanding me and trusting me. I feel safe and protected when I'm with you. Thank you for confiding in me and showing me your vulnerability. I know it was difficult to open your heart to me. You are a strong man, Duncan, and you are a good man."

"I don't feel like I am sometimes."

"You are Duncan, you are. I can see it in your eyes."

Marlo looked into his eyes and she could see and feel his honesty and genuineness.

"Thank you, Marlo."

They both sat in the truck outside the cabin for a long time. They held each other in the peace and quiet. Duncan started thinking about the inconsiderate men that Marlo dated and experienced the senses of fury rush over him, recognizing the truth of these undeveloped men. They knew nothing when it came to a woman scorn. They didn't appreciate Marlo and love her. No wonder Marlo escapes any chance of being with a man, when she has the chance. She's never been understood. Duncan looked at Marlo and thought, *I will be true to her and she will know how special she is.*

"Marlo, I love you." Marlo closed her eyes and leaned into Duncan accepting her fate and the faith of Duncan's words.

She whispered, "And, I love you, Duncan."

Marlo and Duncan decided it was time to end the night. He had to get up early to take some people fishing. Entering Marlo's fairy tale cabin, they walked in, witnessing the roar of card playing rivalry, "Uno!" shouted Brady. "You're totally screwed now. I love this game."

Mandi was thinking, *only because you're winning, otherwise you'd show a display of 'sore loser attitude' . . . the rat.*

"Ha, draw two my friend," said Mandi with a sly look on her face.

"Wrap it up; we need to go. I'm whooped. And, I have to charter a couple tomorrow around noon. I need some serious shut-eye," said Duncan trying to hide the exhaustion he felt from showing Marlo his true feelings.

"Alright, thank you for the card game, Mandi. Next time I'll let you win," said Brady smiling.

"Next time I won't *let* you win."

"Uh huh."

Brady gave Mandi a kiss on the cheek and went out to the truck. Marlo looked at Duncan and gave him a soft kiss and embraced him with pure affection and love.

"Good night love," said Duncan.

Marlo looked into his eyes and reached for his hand. "We'll see each other tomorrow then?"

"Yes, beautiful, we will."

She smiled and told Duncan good night. Duncan and Brady headed down the drive.

Mandi chimed in when she and Marlo were all settled in for the night, "So, what was up with Duncan?"

"Oh, you know, he just wanted to be alone with me for a little before he had to go home. He stops over sometimes unannounced, I'm getting used to it."

"He must really adore you if he comes over after a long night of working just to see you for a few minutes, and then turns around to go home," Mandi replied, wishing she had someone in her life that would do those types of things.

"Well, he normally would have stayed the night, but with both of us here there's not a lot of *privacy*, since this cabin was built for a dwarf."

Marlo didn't want to share intimate conversations between Duncan and her with Mandi, so she decided to promptly change the subject, "How did it go with you and Brady?"

"At first we just looked at each other because him seeing me naked was completely awkward. I mean we just met, you know? Then, we started talking about how he likes living in Alaska and working at the pub. At first I thought he was going to be one of those guys who think women were below Monday night football, eating crunchy cheese balls, and drinking cold beer, shouting at the players like they can hear through the TV, but then I saw a softer side. He's actually exceptionally genuine and talkative too. He doesn't make me hold the conversation. I like that."

"Brady has a soft heart, but it's hard to see when he's at the pub. It's almost like he acts the part for his job and then when he leaves, he's down to earth, loving and understanding. I like Brady, and I think he likes you too, Mandi," said Marlo pulling the covers over her and inching her way down making a nest. "Mandi, thanks for coming out here. I really love that you're here with me."

"That's what friends are for, Marlo. Good night, see you in the morning."

"Good night, Mandi."

Morning arrived faster than Marlo wanted it to since she was overly tired and wanted a few extra hours of sleep. She got up and smelled the aroma of Columbian Blend fill her senses, but didn't see Mandi. She remembered Brady asking her out at the pub before they headed back to the cabin last night. *He probably picked her up early.* She poured herself a cup of remaining coffee from the pot. Rubbing her eyes and staring out the window in her robe and fuzzy purple slippers, she thought, *I need to get a job if I plan on staying here long.*

When Marlo was done getting ready for the day and drinking her four cups of coffee, she hiked up to Sandra and Clay's house, feeling the cold air sting her face. She pulled her coat together to keep the wind from hitting her body. Marlo knew what she wanted to do about work, but she had to talk to Sandra about it first.

She traipsed up to the office, opened the door and said, "Good morning, Sandra. How are you, this morning?"

"Good morning, Marlo. I'm good. Hey, I wanted to talk to you."

Marlo pulled a chair over from the seating area to where Sandra was and sat down.

"Sure, what's going on?" Marlo yawned, "Oh, I'm so sorry, I can't stop yawning. I didn't get a lot of sleep last night."

Sandra looked at Marlo and shook her head, "Because of Duncan?"

"Actually, no, that's not the reason, although, I do have an embarrassing story to share with you."

"Ooooh, I love embarrassing stories, I can wait to tell you what I was going to say," Sandra said with wide eyes.

"Okay, but don't forget what you were going to tell me."

"I won't, now tell me what happened," answered Sandra with her elbow resting on the counter and her chin resting in the palm of her hand.

"Last night, Mandi and I decided to go skinny-dipping in the river. We left our towels hanging over the railing on the porch and when we got out, we remembered we left our towels behind. Just when we were making our way back to the cabins, we saw Duncan's truck. Both of us flipped."

Sandra was smiling at Marlo telling her the story.

"Then we realized Brady was with Duncan. We didn't know what to do. I mean, I didn't want Brady to see me naked . . . how weird. And Mandi didn't want Brady or Duncan to see her naked. Mandi was freaking out . . . anyways, we walked up to the boys and they were totally beside themselves. It was funny to see them squirm," said Marlo, knowing Sandra was in love with this story.

"You've got to be kidding me. Seriously, how did they react?" asked Sandra practically jumping out of her seat.

"They were just standing there, not sure what to say, and looking down. Mandi and I grabbed our towels and Mandi practically tripped over herself trying to get in the cabin as fast as she could. It was kind of comical."

"I can't believe it! You sure do bring excitement to Birch Cabins, girl . . . you need to work here. I could use more of this excitement," said Sandra.

Marlo looked at Sandra and said, "I wanted to talk to you about that actually, but what were you going to say earlier when I came in?" Marlo asked.

"Well, I was going to head over to the pub last night, but then I remembered, Mandi was coming into town. I thought you might want to catch up with her first, so I didn't end up going."

"We did end up going to the pub last night and she met Duncan and Brady there."

Sandra was thinking in the back of her mind, *I wonder what she thought of Brady.*

"I have to ask . . . how did that turn out?"

Marlo knew what she was hinting at and started smiling.

"If you are implying Brady . . . it was interesting. Sparks were flying the second we walked into the pub. Brady noticed her right away. So, that's why it was *really* weird when they saw us naked. In a matter of fact, he picked her up today and went somewhere . . . on a date."

"Oh really, that's interesting. I wonder where he took her."

"I'm not sure, but wherever they went, I'm sure they'll have a good time. Mandi hasn't had a lot of luck in the men department either. I'm happy for her."

"I need to meet this *Mandi* yet. You'll have to bring her by and introduce us," said Sandra.

"I will. I wanted to yesterday, but didn't get the chance."

Sipping their morning cups of coffee and enjoying each other's conversation, Marlo wanted to take Sandra up on the job offer. Since Marlo already had the idea, it's like she and Sandra were on the same page. *Maybe I could work the desk and take reservations,* thought Marlo.

"Sandra, I wanted to talk to you about something you mentioned earlier."

"Okay, what's going on?" I've really enjoyed my time here in Alaska so far and I want to continue living here. I know if I decided to stay, I would have to find a place to live."

Listening intently, Sandra was excited to hear that Marlo wanted to plant roots in Alaska.

"So tell me your plan."

"You and Clay are always taking care of the cabins, cleaning them and keeping them filled, chopping wood and other things. I was thinking, maybe I could be your reservation person and that would free you up to spend more time with Clay. I really like it here and it would give me work and you some free time."

Thinking it over quickly in her mind, Sandra said, "You know, I think that's a great idea. And, if you want, you can stay in the cabin while you're waiting to find something else. We'll substitute the cabin rent with some of your pay; you'll make money *and* have a place to stay."

"You know, that would work. Thank you, Sandra."

Marlo was relieved to know that she had something to fall back on.

"No . . . thank you! Thanks for staying and I'm sure Duncan is going to be thrilled." Marlo thought, *Duncan will be thrilled, but Clare won't be too happy.* "Duncan and I have come a long way even though I haven't been here long. You know Sandra . . . I think I'm in love with him."

"I don't think you're in love with him. I know you're in love with him."

Smiling, trying to hide the truth, Marlo shrugged her coat on and pulled the zipper up.

"You might be right," she said, pulling her mittens out of her coat pocket and sliding them on her hands.

"I know I'm right and he's in love with you, too," said Sandra.

On that note, Marlo gave a wave and said, "I will come by later this afternoon and we can discuss plans for training me, sound good?"

"Sounds perfect; you won't need much. It's easy enough."

"Alright, see you later. I'm going to head over to Seward and talk to Duncan. I know he had to take some people out on the boat today."

Waving at Marlo, Sandra said, "See you later. Have fun." Shutting the door behind her, she heard the click and knew it was closed tightly.

The marina was full of boats and charters; it was a sight to see. She could smell the distinct scent of salt water hovering in the air. It brought on a feeling of comfort. Even though Marlo didn't know many people yet, she still felt like she was in a welcoming place and knew staying here would be a wise decision. She also knew this was something she wanted and she was going to do it. She couldn't wait to tell Duncan the good news and hoped he wouldn't have a negative reaction. *If Duncan doesn't go for this, come hell or high water, he's going to understand this is something I'm doing. I know he'll think it's a great idea and he'll be happy for me. I hope.*

Standing at the end of the dock, Marlo saw Duncan working intensely on his boat. He was moving things around, stowing gear, wiping the boat down and tightening the lines. He had this obscure look on his face like something was bothering him. Wondering what it could be, Marlo slowly made her way to him.

Shouting from the pier, Marlo yelled, "Good morning Duncan." Hearing Marlo, he looked up brightly at her.

Leaping onto the dock from his boat, he jogged over to her and picked her up, nestling his lips into her neck, "Good morning. I've missed you."

Feeling happier than Marlo has felt in a long time she embraced his enthusiasm and held onto him feeling his warmth.

"I was going to stop by this morning, but I knew I had to take some people out today. I've been here about an hour and needed to prepare the boat for a safe trip."

Duncan was thinking maybe something wasn't right. *Marlo never comes to see me when I'm going to take people out on the boat.*

"I had something I wanted to tell you and I'm pretty excited about it, but we can talk about it later."

Wondering what she had to say, he said, "It's okay, I have time. Do you want to go to the coffee shop and sit down and talk?"

"I would love that."

Taking her hand and walking together down the dock to the boardwalk, Marlo leaned into Duncan, and thought, *I could stay with this man forever.*

Nearing the coffee shop, Marlo could see how much time the owner put into the building. The front was covered in cedar shakes, accented with white trim. It had a Nantucket feel to it. The windows had a craftsman design and flower boxes mounted below with evergreen swags and red berries, accented with a few frosted branches. The front door was painted a dark blue, bordering with white trim. There was a sidewalk that led up to the front door and outside the storefront was a white mailbox that had a steamy cup of coffee hand-painted on it.

"This place has the best coffee. You'll love it."

Opening the door, Marlo looked up when she heard a wind chime singing a welcome tune. Duncan led Marlo into the café putting his hand on the small of her back. He followed her, letting the door close behind them. They both ordered their coffee and together, found a somewhat secluded place to sit, where it was quiet. Marlo moved aside so Duncan could take a seat next to her.

"Thank you for taking the time to talk with me."

"Marlo, you don't have to thank me. I love spending time with you." She grinned from ear to ear. Taking a drink of his coffee from an oversized white mug with a huge handle, he looked at Marlo and loved her bright smile. Setting his cup down on the old wooden pine table and adjusting to get comfortable, he had his full attention on her.

"What did you want to talk to me about?"

"Well, Alaska is somewhere I think I have come to appreciate. I've been thinking about relocating here, permanently, but my family is in Minnesota. Even though that is true, I feel like I need a new place to start, and I think that place is here."

Staring at Marlo in a fog and trying to comprehend her wanting to *move here*, Duncan couldn't believe his ears.

"Are you telling me you want to move to Alaska and start a life here and have a home?"

"Yes, isn't that great news!?! I would have to build a home or find another place to live, of course. I can't stay at the cabin forever, but I talked to Sandra and I'm going to manage the office in the evening and Sandra is going to manage the office in the morning. This way she can have time with Clay at night. I told her I would be coming by later in the afternoon to discuss things, but from what we figured out this morning, I'll work for the cost of the cabin rent and have remaining pay to afford other things. This idea would be temporary until I can find a place of my own, then I'll be working strictly for pay."

Thinking that was a good plan, Duncan said, "It seems like you've made a decision already."

"I sure did. I love Alaska and I'm going to make my life what I've always wanted it to be; simple but full of happiness."

Duncan was thinking, *this is awesome, but tread carefully, you don't want to sound too excited.*

"Well then, welcome to Alaska permanently," he said.

Marlo was thrilled with her decision.

"Oh, and the other thing is, I get to be in Seward where my parents loved to visit. I feel close to them, here. I am completely overjoyed with my new plan. I couldn't be happier."

Trying to be quiet, Marlo softly screamed, "Ahhhh, I'm ready to jump out of my skin, I'm so happy!"

Duncan looked at Marlo with a cocked eyebrow. "Now, does this mean I have to see you all the time?"

"Of course."

"Great, I'll never get anything done."

"Mmm hmm."

Hearing Marlo's response, he knew she loved him.

"How could I be so lucky to have found you, Duncan?" asked Marlo while Duncan wrapped his arms around her.

"It's fate, Marlo."

After visiting with Duncan and sending him on his way to charter his boat and slay some fish, Marlo had to run some errands. She thought it would be a wise idea to buy some groceries she needed and do some local shopping since she was in Seward. She stopped off at the post office and mailed out a post card to Clare, Jack, Dilly and Bentley; it read,

> Hello Family,
>
> It's great here in Alaska! I'm really enjoying my stay and have thought about staying longer. I will call with the details. My cabin is up against the mountain and the river flows at the base; it's beautiful. Sometimes I sit down by the river and take in the view. My cabin is small but very cozy and has a lot of character. I love it! Mandi is here, she came to visit me. She's crazy, but I love her. Hello Dilly and Bentley, I hope you are behaving. I miss you two. Okay, I have to go. Take care and I love you.
>
> Love, Marlo

Chapter 12

Marlo was driving back to Birch Cabins thinking in the quietness of her Jeep, listening to the rolling of the tires humming on the asphalt, *is this really happening? I'm actually going to go through with this. I know I can make a life for myself here.*

Starting to talk to her Mom, Marlo said, "You have given me the strength to move forward with my life. You were right, someone has come when I least expected it. I love Duncan James and if it wasn't for you and Dad, I wouldn't be here. I know I have been hanging in the balance not sure where my life is heading. I know I've been struggling with your death and have had a difficult time accepting you not being here. But, I can feel you here, now."

Pulling up to the office, she parked the Jeep and headed inside. "Sandra, I'm here and ready to work," said Marlo, walking in the door.

"Great. It's been a while since Clay and I have been able to go out and have fun and not have to worry about guests arriving in the night."

Marlo took a seat in the back office with Sandra and she started to explain what it takes to run the office.

"Okay, it's self explanatory. When people come to Birch Cabins, we always make them feel welcome and go to extra heights to make their stay a pleasant one. We are well known for our wonderful hospitality and creating a relaxing atmosphere."

Marlo knew that just from being a guest herself. She knew that was important to Sandra and Clay and would not let them down.

"When the guests arrive, they always stop here first. Your job is to take down their information and log them into the computer. Always make them feel welcome when they arrive and when they leave. On their departure date, collect the keys to their cabin. Also, reservations can be made via phone calls or internet." Showing Marlo some forms, she said, "We always log everyone into the computer base, but we also keep paper records in a file cabinet." Sandra sidled a form to Marlo and said, "This form is for general information, including the check in and check out date. We always have the guests pay on their departure to let them know we trust their integrity; we've never been cheated. Clay will do the ground work, like always, and you and I will do the office work. If you have any questions you can call Clays or my cell phone," Sandra said, feeling relieved to have someone take over the office. Sandra asked, "Any questions?"

Marlo was just thrilled that she had a job and being close to her temporary home, was a huge benefit. She was also excited to be working for Sandra and Clay.

"I'm great. I think I've got it, Sandra and thank you. I can't tell you how happy I am to be helping you out."

Sandra could see through Marlo's blissful state and was curious, so she asked, "Why are you glowing?"

"What do you mean?" Marlo asked.

"I know you Marlo and I can see you are hiding something from me, what is it?"

"Well, I went to the dock and told Duncan about living in Alaska . . . permanently."

"And . . ."

"And he made a stinky comment about having to see me everyday, but . . ." Marlo said with a happy sigh, "he was kidding and I ignored him."

"That's awesome, Marlo. I am so delighted to hear the good news. You know, I knew when you came here, something good was going to happen. I knew you would find happiness on your journey to self-discovery."

Giving Marlo a hug, Sandra held her, knowing Marlo was on her way to the good life and starting to heal. *Who knew Alaska was going to be the answer,* thought Sandra.

"Sandra," Marlo said with watery eyes. "Yes Marlo."

"I am in love with Duncan and I will do whatever it takes to make him happy. He deserves that from a woman."

Sandra stared into Marlo's eyes wiping the tears that streamed down her cheeks, "I know you will, sweetheart. I know you will."

Marlo was sitting at the front desk getting familiar with her surroundings and her new job. It was calm and quiet in the office. There was a radio hiding under the counter. She brought it out and plugged it in the socket. She fiddled with the knob until a station came in and to her surprise, only two stations were clear. A rock station and an oldies station; she chose to listen to the oldies. It was uplifting and she started humming to the Beach Boys. She was dancing behind the desk with her back turned when she heard the bell above the door to the office, *ding*. She turned with a startled jolt and feeling like an idiot, she said, "Whoops, welcome to Birch Cabins. I'm Marlo, how can I help you?"

Marlo asked looking at the new, soon to be guests.

"I'm Teresa Holden and this is my boyfriend, Bo Lemke. We were wondering if you have a cabin available. We're staying for a week and are hoping you can accommodate us."

"Let me look at the reservation list and see if we have a cabin available for the week. Sometimes, we can accommodate for a few days, but a week might not work. Let me check," Marlo said, thinking, *I hope we can fit them in. They seem really nice and I want them to be my first reservation.*

Teresa and Bo were nervously looking at each other in hopes of a cabin being free. Marlo stood behind the counter tapping her foot to the music looking at the registration list.

"You have to love the Beach Boys. They can always get me in the mood to do housework," Teresa said.

"Yes, I know, they're great," replied Marlo. Looking up, Marlo said, "We do have two cabins open right now. It looks like you can stay for a week. Cabin A and B are available. Cabin A is closer to the highway so you don't have to travel far on the bumpy drive." Marlo pointed out the window. "Or, you can choose Cabin B which is here, next to the office. Which would you prefer?" Marlo asked, thinking, *I would most definitely take the one closer to the road. I hate getting nausea from driving to Cabin D.*

"We'll take Cabin A. That drive is a little bumpy," Teresa said with a smile.

"Perfect. I would have made the same choice. Just fill out this form and you'll be on your way. You have a woodstove in your cabin so I can have Clay bring you some wood or you can wheelbarrow your own, if you'd like. Which do you prefer?" Marlo waited patiently.

"I'll just wheelbarrow the wood; it's not a big deal. I'll make enough trips to last the week and then Clay doesn't have to worry about it," said Bo with gratitude, thankful they found a place to stay.

"No problem. There's a wheelbarrow by the wood pile and you can help yourself. If you need anything, let me know and I'll be happy to assist you. My name is Marlo and welcome to Birch Cabins, enjoy your stay."

Teresa and Bo left the office feeling liberated and relieved because they found the perfect place to stay for the week. Bo laced his fingers through Teresa's and guided her through the door. Marlo gazed at them walking out, and thought, *what a nice couple. Well, that went well. I think I did great for my first run. Who's next?*

Throughout the day Marlo had little action. She had a couple of guests ask her questions. Surprisingly, she knew the answers, too. She filled the other cabin with another guest, a single guy who looked like he was from the city. He was handsome and had an interesting way about him. His name was Luke Evans and he was everything his name described. He had blonde, short hair, blue eyes and a good disposition. Marlo couldn't figure out why that man would be single. He said he was passing through town, but where do you pass through town here? *Oh well,* Marlo thought, not paying any attention to the thought. Even though Marlo was in love with Duncan, she could still sneak a peek—a little one. She knew no one could take Duncan's place. He was true to her and she welcomed his natural kindness and love for her, whole heartedly.

It was nine p.m. and Marlo was closing up the office. She posted a sign on the door that said, *"We are open again at six a.m. Enjoy your stay at Birch Cabins."* With that, she closed the door and when she climbed in the Jeep, she began questioning where Duncan was. *Why hasn't he stopped by or called?* Not worrying too much, Marlo drove down the same bumpy road back to her own cabin.

Feeling tired and spent from going to Seward to see Duncan, and working the evening shift in the office, she made a hot cup of tea. She lazily went to the bathroom and started her shower to warm the water. Upstairs in her loft Marlo opened her dresser and chose an oversized T-shirt, held it up, and thought, *this will do.* She pulled out a pair of white lace panties to wear to bed. She came downstairs and took a sip of her tea. At the moment Marlo was going to get in the shower, she heard someone knocking. She turned the shower off and walked to the door.

"Just a minute!" she called out. *Please be Duncan, I hope it's him.* She opened the door and there he stood. Marlo had a surprise look on her face and jumped in his arms. "Where have you been? I mean I've been worried about you. Where have you been, Duncan?" Marlo asked with conviction.

"You were worried about me, love?" asked Duncan with humor, but searching for truth.

"Of course I was worried. I was working in the office all day and when I was closing up, I thought, where is Duncan? Why didn't he stop by?" Marlo looked at Duncan with sincerity, "Yes, I was worried about you. Where were you?"

"Well first, I need your lips on mine."

Marlo raised her eyebrow, "I like that idea, come here you big dufus . . . making me worried."

Wrapping his arms around Marlo's waist, he pulled her into him bending her backwards kissing her with passion and heat. Once he let up on the kiss, he brought her up and looked at her with smoldering eyes.

"Marlo."

"Yes, Duncan?"

"I am crazy about you!" Duncan said with purpose. "You don't have to worry about me. I was late returning to port because the crew I took out on the Bay was a bunch of die hard fisherman. I was having too much fun watching them catch their daily quota. It was great! I haven't had that much fun taking someone out in a long time. Then, by the time I flushed the motor, stowed everything, cleaned out the bays and weighed the fish, I went home, showered and came straight here. Plus, I knew you would be busy because I know Sandra, and I know what it takes to run the office. How did that go by the way? I want to hear all about it."

Duncan couldn't wait to hear about her day.

"You came just in time for a cup of hot tea. The water in the tea kettle is still hot. Would you like a cup?" Marlo asked.

"No thank you, love. I would love a glass of water, though," Duncan said, feeling parched.

"Coming right up."

After filling a glass of cold water for Duncan, she took a seat at the kitchen table. He took a seat kitty corner from her in the leather chair, which he was becoming quite fond of. Marlo began telling Duncan all about her day.

"So, after talking to you, I did a little shopping and sent a postcard to my sister, Clare. When I was all done in Seward, I came back and went straight to the office to talk to Sandra. She showed me how to fill out paper work and log in guests on the computer. I checked in one couple, Teresa and Bo, very nice people in Cabin A. Later in the day, I checked a man in by the name of Luke, in Cabin B. I logged everyone into the computer and filled out the proper paperwork."

Duncan listened to Marlo and was relieved that she was on her way to a healthy new beginning.

"Marlo, it sounds like you know what you're doing and I know Sandra is happy to have you working in the office. She needed a break."

Marlo smiled, "Duncan?"

"Marlo"

"Stay with me tonight," Marlo said, showcasing her seductive eyes.

"Baby, I'll stay with you forever." Standing up, he held out his hand.

Marlo took his hand and he pulled her from the chair and said, "Did I hear the shower running earlier?"

Marlo smiled and said, "Yes, it was. I was just about to get in when you knocked."

"Well, I could definitely use a shower since I smell like fish. What do you say, we . . .," signaling to the bathroom, "take a hot, steamy shower together. I could really use my toes cleaned."

"You just said you already took a shower."

"And, I think I could use another one."

Winking at Marlo, he started nudging her to the bathroom.

After a well earned shower for both of them, especially Duncan since he still had a subtle hint of fish lingering on him, they sat at the table and ate a bowl of mint chocolate chip ice cream. It was a long day for both of them and Marlo started to yawn.

"I think we should snuggle under the covers after," smiling at Duncan, "you put a few logs on the fire . . . please?"

"I can do that for you."

"Thank you, I hate getting splinters."

Duncan laughed, remembering how scared she was for him to pull her last sliver out.

Night was quiet and had a mysterious feel to it. When Duncan and Marlo were starting to drift off to sleep, they heard coyotes howling.

"Did you hear that, Duncan?"

"It's just coyotes. Isn't it romantic, but creepy at the same time?"

"That's an interesting way of looking at it," Marlo said.

"Its okay, Marlo," said Duncan. "They're out there and we're in here. You're safe."

Duncan pulled Marlo even closer than she already was and held her tight, feeling her heart beat through her chest. Marlo nestled into him and closed her eyes.

Chapter 13

The next morning Duncan was happy as a clam lying next to the most beautiful woman in the world. He didn't want to leave her side.

"Good morning love, how did you sleep?" Duncan asked in a whispered tone, softly kissing Marlo on the lips.

"I slept great after the third time you woke me up. How did you sleep?" asked Marlo pulling the covers over her mouth to hide her morning breath and laughing.

"What are you doing?"

"I'm covering up my morning breath. Trust me . . . you do not want to experience this. I might make you pass out."

"You are such a nut, come here."

Rolling towards Marlo and covering her body with his, but keeping his weight off her, suspending his weight with his forearms, he said, "Do you know . . . that when I'm not with you, you are constantly on my mind? You fill my heart with so much joy. I love you, Marlo."

Duncan hasn't given himself emotionally, to a woman, yet, but he was ready to give himself to Marlo.

"I love you, Duncan."

Marlo leaned up to reach his lips, softly kissing him and Duncan responded, tasting Marlo and wanting more. She had a delicate sweetness to her and Duncan wanted it all. He made love to her slow and steady, making it last.

Feeling her tighten under his touch and her stomach clench when he slid his tongue over her stomach, Marlo whispered, "I want you. I want you now. I need you inside me Duncan."

"Wait," he whispered.

Marlo accepted what he wanted and withered under his hard body. She moved at every touch. His mouth covered one nipple, and teasing her, sliding to the other breast. He moved down her stomach, kissing her everywhere. Climbing up her body like a jaguar, he knew she wanted him inside her.

She whispered, "I want you. I want you, now, Duncan."

She looked into his eyes with hunger and passion. Duncan took her mouth with his, plunging his tongue into her and slowly slid himself deep inside her. She arched her back feeling him deep inside her. She began rocking with him and feeling her body climax. Duncan waited in anticipation before releasing himself.

Looking into Marlo's eyes, Duncan said, "I feel like I've waited a lifetime for the right woman to come along, but now it was worth every second."

Marlo snuggled into him and together they fell asleep in each other's arms for another couple of hours.

Duncan and Marlo woke to birds chirping and the softness of the late morning light peeking through the curtains. Stretching and snuggling beside Duncan, Marlo realized she hasn't seen Mandi in twenty-four hours.

"Duncan, wake up, Duncan."

Shaking him softly, Marlo said, "I haven't seen Mandi. Do you know where Brady and Mandi went yesterday?"

Duncan rolled towards Marlo.

"I know Brady picked her up from here and he was taking her out for the day. Maybe they had a great time and he took her back to our place. I'm sure she's fine. Brady is a good guy."

"If you think she's fine, then I know she's having a great time. Brady *is* a good guy. I hope I see her though. Since she's been here we haven't spent a lot of time together," Marlo said, climbing out of bed.

Duncan reached for Marlo's arm, "Where do you think *you're* going, Missy?" asked Duncan.

Marlo turned towards him and said, "To get a shower, I stink."

"I thought I got a whiff of something of questionable nature."

Duncan was laughing and rolling on the bed. Marlo jumped on Duncan and started wrestling him, pinning him down.

"I can't believe you just said that! I'm going to . . ."

"You're going to what, huh . . . huh?" Duncan inquired playfully, tickling Marlo.

Wriggling around and laughing, she said, "I'm going to . . ." Marlo had nothing. "I don't know, but you are a rotten man."

Both laughing and playing, Marlo sighed and reluctantly got up and started climbing down the ladder. She made her way to the bathroom and turned on the shower. Duncan sat up on the side of the bed and put his boxers on. He went downstairs and started breakfast.

"Good morning, Man-di . . .," Duncan said in shock to see Mandi walk in the door.

"Well, hello Duncan. I see you had a good time last night," said Mandi looking down at Duncan's boxers.

"It's morning." Trying to hide the obvious reaction of morning, he headed up to the loft to retrieve his clothes.

"I'm home," Mandi said opening the door to the bathroom.

"Hey, I was wondering what happened to you, everything good?" asked Marlo standing in the shower with soap covering her eyes.

"Yeah, everything is great."

"Did you have a good time?" Marlo asked. "I did. We had a lot of fun."

Duncan came downstairs feeling a little more prepared for Mandi's surprise arrival.

"Good morning Mandi, did you want breakfast?"

"No, thank you. Brady and I went out for breakfast this morning. But, thank you for asking."

Mandi sat at the table waiting for Marlo to get out of the shower. Marlo came out of the bathroom with her hair up in a towel and a towel wrapped around her body.

"Mmm, smells good. I'm starving."

"I figured you would be after exerting all your energy last night and early this morning."

Duncan winked at Marlo and her face turned red.

"Okay then, I'll be getting dressed. I would love an egg over medium and a side of toast, if that's okay," said Marlo starting up the ladder to her loft.

"On its way," Duncan said while cracking the egg into the pan. Coming back down, Marlo took a seat at the table with Mandi and Duncan.

"I'm really glad I came to Alaska. It's a magnificent place," Mandi said, watching Duncan dip the corner of his toast into his runny yellow yolk.

"Mandi, cut the crap, I want to know about your date with Brady," said Marlo taking a bite of her jellied toast.

"Okay, so, I was sleeping yesterday morning and you were out like a light and I didn't want to wake you. Brady came over and said get dressed I'm taking you on a tour of Alaska. So, I jumped in the shower, got dressed, and we left. We went all over the place. We ate breakfast, lunch and dinner out in different towns and went sight seeing. We took a hike, we went shopping, we went whale watching, it was amazing. We rented a two-seater bike and went bike riding. It was crazy, I loved it. Then, he asked me over. I said yes and we ended up falling asleep to a movie on the couch. We had a great time," Mandi said with excitement in her voice.

Brady was fun, but she knew she had a career and couldn't leave it. "So, what's going to happen now?" Marlo asked, watching Duncan sit quietly at the table waiting to hear her answer and eating his toast. "Well, Brady has the pub and I have my career back in Minnesota.

We talked about it and agreed we had fun and we'll see what happens when I come back next spring or summer."

"Well, it sounds like you guys hit it off," Marlo said confused, and thought, *had fun, what does that mean?*

"Oh, we did, but I'm not ready to up and leave Minnesota, yet. I love my job. It took me a long time to achieve my goals. He understands," Mandi said with certainty.

"Okay, well as long as you both are good with the decision you made, it sounds like you both enjoyed each other's company."

Marlo looked at Mandi with the 'we're going to have some fun today,' look on her face.

"Okay, so here's what I was thinking. You and I could go into Seward and do some shopping. They have the cutest stores. They have all sorts of different things we can look at and they have antique stores . . . our favorite."

Mandi looked at Marlo with a saddened expression.

"What's the matter Mandi? I thought you would love to do that, today?"

Mandi looked at Marlo and then looked down at her feet. "I have some bad news, Marlo."

Before Mandi could say another word, Duncan said, "Marlo, Mandi, this would be a good time for me to head out. I have some things to do." Walking over to Marlo he said, "I'll come back later when you're working and maybe we can hang out for a bit before I go into the pub. I had a wonderful time last night, thank you. I'll see you later."

"Alright, love. I can't wait."

Marlo smiled at Duncan and gave him a kiss. Duncan slowly closed the door behind him.

Marlo turned to Mandi and asked, "What bad news? You just got here."

Marlo was extremely disappointed and frustrated. However, she immediately felt remorse for how she sounded.

"When Brady and I were out yesterday, I received a phone call from my boss, Jim, back in Minnesota. We're in the process of merging with another company right now and I was under the impression it was going to be a couple of weeks before the other company made their final decision. They even told Jim they wanted to go over the figures amongst themselves one more time, but they decided sooner than we were expecting. Now, I have to go back to Minnesota to settle the merger with him, and I'm not looking forward to it. I called Jim and told him that I just got here and maybe I could do it over video conference, but he said no. He wants me there in two days."

Marlo looked completely forlorn and was disappointed beyond measure, but knew how important Mandi's job was to her.

"This is totally unexpected. I wanted to enjoy your company and hang out. I wanted to go shopping and go out to dinner and laugh at our stupid jokes. I don't know what to say. I'm shocked that this is happening. I can't believe this."

"I know, Marlo, I'm sorry. I'm really sorry, but I'll be back. I promise. Please forgive me."

"Oh Mandi, I'm not angry with you. I'm angry with this other company. I know you have to go."

Marlo was disappointed and frustrated with Mandi leaving, but knew she wouldn't leave unless it was serious.

"I understand. Look, when you get home, we can start planning for your real trip out here. Just make sure you don't schedule it in the middle of a merger."

"I won't Marlo and thank you for being so understanding about this. You are truly a wonderful friend," said Mandi.

Later that day, Mandi packed up her things and got ready for her flight back to Minnesota, the Viking State. She felt like she didn't even arrive and now she had to leave, but she knew she was coming back. She looked around and thought, *this place is so warm and inviting. I wish I could pack up my life in Minnesota and move out here. No worries;*

just relax and live a slow life. No morning rush hour traffic, no sirens, no trains, just peace and quiet.

Marlo worked all day and didn't get to spend any time with Mandi. She locked up the office and started down the path to her cabin and saw Luke coming towards her.

"Excuse me, Marlo is it?" asked Luke.

"Yes, is everything okay, Luke?" asked Marlo wondering what he needed.

"Yeah, everything is fine. I was thinking about switching my cabin if someone departs before me. Would I be able to do that?"

Luke stood there looking at Marlo thinking how she glowed in the moonlight.

"Yes, that wouldn't be a problem, but all the cabins are rented until after your departure date. I'm sorry. Is there something wrong with the cabin you're staying in?" asked Marlo.

"No, it's just . . ." looking around he continued, "Don't take this the wrong way, but I can see you through the window all day and you're dancing distracts me. I love the dancing but I'm working and it's hard to not look over and see you rock out to your jam sessions," said Luke with a smile on his face.

He thought she was adorable with all her dancing and what not.

"Oh, I'm so sorry. I will close the blinds on that side of the office," replied Marlo thinking, *okay, just shoot me. Shoot me now.*

"Thank you. I really enjoyed your dancing moves, but I am easily drawn to things that grab my attention. I really need to focus on my work," said Luke smiling, enjoying her squirm with embarrassment.

"No problem, I will make sure I don't distract you anymore. Oh, and I'm sorry you had to see me dancing."

Marlo saw laughter in Luke's eyes and new he thought she was adorable.

"Well, good night Luke."

"Good night Marlo," replied Luke turning on his heels back up the hill to his cabin. *That woman is quirky and adorable. She's a nut,* Luke thought to himself.

Marlo opened the door to her cabin and shut it behind her, seeing Mandi sitting at the table.

"There is someone I want you to meet before you leave," Marlo mentioned to Mandi.

"Who?"

"Sandra, the woman who owns Birch Cabins, and her husband, Clay; they're really great. I know she's at home and I want you to meet her before you leave tomorrow. Both of them have helped me tremendously since I've been here and Sandra has become a close friend," said Marlo grabbing her coat.

"Okay, let's go. I don't want to stay long though because I have to get up early," said Mandi walking behind Marlo.

"Sure, that's fine," Marlo replied.

Knocking on the door, Marlo and Mandi waited for Sandra or Clay to answer.

"Hey Marlo, come on in. I'll get Sandra for you," Clay said shutting the door.

Clay walked in the kitchen and told Sandra Marlo was at the door. She came walking over.

"Marlo was everything okay tonight at the office?" asked Sandra. "Yes, everything was fine." Gesturing towards Mandi, Marlo said,

"I want you to meet my best friend, Mandi." Looking back to Sandra and Clay, Marlo said, "This is Sandra and her husband, Clay. They've been a huge support to me since I've been here," said Marlo introducing them.

"Hello, it's nice to meet you. Marlo has told me all about you," offered Mandi stretching her arm out to shake their hands.

"And, we have heard all about you, Mandi," Sandra replied with a smile.

"Good, I hope."

"Yes, it was and is, all good. Marlo thinks very highly of you. You are a huge part of her life," said Sandra looking at Marlo.

Mandi glanced over at Marlo and showed her affection and gratitude, "Thank you."

Marlo returned the gesture and said, "Well, I don't want to keep you. Mandi has to get up early to catch her return flight in the morning."

"Alright, well, it was great to meet you, Mandi. You come back again and visit, anytime," Sandra told her as they were getting ready to leave.

"I will and thank you for taking Marlo under your wings."

"We didn't. She did it all on her own."

Heading back to the cabin, Mandi said, "Wow, you're right, they are really wonderful people. I can see why you like it here, Marlo. I'm proud of you and your decision to stay."

Marlo showed her appreciation to Mandi.

"Thank you for understanding. Now, I have to break the news to Clare. That's going to be tough. She thought I was just taking a vacation. However, I did tell her that it could be a few months before I came home. I think she'll be okay . . . I hope. She knew I needed a change," Marlo told Mandi.

Not wanting to waste what little time they had left, they sat up for a long time and talked, laughed, and ate, and ate, and ate. Nearing midnight, Marlo and Mandi decided to call it a night and head to bed. Morning would soon be upon them.

Chapter 14

The following morning, Mandi saw Marlo sitting at the kitchen table drinking a cup of coffee and asked, "Would it be okay if Brady took me to the airport? I know you have to work and he asked me yesterday. I told him it would be okay."

"Yeah, I guess so. That's fine, Mandi. I don't mind." Just then, Brady pulled up to the house.

Walking in the door, he said, "Good morning girls."

Marlo smiled, "Good morning, Brady. Thank you for taking Mandi to the airport. That's very nice of you."

"No problem. It's my pleasure."

Brady saw Mandi standing by the wood stove and asked, "Are you ready, Mandi?"

"I am. I just need to load my luggage into your truck."

"I'll get it. You can say your goodbyes," Brady told Mandi, taking two bags to the truck.

"Well Marlo, it was a mini adventure. I will see you again soon, though. I promise. You be careful and hang on to that man of yours; he's a keeper."

Hugging Mandi good bye, Marlo said, "Call me when you get home so I know you made it safely. I'll see you soon. Take care of yourself. Oh, and I need to make arrangements to cancel my lease on my apartment and get my things shipped to me when I find a place," said Marlo.

"Don't worry, we'll get all that figured out later. Just get settled in first."

They gave each other a tight sisterly hug and Mandi walked to the truck. Waving goodbye as Mandi and Brady started up the drive, Marlo thought, *this totally sucks. I hate that Mandi had to leave. I need to call Clare.*

Marlo went inside and thought how she was going to break the news about staying in Alaska . . . *permanently,* to her one and only sister. *Clare would understand. She knows I'm a 'fly by the seat of my pants' kind of girl. I can't see her not responding to this well. Hmmm, maybe I should wait another few days to call her. No, no, I need to tell her now otherwise the waiting will eat at me and I'll get distracted. Okay, I'm calling. Wait, Yes, I'm calling.*

Marlo started pushing buttons on her phone and was contemplating whether to call her now or later, but it was too late when Clare picked up the phone and said, "Hello?"

"Hey Clare, how are things going?"

Clare was ready to strangle Marlo through the phone.

"Good, you mind telling me why you waited so long to call. I was a little worried."

"I know. I wanted to call, but things have been coming up and I kept putting it off, but I'm here now."

"Tell me what's been going on. What have you been doing?"

"Well, you know that guy I told you about when I first arrived?"

"Yes," Clare said, thinking, *I know where this is going.*

"You know, Duncan?"

"Yes." *I knew it.*

"We've kind of fallen in love with each other," said Marlo and winced, waiting.

And, the bomb drops.

"Ah, Marlo, you just met him. How could you be in love with him?" asked Clare.

"We just fell in love. I know it's soon, but it just happened. I love him and I've decided to stay in Alaska." Marlo started speaking quickly so Clare couldn't interrupt her. "I found a place to stay and a job that covers my rent and utilities and I would still have money left over. Sandra and Clay, the owners of Birch Cabins, gave me a job working the front office and I can stay in the cabin for free until I find a place of my own. And, Duncan is a wonderful man. He treats me with respect, kindness and love unlike the other men I've dated and I'm happy, Clare. I'm really happy and I want you to be happy for me."

Listening to Marlo, Clare knew Marlo was really truly happy. She could tell. How was she going to give Marlo grief when she hasn't been this happy since their parents died?

She thought about it and said, "Marlo, you are one of the craziest people I know. And, that's why I love you. I love you as a sister, but also as the one person who never lets anything stand in her way of getting what she wants. You're a fire that needs to be put out. If he's the one, then . . ."

"Hey—"

"You know what I mean, Marlo. He's your rock. If you love him and he loves you then it's meant to be," Clare said with heartache, but knew Marlo was desperately in need of finding her happiness.

Clare didn't want to stop her from finding peace in her life. "Marlo, I just want to remind you of one important thing."

"What's that, Clare?"

"Remember when you were sitting in the chair down by the lake, thinking about where you wanted your life to go?"

"Yes."

"It sounds like you are definitely in a relationship and the whole point of going to Alaska was to find yourself and come to terms with Mom and Dad's death."

"I know, you're right, Clare. I wasn't expecting to find Duncan. And, I had him at arms length until"

"Until what, Marlo?"

"Until, I fell in love with him. I know this looks like a pattern repeating itself, but it's not. Duncan is different. You'll see. Please trust my judgment, Clare. I won't let you down."

"Marlo, what am I going to do with you? I trust you to know what you are doing will be right for you, since I'm not there to watch over you, like I always do. Please know that I am here for you. If something goes off kilter, call me. I'm right here. You will always have me."

"I want you to know that I am searching out answers and trying to come to terms with Mom and Dads' death. I have been thinking about things and I think, eventually, everything will be okay, Clare."

"Well, that's good news. I know you'll figure things out, Marlo. You're a fighter."

"Thank you, Clare." Marlo was thrilled that she had Clare's blessing. "This means so much to me and don't worry, we'll go on holiday. I promise. Duncan and I will come down so you can rally the family up and make him feel embarrassed."

"Very funny," Clare said into the phone.

"Just kidding, I mean welcomed. I don't know when we'll show ourselves, but we will. He wants what's best for me and he knows how important you are to me. I love you, Clare."

"I love you, too, Marlo. Be careful and call me soon. Please don't linger and get caught up in your love life and fail to remember your sister," Clare reminded her, almost in tears.

"I won't. I love you. Talk to you soon."

Hanging up the phone and thinking, *that went better than I expected,* Marlo picked up a wash cloth and rinsed it with soap and water. She started wiping down the counters and the kitchen table, humming to the Beach Boys; they were stuck in her head. *I think I'll go for a walk today, and then when I come back, I'll shower and head over to the office.* After Marlo tidied up her cabin, she eased her coat and boots on. She took one last glance at the inside and was satisfied with her hard work.

Marlo headed up the drive for a relaxing walk in the coolness of early afternoon. She was coming up to the office and saw Sandra working away on the computer. She couldn't help but peek in Luke's cabin when she walked by. Marlo couldn't see him in his cabin and kept walking. Talking to herself while she dodged ruts and avoided pot holes she said, "Maybe I'll stop by Luke's cabin this afternoon when work is stagnant. I'll ask him if the blinds obscured my foolish dancing moves." Marlo let out a chuckle and kept walking. Her arms were swaying to and fro; she had a skip in her step. She was full of self-gratification and in high spirits. Further up the road, she saw someone walking towards her. "Who is that? I can't tell . . . oh, that's Luke."

Marlo gave a shout, "Hey Luke, what are you up to?"

"Roasting marshmallows, want to join me?"

"Ha, very funny," said Marlo thinking, *what a smartass*! "What are you up to, Marlo?" asked Luke.

"I was just taking a walk. I thought it would refresh me if I got some air."

Luke couldn't help but gaze into her eyes and feel her energy. "Would you like to walk me back to my cabin?" asked Luke, piercing her insides with his stare.

"Um . . .," thinking quickly, *its okay Marlo. A walk isn't a big deal.* "Sure, but then I didn't get a very long walk."

"Okay, well, let's keep going then. I don't mind heading the same direction I just came from."

Luke looked down at Marlo and the corners of his mouth turned up. Marlo returned the look and smiled. *It's just a walk. Don't panic. You're just walking with a guest from Birch Cabins whom you happened to bump into. No biggie.*

"Are you sure, Luke? I don't want to keep you from your work."

"It's okay. My mind has been wrapping itself around things I have no control over. I needed a break anyways."

Marlo took bigger strides than normal, trying to keep up with Luke, making sure she kept her distance to avoid bumping his hand or brushing his arm. She kept telling herself, *it's just a leisurely stroll.*

"Can I ask what brought you to Birch Cabins, Luke? I mean, I don't want to pry."

Staring out in the distance, he said, "Oh, sure you don't," laughing and nudging her with his shoulder.

"Hey now, I was just wondering," replied Marlo, laughing and thinking how friendly Luke was. "Seriously though, never mind, it's okay. I shouldn't have asked." Marlo felt like he may not have wanted to share with her the reason he was staying at Birch Cabins.

Then he offered, "I live in Alaska, near Fairbanks. When I was younger, my parents and I would vacation here, in Seward. They always loved this place and it's not too far from where we live."

Marlo was keeping in step next to Luke listening to him and looking at how the sunlight captured his blue eyes, giving them a turquoise color.

"Mmm hmm," she said letting Luke know she was listening.

"Lately, I've been thinking about my parents a lot and thought maybe coming back here would put my sadness to rest."

"Luke," Marlo said putting her hand on his arm to stop him, "what do you mean, 'put my sadness to rest'?"

Luke didn't say anything.

Marlo stared at the road and said, "I'm so sorry. It's none of my business."

Thinking he made Marlo feel like she was trespassing, he said, "That's okay, you're fine. It might help if I tell someone about my feelings."

Marlo stopped and glanced up at Luke's eyes and said, "I'm a good listener, if you'd like to talk to me. If you choose not to, that's okay."

He thought she was a kind hearted woman and knew she was being sincere. He decided to tell her because he didn't have anyone else to share his past with. "Well, four years ago, my parents passed away. They were in a freak car accident, right here just outside of Seward. I thought maybe being here where they loved to come would open my heart and help me remember the good times we shared. I thought maybe it would help with my heartache. I'm an only child and it's hard to know that, without your parents, you're all that's left. I feel alone."

Marlo stared at Luke and didn't know what to say. Thoughts were rushing through her faster than she could grasp. She stood on the path with one foot in a rut and the other in a pot hole and looked at Luke, but words could not escape her.

"Marlo, are you okay?"

"Uh, yeah, I uh . . . I need to get going. I just realized I work in the office in a bit, maybe I'll see you later."

"But, Marlo . . ."

"I'm sorry, I have to go." Turning on her heels and jogging back to the office, Marlo couldn't help think, *what was that all about? His parents died in a car crash four years ago? If that's not a coincidence, I don't know what is. Holy shit! Marlo relax a minute, it could be a coincidence. Or, maybe it's not. What if his parent's car was the car that was involved in my parent's accident? I should talk to him, for sure, but . . . ah, that might not be a wise idea. I don't know. Think Marlo, think.*

Marlo slowed down to a brisk walk and when she reached the office she started to pace. She didn't want to go in until she cleared her mind.

Five minutes later, Marlo opened the door and went inside. "Hey, Sandra, how was the morning shift? Busy?"

"Well, not really." Sandra was tapping her pen on the counter. "I saw you walking with Luke. What did he say?"

"Oh, he's just visiting. I didn't talk to him long because I knew I had to come into work."

Sandra gave Marlo a suspicious look, but let it go.

"Alright, then, if everything is fine, I'll be on my way. Clay and I are going to go out for a late lunch today. Have a relaxing afternoon, Marlo, and be sure to lock up tonight on your way out."

Sandra opened the door to head out.

"Always do. Enjoy your lunch with Clay, Sandra."

Marlo took her coat off and hung it up on the wooden peg by the door. She started to brew a fresh pot of coffee and turned the radio on to the Oldies station. It was getting cloudy outside. Marlo decided it would feel inviting if she lit a candle. She found a lighter and lit the candle.

"Mmm, Warm Vanilla Sugar, I love that smell. This will make it feel cozy in here," said Marlo and set the candle down. She started to look over what Sandra did for the morning.

When Luke was almost to his cabin he saw Marlo in the window and felt uneasy about how Marlo and his conversation ended. He sauntered up to his door when he noticed Marlo pulling the blinds on the one side of the office by his cabin.

"Maybe I should go talk to her," Luke said out loud.

"No, maybe not, that was an interesting way to end a conversation. Why did she react that way?"

Marlo was pulling the last of the blinds in the back room and saw Duncan's truck pulling into Birch Cabins.

"Luke, you are going to talk to her," he said to himself. "She acted like something clicked in her brain."

He knew this was going to fluster him so he turned and walked to the office. He opened the door and saw Marlo pulling the last shade down on his side of the office.

"Why did you react that way outside?" asked Luke.

Marlo turned, "Oh, you scared me, Luke. Um, I don't know. I was in shock to hear it, I guess."

"Well, you looked like you . . ."

Luke turned around and saw a tall, broad shouldered and muscular man who looked like a hard worker, smile when he walked in.

"Hey Marlo, sir," Duncan said closing the office door. "Hello," said Luke, looking at Duncan.

"Duncan, I'm glad you came to visit. This is Luke Evans. He's renting the cabin next to the office."

"How do you do?" asked Duncan. Luke looked over and nodded.

Marlo looked at Luke and said, "Mr. Evans, if you have any more questions, I'll be here until nine tonight."

Luke took that as, *it's time to go,* and said, "Thanks again."

Nodding his head at Duncan, Luke left and went back to his cabin.

Marlo walked over to Duncan from behind the desk, teasing him with playful eyes. "I'm happy to see you, love." She put her hands on his waist and pulled him into her. Duncan leaned in and lowered his lips to hers and softly kissed her.

"Who was that?" asked Duncan.

"That's the guy I checked in. Remember I was telling you about him my first day?"

"Oh, right. I wonder what brings him to Birch Cabins."

Marlo smiled and asked, "What time are you heading into the pub?" She ignored his question for reasons she did not know.

"Soon, I just wanted to come over and give you a kiss before I went to work. What happened with Mandi? I felt like it wasn't my place to be there when she was laying bad news on the table."

"She had to go back to Minnesota for work. Her boss called her and she didn't really have a choice."

"That's too bad. I know you wanted to spend some quality time with her."

"At least Brady had the chance to show her Alaska and all its beauty. I wish it was me, though," said Marlo looking down.

"I know, Marlo. I'm sorry. I know how excited you were to show her Seward and spend some girl-time with Mandi," replied Duncan.

"She said she was going to come back soon. It'll be okay." Marlo was walking over to the coffee pot.

"Do you want me to pour you a cup of coffee?"

"Sure, that'd be great. I can only stay for one cup and then I have to head over to the pub."

Marlo and Duncan relished in each others company for a while, talking and drinking their coffee. Marlo couldn't help daydreaming about what Luke said about his parents and what significance ties Luke's parents and her parents' death. Duncan stood, running his hands down the front of his jeans.

"Well love, I have to go. Have a good evening. I'll come by tonight and we can make chocolate chip pancakes for a late snack."

"That sounds wonderful. I'll see you later." Marlo watched Duncan get in his truck and drive down the road.

Marlo went behind the desk and was pacing back and forth talking to herself about what Luke said.

"Could this be true? Could Luke's parents have died the same day mine did? He had the same idea I did, coming up to Seward and trying to figure things out. Maybe I should go talk to him, but what would I say? *Oh, hello again, yeah, I'm sorry I freaked out on our walk and by the way, my parents are possibly the reason your parents are gone.* That would go over well with him, I'm sure."

Marlo continued to pace.

Luke was in his cabin and could see Marlo's shadow from behind the blinds.

He said to himself, "She's pacing. Why would she be pacing? She was acting stand-offish and now she seems worried. Maybe I should go over there and sit down and have a calm discussion with her."

Marlo was getting ready to go next door and talk to Luke. "I'm just going to go over and calmly ask him if we can talk."

She opened the door and saw Luke standing on the stoop with his hand raised, ready to knock.

She smiled, "I was just coming over to you."

"I guess I beat you to it." He looked at her and asked, "Can I come in and talk to you, Marlo?"

"Yes, come in, Luke. Would you like a cup of coffee?"

"I would, thank you. It smells good in here."

"That would be Warm Vanilla Sugar, a candle I lit because I think it's the perfect day for a candle."

Luke listened to Marlo and felt like he's known her forever. He sat at the table and watched Marlo.

Duncan was driving to the pub and couldn't help, but think how awkward it felt when he walked into the office, this afternoon. He sensed something odd between Luke and Marlo. *It looked like they were in a discussion or there was tension in the room. I'll have to talk to her about that guy. Something doesn't seem right.*

Duncan went to work that evening and was distracted by what happened in the office earlier. Brady kept looking at Duncan making simple mistakes and was questioning what the heck was going through Duncan's mind.

"Are you okay, Duncan? You seem distracted or upset about something."

"I'm a little of both."

"What's wrong? Talk to me?"

"Well, I'm probably over reacting in the first place, but this afternoon when I went to see Marlo, some guy was in the office with her and something seemed . . . off."

Duncan was wiping the bar down and Brady was drying glasses with a white hand towel.

"What do you mean, something seemed off?" asked Brady.

"Like they were in a conversation and then when I walked in, she said, "Ok then, if you have any questions, I'll be here until nine tonight. It was just bizarre."

"Maybe she was caught off guard and surprised to see you," Brady threw out.

"Yeah, maybe, I don't know. I'm not usually the protective type and I know Marlo loves me, but that guy better back off."

Duncan could feel his body becoming stiff. Talking about Marlo with Brady and bringing up this guy, was making him upset.

"You need to relax, Duncan. There's no reason for you to get your undies in a knot. I'm sure you're just over reacting."

"I hope you're right because I have this uneasy feeling something else is going on."

"If you feel troubled by what you felt or saw, maybe you should just talk to her."

"Yeah, maybe," replied Duncan.

Luke sat in a chair across from Marlo at a round wooden table, up front in the corner. After he took a sip of his coffee, he said, "I think I may have said something to upset you and if I did, I'm sorry."

Marlo just sat there and looked nervous, bouncing her knee. Luke continued when he realized she wasn't going to say anything.

"I'm just a little confused why you left."

He waited for her to offer up something, anything.

A few moments later, she said, "There is something I should talk to you about."

"What is it?"

"I know I don't know you and what I have to say, might shock you a little."

Luke sat at the table looking at Marlo and waiting for what she about to say to him.

"You're not going to believe this, but that's why *I* came up here."

"What do you mean?" asked Luke.

"Four years ago *my* parents died as well, just outside of Seward, heading to the airport in Anchorage. Their death has been weighing on me since that day."

Marlo paused and waited for Luke to reply. "What?"

"I know it sounds like a coincidence, but I think our parents hit each other."

"Wow. You're right, I'm in shock. I don't know what to say," replied Luke.

"That's why I couldn't talk to you and had to leave; it was all too surreal. When I came into work I was pacing and contemplating whether or not I should talk to you about it. And then I thought if it was the other way around, I would want you to talk to me."

Marlo took a sip of her coffee and asked, "What did you think you were going to find, Luke?"

"I don't know. Maybe a reason to put all this behind me, maybe a sense of closure, I'm not sure." Luke was just staring into his coffee.

"How long are you going to be here, Luke?" asked Marlo.

"I don't know, now. I don't know what I'm looking for anymore," said Luke lifting his eyebrows and unsure of his next move.

"Do you want to go to the café in Seward, tomorrow?" asked Marlo. "Maybe just talking about it would help."

"That sounds great. I would love to do that," said Luke. "I have to work in the afternoon. Does morning work for you?" asked Marlo.

"Morning is perfect."

Luke got up from his chair and pushed it in. He grabbed his Styrofoam cup of coffee and headed back to his cabin. Marlo remained sitting in the chair, thinking, *that went well . . . maybe.*

After a long night of doing nothing, except listening to the oldies and wishing she was with Duncan, Marlo locked up the office and turned the lights off. She walked back to her cabin feeling exhausted and nervous about meeting Luke at the café tomorrow. She looked up from the ground and saw Duncan's truck outside her cabin, but Duncan wasn't in it. *Oh, Duncan is here. I didn't see him drive by. I wonder why he didn't come to the office. Where is he?*

Marlo yelled, "Duncan, where are you?"

He came walking up from the river and Marlo headed over to him. "Hey you, I didn't see you drive by. I'm glad you're here."

Marlo looked at him and gave him a soft kiss on the lips.

"What's wrong?" asked Marlo, sensing Duncan was upset about something.

"Who was that guy in the office, this afternoon?"

"I told you. That was Luke Evans, the guy I checked in the first day I started working the evening shift, remember? Why does it matter?"

Marlo looked at Duncan with a suspicious stare.

"Well, when I came in the office, the conversation seemed peculiar to me. That's all."

Marlo wanted to tell Duncan about her discovery, but figured she should keep this new found information to herself until she had all the information. Then she would share it with him.

"Everything is fine. Why don't we go inside and get out of the cold." Duncan followed her inside.

She said, "Ooooh, it's so warm in here," rubbing her hands together. "I love having a woodstove." She took off her coat and boots and set them neatly by the door. Marlo went over to the kitchen counter and pulled a cup from the shelf. She opened a packet of Swiss Miss Cocoa and started a kettle of water on the stove. "Would you like some hot chocolate, Duncan?"

"Sure, don't forget the little marshmallows," said Duncan, with a smile and a wink. *I'm not going to worry about anything. I'm sure I'm over reacting and acting like a fool in love. I'm just going to drop it. I love Marlo and I know she loves me, too.*

"I would never do that. Hot chocolate isn't hot chocolate without the little marshmallows."

Marlo and Duncan snuggled up for the night and enjoyed each others company. Later, they went up to the loft and fell asleep in each others arms.

Early the next morning, Duncan opened his eyes to Marlo sleeping soundly and the covers pulled up to her ears. He smiled and shook his head. He was in love. He didn't want to wake her, so he tiptoed through the cabin and gathered his things. He left a note:

Love,

I have to go into Seward today, but I'll be back later.
I didn't want to wake you. I love you.

Duncan

Soon after Duncan left, Marlo opened her eyes, slowly. Stretching her arms over her head and arching her back letting out a stifled yawn and moan, she turned to give Duncan a kiss, but he wasn't there. She sat up looking around and peeked over the railing. She saw a note. Marlo threw on some sweats and climbed down the ladder. She walked over to the table and picked up the note.

After reading it, she smiled and said to herself, "He's going to be the man I marry," and proceeded to hum. She took the kettle from the stove and filled it with water. Marlo was in the mood for some tea. She ate a light breakfast that consisted of oatmeal and chopped fruit with a side of jellied toast and, of course, her hot cup of coffee. It was getting chilly in the cabin. She opened the damper to the woodstove and put a couple of logs on the smoldering coals. Then, she closed the door to avoid any smoke escaping into the cabin and set the damper.

She loved having a woodstove. The warmth it put out was soothing and comforting. And, the smell was heavenly. She felt her hands were getting a little dry, so she filled a kettle of water and put it on the top of the woodstove. "There, that's perfect," she said. Marlo figured by the time she got dressed and drove to Luke's cabin, he would be ready to go to the café.

Marlo stood at Luke's door and knocked. He opened the door with a smile on his face.

"Good morning, Marlo."

"Good morning, Luke. Are you ready for that cup of coffee?"

"I am. Let's go."

Shutting the door behind him, he followed her to the Jeep and got in. They parked in the municipal parking behind the shops where the café was located.

"I haven't been here yet," said Luke.

"They have really good coffee and pastries. You'll like it." Luke held the door for Marlo and followed her inside.

Looking back at him, she said, "Duncan and I just came here the other day."

"That's good to know," said Luke with a speck of sarcasm.

The weather was brisk and the wind was a little breezy, but Duncan worked on his boat and wasn't fazed by the chilly air. A couple hours later, he thought about going to the café and getting some lunch before heading over to Marlo's. He wanted to apologize for acting like a jerk. He finished stowing his gear and securing his boat. He lifted his backpack onto his shoulder and trekked up to the café.

On the way there, Duncan was mumbling to himself, "I can't believe I actually assumed Marlo would have something to do with Luke. What was I thinking? I've never been one to be insecure. Brady was right, I was just over reacting."

Duncan walked up the sidewalk to the entrance of the cafe and smiled when he thought about Marlo and him having coffee here not too long ago. When he was ready to go inside he saw Marlo and Luke sitting on a couch drinking coffee and talking. *What the . . . I knew something was going on. I knew something smelled fishy when I walked in the office yesterday; so much for talking to Marlo. I was dismissing all the 'foolish thoughts' I was having and for what? My initial instincts were right on the money. Why didn't she say anything when I brought it up? She just acted like nothing was wrong and dismissed it. Fine, if you don't want to tell me what's going on, then I don't want to know. Have fun with Luke!*

Duncan closed his eyes and shook his head in anger and disappointment. He slowly turned around and headed towards his pick up, feeling pale and betrayed and full of anger.

"I just can't believe how you and I, just a tiny fragment of the earth's population, ended up in the same place for the same reason. It's truly, too hard to believe," said Marlo.

She looked around the café and distracted by other conversations, Marlo refocused on Luke.

"Tell me about your parents, Marlo. Why did they visit Alaska all the time?" asked Luke, completely into Marlo and patiently waiting for her response.

"Well, I guess because they loved it here. My Father was a great fisherman. He loved to fish for Salmon. My Mother just loved the beauty Alaska provided for her; it cloaked her."

Marlo spoke with honesty in her voice. Her expression was sincere and full of vitality. Luke just sat there and absorbed Marlo's admiration for her parents.

"She used to say it would nourish her soul, rejuvenate her. The both of them truly admired Alaska. Reflecting on who they were, I know what they treasured most, was each other. Sharing their life and adventures together, no matter where they were in the world, is all they needed to be happy."

Marlo glanced up at Luke and smiled softly. She was savoring the feeling that came over her when she was speaking of her parents' happiness. Studying Marlo, Luke was amazed how she conveyed this infectious dose of passion when she talked about her parents.

Marlo wasn't sure how Luke was taking her, until he said, "Marlo, when you speak of your parents you have this energy, this glow around you. When I listened to what you said and saw how you lit up, it was almost like you had this connection with them. It was really amazing. I would love to be able to share my parents' past with someone and be able to hold it together."

Marlo was still. She didn't realize it until just now when Luke mentioned it, but she has come to terms with the death of her parents. *He's right. When I was telling him about Mom and Dad, I didn't cry. I know they are in a wonderful place and I'm okay. I have actually crossed this massive hurdle and its okay. I'm going to be alright.*

Marlo came back from her moment of thought and said, "You're right, Luke. And, you know, it was just *now* that I have finally come to terms with my loss. It was just *now* that I feel whole again. Thank you, Luke." Marlo looked at Luke and showed him her empathy, "And you will get there, too. I promise."

"Marlo, I'm not as strong as you. I haven't been the same since I lost them. It's funny, but no matter how old you are when your parents die, you are still a child, inside. I hope one day, I can live a joyful life through the memories of my parents, like you."

Marlo knew how Luke felt . . . alone, sad and just existing, not living.

"I want to tell you something, Luke."

Luke adjusted himself on the couch and stared into Marlo's eyes. "The reason I came to Alaska, was to be with my parents. I know that sounds crazy," running her fingers through her hair, "but it was the first place they loved and it was the last place they were, when they died. This is my new home and I know I will live a lifetime of happiness, sharing the one thing my parents desired most, Alaska."

Luke and Marlo sat for a long time and enjoyed each others company while opening up to each other. They realized living a lifetime of sadness wasn't going to bring their parents back, but living through their memories . . . would bring a lifetime of happiness.

Marlo stood up and said, "Luke, I should be going."

Just then, Luke looked at Marlo and said, "Omigod, you're her."

"I'm who?"

"The woman in the hospital I passed in the hallway that day."

"What are you talking about, Luke?"

"You were walking with someone and you were both sullen and had your heads down. When I walked past you you looked at me and I looked at you."

Marlo stood there, thinking back to the day she and Clare went to the hospital, retracing every moment. And, it hit her.

"Luke, I can't believe it, you *are* him. You were the one I made eye contact with."

She shook her head with amazement that they've seen each other before.

"Omigod! It's true then. It was our parents who hit each other." Marlo sat back down holding her head up with her hand. "Marlo, are you okay?" asked Luke.

She looked up at him, "Luke, what happened to your parents? I mean you were at the hospital before we were and left after us."

Luke crossed his fingers in his lap and said, "My parents were alive when they made it to the hospital, but then one day later my Mother passed away and on the second day my Father passed away. It was just a matter of time. They couldn't do anything for them."

"I am so sorry Luke."

Marlo reached up and gave Luke a hug and held him for as long as she could. When she let him go his face was wet with tears and Marlo's tears fell when she saw the sadness in Luke's eyes.

He looked up and said, "Where are you going to go?"

Not remembering she was going to leave, she said, "What do mean, where am I going?"

"You were getting ready to leave when I figured out you were the woman at the hospital who I passed in the hall."

"Oh, right. I'm sorry. I'm a little thrown off right now. Remember that man who came in the office yesterday when we were talking?"

Luke thought about it for a second, "Yes."

"Well, I'm in love with him and he might get the wrong idea if he sees me here, with you. He's working on his boat today. I'm going to stop in and see him."

Marlo stood up and reached for her purse, "Are you going to be okay, Luke?"

"Yes, now that I've met you, I'll be just fine. Thank you for talking with me. I think I'm going to head home; my stay here is done. It's time for me to start my life where I left off. I'm glad I met you, Marlo. You've made me see things through a new set of eyes, thank you."

"I'm glad I met you, too, Luke. Good luck on creating and discovering your new adventure. Safe travels and come back to Alaska one day; it would be great to see you, again."

"I will. I'll see you, Marlo."

They gave each other a friendly hug goodbye and parted ways. Marlo dropped her cup off at the front on her way out. She was thinking back when she saw Luke in the hospital and remembered it clearly, now. She knew it was him. *Wow, I never expected to run into him, but I'm so thankful I did. I think he found his way by talking to me and opening himself up. You did good, Marlo. You did good.*

She walked down the boardwalk and saw Duncan's boat. She was squinting her eyes and looking for him, but didn't see him. *I thought he was going to be here. Maybe he was here and left already.* Marlo walked back to her Jeep and drove back to Birch Cabins thinking, he may have stopped by the cabin. On her way home, she was thinking about her conversation with Luke. She did speak with passion and happiness. She didn't cry. She knew she was healing. Marlo smiled and turned into Birch Cabins.

When Marlo was slowly riding the ruts and unavoidably hitting the potholes, she didn't see Duncan's truck. Wondering where he could be, but not worrying, she knew she had a couple of hours before going into work. She decided to drive to the pub; maybe Brady would have some insight.

Marlo saw Brady at the bar getting ready for tonight's crowd. "Brady, have you seen Duncan?"

"I saw him a few minutes ago. He left and said he was going somewhere, but didn't tell me where."

Marlo was unsure where he could have gone.

"Okay, well if you see him, could you tell him I'm looking for him?"

"I sure will, Marlo."

"Thanks Brady."

Marlo left the pub and headed back to her cabin. She started thinking, *that's strange. He never goes anywhere without telling someone where he's going. I have to get to work. I'll just talk to him later.* Marlo returned to her cabin and got ready for work. She didn't put too much thought into what was wrong, if anything, because they had a wonderful time the night before.

After a long night of work and wondering where Duncan might be, she headed home. She wasn't home for more than fifteen minutes and heard a knock.

"Coming," she called out.

Opening the door, Marlo's face expressed relief and finality. "Duncan, where have you been? I've been worried. I stopped by the pub earlier and asked Brady where you might be because I went to see you on the boat and you weren't there. Brady said you went somewhere, but you didn't tell him where you were going."

"I had some things to take care of. Look, Marlo, I need to talk to you."

"Okay, what about?"

Marlo was nervous why Duncan was acting like this.

"I need a little time to think about things. I think we're moving too fast and I just need some time."

Duncan was holding back the anger he felt. He wanted to rip Luke's limbs off.

"Duncan, what's wrong?"

"I just want to slow down for now."

Tears started to fill Marlo's eyes. She didn't know what was going on and her stomach was churning.

"How long do you need?"

"As long as it takes to figure things out," said Duncan, not looking into Marlo's eyes.

He's running away, but why? Let him go Marlo or he'll get defensive and angry and maybe not come back at all.

"Duncan, if you need time, then I understand. I hope you can figure out what's bothering you."

"Thank you, Marlo."

That's all Duncan said and then left; sadness filled his eyes. Marlo stood by the door in a daze trying to figure out what the hell just happened.

A few weeks went by, and except for hearing little things here and there from Sandra, Marlo hasn't seen or talked to Duncan. Marlo was working in the office staring out the window thinking about him. Sandra came in and asked Marlo if she wanted to go to the pub for dinner, but Marlo turned her down. She wasn't in the mood to do anything.

"No thanks, Sandra. I think I'm going to close up and stay in for the night."

"Are you sure you don't want to get out and do something? You've been sitting around in your cabin and working, not doing much of anything else," said Sandra, concerned for Marlo.

"No, I'm fine. I'm going to take a long hot bath and go to bed. Thanks anyways, though."

"He'll come around, Marlo."

"I hope so, but it's not looking very promising."

"Sometimes men can't see what's right in front of them, until they've lost it," offered Sandra.

She gave Marlo a reassuring look and left the office. Marlo just sat there. She sighed and decided, worrying about Duncan, was pointless. *If he can't see what's in front of him then he'll lose what he can't see.*

Brady and Duncan were behind the bar serving customers like usual and Sandra decided to have a little talk with Duncan. *It's been a few weeks now, maybe I can find out what's going on.*

"Hey boys, I'll take a Captain and Diet Coke." Sandra took a seat in her reserved spot at the bar. "Coming right up, Sandra," said Brady.

Sandra looked over at Duncan, "How's it going Duncan?"

"Good. How are things for you?"

"Oh, things are fine. What have you been up to, lately? I haven't seen much of you?"

Sandra could tell Duncan wasn't happy at all. He was purely miserable in every sense of the word. He didn't smile. He wasn't very talkative or social. *He's a mess*, thought Sandra.

"I've been around. I've been working on the boat and taking people out fishing. I've been tending bar at night and trying to do paperwork during the day."

Duncan was being short.

"It sounds like you've been keeping yourself busy," said Sandra.

"Yup. Staying busy," said Duncan with less than zero enthusiasm.

Brady looked over at Sandra and rolled his eyes. Sandra smiled a weak smile and walked over to Brady at the other end of the bar.

"Brady, what's up with your brother?"

"Beats me, I haven't figured him out."

"Well, Marlo is miserable; she doesn't know why Duncan is acting like this. And, he's miserable . . . so whatever is wrong, Duncan and Marlo need to fix it."

Sandra looked at Brady and smiled.

Brady returned the smile and offered up, "I've tried to get him to talk, but he's got a closed sign hanging around his neck."

"Hmmm . . . well, I hope he talks to her soon because she's sick about this," said Sandra, wishing she could have the old Marlo back.

Chapter 15

It was the beginning of November. The trees that displayed marked brilliance in lemon yellow, burnt sienna, copper and various shades of green in September are now bare and stick like towers. The weather continued to become more frigid and Marlo's wood stack was confidently stock-piled, thanks to Clay. All the cabins were filled with vacationers, chipped stone leveled the nauseating ruts of Birch Cabin's drive and winter was well on its way.

Marlo kept true to her promise and was keeping Clare updated on her new-found adventure in Alaska. Sandra was living the life, now that Marlo was in charge of the afternoon shift at Birch Cabins and Clay was taking full advantage of the new arrangement. He thoroughly enjoyed spending time with Sandra, it was *their* new adventure; to have more time together. And, Duncan hasn't talked to Marlo . . . at all.

Knock, Knock, Knock echoed throughout Marlo's cabin, "Coming, just a second."

Marlo pulled her pan of soup from the stove and walked to the door with a red and white striped oven mitt on her hand. Opening the door, she saw Sandra and offered her to come in.

"Sandra, come on in, I was going to head up to the office, shortly. I just wanted to quickly eat something."

Sandra looked at her with worry and said, "That's not why I'm here. I was coming over to talk to you; I have some news."

"What news? What is it Sandra?" Marlo said, with a concerned tone in her voice.

Marlo waited for Sandra to speak and saw the 'look'.

"I heard on the weather station, a massive storm is coming and we are under a blizzard warning for a week, starting tonight. I know this is your first time here in Alaska and that's why I want to go over things and make sure you have plenty of supplies on hand. We get snowed in for up to a week sometimes."

Marlo was thinking, *a storm; I'm not prepared for a storm. I'll need to go into Seward to get supplies.*

"What do I need to get from Seward?" asked Marlo.

"Well first, I want you to know you can always stay by Clay and me if it gets really bad. You need to have plenty of wood because Clay won't be cutting any and the snow will be too deep to haul wood to your cabin." Then Sandra remembered, "But, I think you have enough to get through the storm. Didn't Clay make quite a few trips the other day?"

"Yes, he did. Clay must have felt a storm coming," said Marlo, thinking Clay had a sixth sense.

"Have enough wood," Marlo said, checking it off in her mind, *"check."*

"You will also need . . .," thinking this is a lot, "actually, you should probably write this down; there's a lot," said Sandra, motioning to a pad of paper and pen on the counter.

Marlo retrieved her paper and pen and sat down, listening attentively with her pen erect, waiting to write.

Sandra pulled up a chair across from Marlo and folded her hands. "Alright, you'll need . . . bottled water and kerosene lamps; at least three, one for the kitchen, upstairs in your loft and the bathroom. You'll need kerosene oil to keep them filled; probably four large bottles worth. You'll need plenty of matches, batteries for a small radio; which if you don't have, you need to get one. Also, three plastic tubs; one for washing dishes, one for rinsing dishes and one for bathing. You'll need a couple of flash lights, some extra warm wool blankets, good reading material and stock your shelves with plenty of canned and boxed food. In addition, you need to get a couple of coolers and keep your refrigerated items in the coolers with ice. The power always goes out during storms."

Marlo was writing down everything Sandra was saying, faster than her mind could process, and said, "Wow, this must be some storm. I never had to buy supplies like this in Minnesota."

"Around here, we never take snow storms lightly. They're dangerous and we always have a high death toll because some people don't realize how severe the storms can be. Most of the time it's people that just moved here and don't have someone to tell them to get prepared. And, the people who think driving in a snow storm, is safe . . . aren't very wise."

Sandra smiled at Marlo and thought of her as family.

"You're going to be prepared," said Sandra. "Oh, and one more thing . . . make sure you fill your bathtub and pots for your water supply so you're able to flush the toilet."

"I'm going to head into Seward and buy everything on this list."

She put her list in her pocket and grabbed her purse. Sandra stood in the doorway, hesitant to leave and Marlo knew something wasn't right. "What's the matter Sandra, what's wrong? Is there something else you want to tell me?"

Sandra looked forlorn at Marlo and said, "Duncan is going to pull his boat from the marina. He said he'll be there for another two hours getting things ready for his departure. I suggest you round up your supplies, first or they'll be completely gone and you won't have anything to weather the storm. Then, I think it would be a good idea to go see Duncan before he leaves. I know he hasn't talked to you, but I think this would be a good time to talk to him. He'll still be there after you get all your supplies."

On her way into Seward, Marlo was thinking of the storm and desperately wanting to talk to Duncan. She didn't know what to think.

Thoughts consumed her mind and Marlo unavoidably began to get nervous. *Why is Duncan risking his life for his boat? Is he crazy? I can't let him go. I'm going to try to stop him. I don't want to lose him, too.* Pulling her thoughts to a halt, Marlo composed herself. *Sandra said; get the supplies first, then go see Duncan. That's what I'll do.*

Rewinding in her mind what she needed to buy and what stores she needed to stop at to purchase her supplies, she pulled out her list to help her remember. *Good thing Sandra had me write it all down. I wouldn't have been able to remember everything.* Arriving in Seward and parking her Jeep in the overflow parking area, Marlo was aware that everyone conjured up the same idea she did; there were people everywhere. *Crap, so much for being on top of my game. Everyone must have heard the news. This should be fun. I need to hurry before all the kerosene, batteries, flashlights, matches, and bottled water is gone.*

Swiftly walking, actually jogging, into Seward's local outfitting store, Marlo acquired her kerosene lights, fuel, flashlights, batteries and wool blankets. She looked to the local grocery mart for her bottled water; she searched out purified, Marlo despised spring. She found matches, some candy she spied and a few books. She also spotted two medium sized red coolers to hold her groceries once the power decides to take a nose dive. And, she made a last minute decision to pick up five large bags of ice for keeping her drinks cold; Marlo didn't like warm pop.

She said to herself, *I'll keep the bags of ice outside for the coolers, they'll stay frozen.*

Feeling relieved and accomplished, Marlo escaped the local chaos with victory. She urgently headed to the marina to see Duncan. Walking down the dock, Marlo noticed all the boats in the marina were pulling out, *what is going on? Why are all the boats leaving port?* Marlo increased her strides and panic started to set in. When Marlo reached Duncan's boat slip, she saw Duncan look at her and he immediately gestured he was coming over.

Approaching Marlo, he asked intensely, "Marlo, What are you doing here?"

"I needed supplies for the storm and I figured you would be here. What are you doing?"

Marlo felt sick to her stomach seeing Duncan for the first time since he decided he needed to 'figure things out.'

"There's a severe heavy storm on its way and I'm taking my boat out to avoid it."

Marlo saw determination in Duncan's eyes. She tried to convince him to stay.

"Duncan, I know we haven't talked and I don't even know why, but I still love you and I think this is a dangerous idea. Don't go."

Duncan stopped her, "Listen Marlo, I need to take the boat out to sea and get a head of the storm and then make my way around and come up behind it."

Marlo looked at Duncan with worry thinking, *there is no way I'm letting you head out in this storm or ahead of it or whatever. You're staying right here.*

"Duncan, I can't let you go out."

"Why does it matter to you anyways? You don't care about me. Just go home, Marlo!"

Duncan knew Marlo was becoming worried and she was scared for him. He loved her so much, but seeing her was making him angry and he didn't want her near him.

"Duncan, what is going on? Why haven't you talked to me about what's been bothering you? Avoiding me and keeping me in the dark is not fair to me or to you. Will you please just tell me what the hell is going on? I deserve an answer!"

Duncan looked into her eyes and knew what she said was true, he started again, cupping her shoulders with his hands, "Marlo, if I don't go out, the storm will destroy the boat. It will rip the boat to shreds pushing it into the docks. The mooring lines will rip loose and the storm will throw it around like a toy. I have to take it out and get a head of the storm or I will lose my boat!"

"You care more about that damn boat than you do me! I'm right here! Tell me what your problem is and why you've been ignoring me!"

Marlo's eyes were filled with anger and Duncan knew it. He couldn't talk to her now if he wanted to.

Their long over due discussion would have to wait.

"Marlo, I don't have time for this right now! The winds are picking up!"

Duncan was shouting over the wind. They could barely hear each other with the water hitting the boat and the wind whistling in their ears.

"Don't go Duncan, please! Stay with me and we can talk about what's bothering you, please!"

Marlo pleaded with Duncan to stay, but his mind was made up. She stood there, thinking and willing herself to suppress her tears.

"Marlo, look around."

Duncan was pointing to everyone around him in the marina. "Everyone is taking their boats and getting them out of the marina before the storm hits."

"I'm scared," was all Marlo could muster.

"I know you're scared, I am too, but this is something that has to be done."

Marlo knew she had no choice, but to let him take his boat and get ahead of the storm and then interjected, "I'm coming with you then, we can go together."

Frightened for her, Duncan immediately stomped the idea.

"No way Marlo, it's too dangerous! You can not come with me. There's too much risk out at sea. I'm not taking you. I will not risk your life on the open seas. The swells can get up to twenty feet. They probably won't reach that height because I'm going out early, but the longer I wait the higher the risk will be."

Marlo started to protest, "But . . ."

"Look at me, Marlo." Holding her head in his hands, he needed her to understand. "I will be fine. Now, go back to the cabin and let me be."

Marlo couldn't hold back her tears and let them fall with the feeling of hopelessness filling her soul. No matter what she did, she couldn't change his mind. He wouldn't even talk to her. She felt defeated. She knew he still loved her; she could feel it inside her. Marlo was not going to give up on him. She was going to be strong and pray for his safe return so she can make him realize whatever he's thinking, is wrong. She loves him and only him.

Seeing Marlo stand on the dock made Duncan realize he's never been sent off by a woman he was madly in love with. Duncan started the engine and with a roar, it came to life. He moored the lines and slowly backed out of his boat slip. Marlo stood on the dock trembling inside, watching him and seeing him off and praying for his safe return.

She yelled to him, "I love you, Duncan."

He looked at her, but didn't say a word. She broke into tears.

Duncan turned the boat towards the mouth of the sea, reached up and held the one thing he holds dear and said, "Please protect me during the storm and for my safe return, to Marlo." Increasing his speed a little more, Duncan neared the open sea and when he was free of the bay he put the throttle down entering the Gulf of Alaska. Breaking other boat's wakes he started off on his own path and knew he had no other option. Leaving Marlo behind was the hardest thing, but he had to do it. Duncan knew Marlo would be safe at the cabin.

Sandra and Clay were there to help her if she needed it. He talked to Brady before he left and Brady said he would keep Marlo from worrying. Also, Brady was taking over the pub until Duncan returned home. With everything on his mind checked off, Duncan called into the Coast Guard to let them know he was on his way, reporting to them the direction he was going. Granting him a safe voyage, Duncan was off and hopefully he had time to get far enough ahead of the storm. The swells were already four feet and Duncan knew they were going to get a lot worse.

Marlo stood on the dock and stared out until she couldn't see Duncan's boat any longer. She was in a trance and was jolted back when the boat a couple docks down from her roared *its* engine. Marlo wiped at her tears, standing there, feeling helpless, like a small child lost in the woods. She was separated from Duncan and had no control over his decision. All she knew was she believed in him and knew no matter what, he would come back to her. She had to have faith. She told herself, *Mom would not have been right if Duncan doesn't come back. He's going to come back. Mom will protect him, I know she will.* Realizing her fate, Marlo composed herself as best she could and sluggishly walked back to the parking lot. She sat motionless in the quietness of her Jeep, watching people on the streets of Seward thinking, *those people are worried about a storm and I'm worried about the man I love.*

Marlo returned to her cabin after an agonizing drive back and unloaded the supplies she purchased. She stretched across the front seat for one last bag and shut the Jeep door.

Sandra was standing behind her, "Did you get everything on your list?" Marlo turned and saw Sandra, dropped the bag she was holding and wrapped her arms around her, crying into her shoulder. Sandra held her.

"Duncan will be okay, Marlo, I promise. He's done this more times than I can count."

Marlo pulled back and looked up at Sandra, "What if he doesn't make it? I can't lose another person I love."

"He will make it home safely Marlo, he will. He is an experienced fisherman. This isn't his first time he's gone around a storm. Duncan is well aware of what he's doing and he will be back in your arms before you know it."

Marlo inhaled a deep breath and let it out slowly.

"I believe you, Sandra. I have to have faith that he will make it home safely."

"I know you are new to all of this, but this is very common amongst fishermen. They do this every time a heavy storm approaches. You are safe *here* and he is safe out *there*," Sandra said, hoping she knew what she was saying, was going to comfort Marlo. "Why don't we get all your things put away and then we'll take some coffee up to the office. I'll stay with you for a while."

Marlo thought that was a welcomed and comforting idea. She picked up her bag then headed inside.

"Thank you Sandra, that's very thoughtful of you. If you have other things to do, though, it's okay. I'll be fine."

"Nonsense, I want to visit with you. Anyways, it will be relaxing. You do all the work and I'll watch."

Marlo looked at Sandra with eyes that revealed a hint of sarcasm. "That sounds . . . perfect."

After Marlo brewed their coffee, put her supplies away and finished what she needed to do to be prepared for the storm's arrival, Sandra said, "Well, you're all set. Are you ready to go to the office?"

"I am," she was looking around, "let's go."

With coffee in hand, Sandra and Marlo headed to the office for a 'relaxing' days work.

Since all the cabins were full and Sandra previously put an announcement out that a storm was coming, there wasn't much to do. Sandra and Marlo were only there for phone calls, questions or guests needing supplies, like towels and such.

"It's going to be slow for the next week or so, but we can keep busy with filing paperwork, logging information in the computer and cleaning the office," said Sandra trying to distract Marlo from worrying about Duncan.

"That sounds good. I think the office could use a good cleaning," replied Marlo winking at Sandra.

"Hey now, the office isn't dirty, it just needs a little more organization."

"I know, I was just kidding. Instead of sitting here and sulking over something I can't change, where should we start?" Marlo asked, wondering if she said that to make Sandra feel relieved or to relieve her own unsettled thoughts about Duncan.

Sandra stayed the shift with Marlo knowing she needed support and a friend. They tidied the office and filed the remaining paperwork, organizing what they could as they worked. Clay came in and thought it would be nice for them all to head to the pub and get dinner. Since it was the last day this week they would be able to venture out and do something, Sandra and Marlo were on board with the idea. They all piled into the truck and drove to the pub.

Walking in, the first person Marlo saw was Brady, "Hi Brady, how's everything going tonight?"

Excited to see Brady since he resembled Duncan in a lot of ways, she felt soothed.

"Well, because of the storm, everyone is out and about getting their last minute essentials and I'm sitting here ready to go out of my mind."

Marlo smiled at Brady and said, "Well your friends are here now . . . so, you don't have to enjoy being bored anymore."

"This is true; you did come to my rescue," said Brady, glancing up and noticing Sandra and Clay selecting a table by the front window.

"We're going to eat here tonight because it might be the last time we go out for a week. We thought we'd come see you and have a nice dinner. You should join us; we'd love to have you eat with us."

Thinking that was awfully nice, he grabbed four menus and walked with Marlo over to the table.

"I told Brady he should join us for dinner tonight since the bar is totally empty," said Marlo looking at Sandra and Clay.

"That's a great idea," offered Clay pulling out a chair next to him. "Have a seat Brady. What are your specials tonight?"

"Whatever you want tonight is on me. That's our special," offered Brady, just happy they came in.

"You can't beat that special."

After they enjoyed a fun dinner, they sat and talked for a while. It was nice to unwind in good company and not have any chores to rush home, too. Sandra and Marlo closed the office down early and Brady didn't have anyone to service. All in all, it was just a slow night. And, where better to spend time, then at James' Bros. Pub with close friends.

"It's starting to snow," said Sandra looking outside.

Marlo glanced over, too, and thought, *I hope Duncan is far ahead of the storm by now.*

Seeing Marlo and knowing she was having thoughts of Duncan, Clay said, "Don't worry, Marlo. Duncan is just fine. He knows what he's doing."

"I know. I'm just worried. I love him and I want him to come home to me, hopefully, *to us*."

Sandra patted Clay's knee looking at Marlo, "He will Marlo, he will."

"Is anyone ready for another beer?" shouted Brady up at the bar taking care of the dirty dishes.

"Not for me, I'm going to head home," said Marlo, yawning. "We are too," Sandra chimed in.

"Well, I'm not staying any longer than, either. No one has been here since you guys arrived two hours ago."

Deciding on closing the pub early, Brady started putting chairs up and cleaning.

Brady asked, "Do you guys mind if Marlo stays and keeps me company until I'm ready to leave? I'll bring her home."

"Sure, if Marlo wants to do that."

"That's fine. I can stay here with Brady and keep him company. We'll be along shortly."

With that, Sandra and Clay said their goodbyes and headed out the door, locking it behind them. Brady pulled the open sign string and it flickered off.

Swabbing the floors, moving the mop in a side to side motion, Brady was talking to Marlo, "I've gotta say, Marlo. You and Duncan sure have something great going for you. I think you'll be my sister-in-law soon enough."

Marlo smiled, "Yeah, which would be great, if I can get him to talk to me, again. If that happens, I think you might be onto something, Brady."

"He will, Marlo. I don't know what got into him. One minute he couldn't stop talking about you and the next minute he wouldn't talk about you at all."

"Thanks for that, Brady. That helps a lot."

Marlo looked at Brady with sarcasm all over her face.

"He'll be back for you, don't worry. I know my brother and he loves you."

"He hasn't shown it for a long time," said Marlo beginning to feel Duncan's love for her, fading.

"He gets in these ruts and sometimes it takes him a while to realize how stubborn he's being."

"Well, when he's finally over his stubbornness, I might not want him back."

"I doubt that, Marlo."

"How can *you* be so sure about that, Brady?"

"Well, little miss; you're in love with Duncan. That's how sure I am."

Marlo looked down at her feet and knew Brady was right. If Duncan asked her back she'd jump at the chance. She was in love.

"You think Duncan will be okay out there? He said the swells can get pretty high."

Brady watched Marlo and chose his words carefully.

"Marlo, Duncan has done this a dozen times. He knew you would be upset, but he'll be fine. He's a survivor and now that you're in his life he actually has a reason to want to come home."

"Well, I don't know about that. I yelled, 'I love you' to him when he was pulling away from the dock and he just looked at me."

"Oh, Marlo," Brady said, frustrated with Duncan, "he loves you, trust me. I've never seen him act this way . . . ever."

"And, he loves you, too, Brady."

Marlo knew Brady was worried about Duncan as well, even though he was being strong, for her.

"Yeah, you're probably right. Even though I'm a pain in his ass, he still loves me."

Trying to avoid showing any sign of worry, Brady quickly thought, *the boat is old and in need of some fixing up but he should be fine.*

Brady cast the thought aside and said, "Well, I'm done. Are you ready to hit the road before the snow gets too risky to drive in?"

"I'm ready," replied Marlo, putting her new heavy winter coat, hat and scarf on.

"With all that gear I'm going to have to roll you to the truck," said Brady laughing then swiftly threw on a light jacket and guided her through the entry way, locking the door behind him.

Brady dropped Marlo off at her cabin.

"Are you going to be alright tonight? Do you want me to stay?"

"No, that's okay, I'm a big girl. I'll be fine Brady, thank you. You head home and drive safely, please.

The roads are starting to get slippery."

"Alright then, if you need anything or something happens, you call me immediately and I'll be right over."

"Thank you Brady, you're the best."

Brady put the truck in reverse and headed out to the highway. It was snowing heavy saturated flakes and was almost too hard to drive in. A thick blanket of snow was already covering the frozen ground. Marlo thought watching him leave, *it's a good thing he has four wheel drive.*

Turning away and opening the door to her cabin, Marlo went inside and was greeted by the heat from her wood stove. *That heat feels amazing. I love woodstoves,* thought Marlo. She made a warm cup of hot cocoa topped with little fluffy marshmallows, her specialty, and settled in for the night. Marlo, overwhelmed by her feelings of Duncan out at sea, cried herself to sleep.

It was dark out on the ocean; almost mystical. The winds were whistling in the dark void. Duncan was hoping not to endear any of the storms fiery, but the storm was moving faster than his boat could travel, considering the rough seas. They were becoming more and more prominent. Duncan was monitoring his gages and making due, southeast, away from the storm.

In his cabin on the boat, the light was dim, a soft golden glow. It was his only comfort besides the thought of coming home to Marlo. Duncan was moving the boat through six foot swells carefully, to avoid water spilling onto the boat. The snow was falling in a sideways pattern while Duncan's vessel was moving forward at a racing ten knots. Keeping the Marine Band Radio open and listening for dispatches from the Coast Guard, he kept his hands steady on the wheel. The winds were increasing. The weather was not going to let up and could possibly get worse.

The fishing boat was an older vessel and he didn't want to push forward because he was worried his boat wouldn't be able to handle the unforgiving seas and forceful winds. Even though he knew the boat was old, Duncan wasn't giving up on her anytime soon. *If I can make it until morning, tomorrow will be easier to navigate. I hope Marlo is okay. I wish I didn't leave, angry with her. I love her and I hope she can forgive me for how I was behaving. I should have said I love you, back to her. Dammit, Duncan . . . you're an idiot!*

Thinking about leaving Marlo standing in despair at the end of the dock and knowing she doesn't have any idea what an Alaskan storm can bring, he felt awful. All he could hope for, was she was going to be alright.

The night was rough and draining. The first winter storm of the season was relentless. It was dominant and ruling the seas with enormous power. The swells were increasing and the snow was skewing his vision. Duncan could feel fatigue setting in. He needed to get some rest. He exchanged blows with the storm all through the night and was determined to keep the storm from trouncing him. He stayed strong mentally and physically. He had to return to Marlo.

Morning was upon him and the skies were invisible. The seas were not forfeiting and it was snowing with zero intentions of letting up. He was in desperate need of sleep since he navigated through the night. Duncan set the vessel to autopilot, thinking how thankful he was that he updated all the electronics on his boat, and headed below deck to get some shuteye. With the seas beating the sides of his fishing boat, he lay under the covers; *this is going to be fun, thought Duncan before he drifted to sleep.*

Chapter 16

Marlo awoke to soft light filling her cabin, no sunshine and a few smoldering coals. She rolled to a sit up position with her elbows on her knees and ran her fingers through her hair. Rubbing her eyes, she slowly stood and stretched. She pulled her plaid robe and fuzzy purple slippers on. She carefully descended from her loft and peeked out the window. To Marlo's surprise, there was a good foot of snow covering the ground. *Wow, it's been a long time since I've seen a foot of snow in one snow fall and it's still snowing. Sandra warned me.* When she saw her wood in the cabin, was low, she decided to use a section of the cabin next to the woodstove to stack some wood; a few days worth. This way she didn't have to go out into the blustery conditions every time she needed to stoke the fire.

Marlo started the coffee pot for her usual morning caffeine kick and went upstairs to get her clothes for the day. She came down and took a shower, got dressed and put on her winter coat and boots, hat, mittens and her scarf, then opened the door. Well, tried to anyways. She started pushing with all her might.

"Why isn't," Marlo grunted . . . *the door barely moving an inch,* thought Marlo and said "the door," grunting some more, scrunching her cheeks and pushing, "opening!?!" Finally, with one more push and a lot of effort, it opened a quarter of the way. Panting, Marlo peeked out and thought, *no wonder it's not opening, its snowed shut! Crap!* Squeezing through the small opening, thinking, *what if I didn't fit? I would have frozen to death.* Marlo was finally free of the cabin and started to move the snow away from the entrance.

The ghastly winds were blowing the snow half way up her door. She began moving the snow with her hands and using her boot to push the snow from side to side and thought, *this sucks. Where's a man when you need him, oh yeah, on a BOAT!* Marlo kept on moving snow and not getting very far because as soon as she would get some cleared, the winds were swift in aiding the snows return. Marlo wanted to give up and just say, *forget it,* but Clay appeared with a shovel.

"Marlo," Clay shouted above the wind, "Would you like some help?"

Marlo looked up and her hood hid the side of her face. She kept trying to see who was next to her. Finally, Clay saw her struggling and started giggling to himself, moving into her view.

"Clay, thank goodness. Can you help me?" asked Marlo, not hearing him offer the first time because the winds were deafening.

"That's why I'm here. Sandra was heading to the office and saw your door was drifted shut," shouted Clay while he put the shovel to the ground and began shoveling in long bands to keep away as much accumulating snow as possible.

"Thank you. I was making a noble attempt, but was getting nowhere."

Marlo was struggling to keep her hood on, so she let it blow off and started towards the side of her cabin to haul wood. As soon as Clay saw Marlo with more wood than she could handle and barely seeing the top of her hat, he opened the door. Marlo walked over to the bottom of the loft next to the bookshelf and dropped the wood. She stacked it neatly next to the woodstove and saw Clay coming with another load. She went out for one more trip and Clay followed. After four trips of wood, Marlo felt she had enough wood in the cabin for a couple three days.

"Oh my goodness, it's a blizzard out there. Thank you, Clay. I don't know what I would have done without your help. The snow just kept blowing and I couldn't get the door cleared," exhausted Marlo, panting while pulling off her hat and mittens.

"Yeah, it's going to be an ugly one this time. Sandra told me you went out yesterday and loaded up on supplies. That was smart."

Marlo wanted to be the smart one, but said, "If it wasn't for Sandra I wouldn't be prepared for anything. She came to me and informed me of a bad storm coming and we made out a list of what I would need."

Just then the power started flickering on and off.

"Great, there goes our power," said Clay, annoyed. "It takes the electric company forever to get the power up and running. Don't expect it back on until the storm is over."

Marlo smiled and said, "Don't worry, I'm prepared, thanks to your one and only."

Nodding to Marlo, Clay put on his gloves and hat and told her he was going up to the office to see Sandra. Clay shut the door behind him with a loud, *SLAM!*

Marlo shook her head because she couldn't believe how strong the winds were; they had to be blowing sixty miles an hour. Marlo stoked the woodstove with a few logs and shut the door, setting the damper perfectly. She lit the oil lamp that was sitting in the middle of the table then lowered the wick to keep it from smoking. Walking over to her stove, she lit a match and held it to the burner, lighting the stove and cracked an egg into a cast iron pan. She made an egg on toast and a side of fruit for breakfast.

After eating her well earned breakfast because her energy was spent fighting with the door, and competing with the wind, and hauling wood; she sat at the table staring at a dirty breakfast plate wondering where Duncan was. She was beginning to doubt his return, worrying if he was going to make it and then pushed the awful thought aside.

Don't think about it, he's fine. Go up to the office and visit with Sandra. You can't go anywhere and all the roads are closed. And, even if they were open, the businesses would all be closed. And, you'd be stupid to try to drive anyways, so just relax. With that thought, Marlo made up her mind and put her winter gear on and pushed the door as hard as she could to open it. Then the inevitable, *SLAM!* Looking back at the door she thought, *crap, the snow is already starting to pile up against the door. It's freezing out.* Marlo picked up her feet and trudged through the foot of snow that has complicated her life and made for a strenuous trek up to the office.

The waves crashing against the boat startled him from a sound sleep. *Where am I,* thought Duncan. Coming back to reality, he jumped up and threw the covers off of him, diving for the stairs that led topside. Hastily moving up the stairs, Duncan was scanning for anything out of the unusual. He checked his compass. He was still heading east towards Chugach National Forest, the direction he started on. *Good, I'm still on the right track,* thought Duncan.

Hearing something on the radio, Duncan turned it up. Trying to listen to the Marine Band and hoping to be out of the storms path soon, he realized he wasn't going to get ahead of the storm. Duncan saw a swell of water crash over the bow of the boat. The boat listed port and water was being thrown from side to side. Duncan couldn't go out on the deck to inspect anything, for fear of being thrown from the boat, so he stayed in the cabin and feared for his life.

The snow was coming down in heavy bands. The sea was cold, very cold. Trying to keep the boat steady, Duncan had a tight grip on the steering wheel. He stared out the window, wide eyed at the unforgiving sea and feeling very small. He could hear the Coast Guard's dispatch taking calls and hearing people calling in for rescue. Duncan was coasting and manipulating his boat to steer through the swells, but no matter what he did, the swells were beginning to consume it. Duncan feared they were going to confiscate his boat and possibly his life.

The charter wasn't battling the storm with promise, in a matter-of-fact; Duncan began to reluctantly acknowledge his boat was making its final voyage. The charter, being an older vessel and not as large as some, wasn't supporting the weight of the water. The water was beating against the battered planks and cracking the sides allowing water to seep in. Duncan was taking on water and fast. The boat was swaying from starboard to port, swooping with the swells. Duncan's boat was taking on water quickly. He was holding on for life. He felt like a play toy being tossed around. The snow was blinding his way, he couldn't see a thing. Thoughts of Marlo rushed through his mind, thanking God he didn't bring her. He needed to get back to her. He loved her and knew now, more than ever, he needed her. Trying to make a last minute decision, he was thinking, *do I try to make it out here in the storm and try to salvage my boat? Are you crazy? Your boat is half underwater! Forget the damn boat and call it in!* He picked up the radio receiver and called into the Coast Guard, "May Day, May Day, vessel 217644 is taking on water! May Day, May Day, I repeat, vessel 217644 is taking on water! My location is 289 kilometers from the entrance of Resurrection Bay heading east towards Chugach National Forest! The vessel is taking on water! I'm going down. Look for flashing beacon! I'm 289 kilometers east of Resurrection Bay south of Chugach National Forest!" Duncan grabbed his life vest and fastened it, turned on the strobe light and reached for the one thing that was going to save his life.

 Duncan went out onto the deck searching for the Coast Guard in the distance. The wind and snow were thrashing and swirling over the seas, it felt like glass cutting his face. The towering swells were spraying salt and dumping water, drenching him, restricting his movements. Duncan was struggling to cling to whatever he could get hold of. He was fighting for his life, but the vigorous storm was weakening him. The water was heavy and forceful with every swell crashing onto the deck of the boat. Sliding and falling, reaching for whatever he could, to hold on. The boat was flailing around like a tinker toy. He had no control over his fate. Duncan was scared for his life and didn't know how it felt to be knocking at Death's Door, until now. He couldn't wait anymore, he had to jump or he would be pulled under with the boat. Duncan closed his eyes and said, "I love you, Marlo." His life flashed before his eyes, then he jumped. Duncan surfaced the dark water and a swell came crashing down on him. Trying to catch a breath and feeling the shock of the cold water, Duncan didn't know what was going on and then realized what was happening. He didn't see his boat and remembered he had alerted the Coast Guard. He quickly thought, *I have about fifteen minutes if I stay calm, and keep my extremities close to my core. Breathe Duncan, breathe. Deep breaths, you can do this. Stay calm.*

On the horizon Duncan could see the Coast Guard coming, but they were a half a mile out, at least. With the swells, it could take them awhile to get to him. He didn't think he was going to make it, but he was going to die trying. Another swell crashed over Duncan like a Cheerio in a bowl of milk. He came up again, fighting for air. A few moments later another swell came. Again Duncan surfaced, but this time, he was unconscious. Floating with his beacon light flashing and being swallowed by the deep swells, the Coast Guard spotted him and divers were sent to rescue him. The Coast Guard Rescue Swimmers were equipped with a coverall flotation dry suit, a rescue swimmer harness, dive gloves, boots and mask, fins and snorkel to swim quickly through the waves without having to struggle for air. When the rescue swimmers reached Duncan, one of the men wrapped his arm around his shoulder, crossing his chest and hooking underneath his underarm. The diver pulled Duncan through the water on his back towards the boat and crew. When the divers returned to the boat with Duncan, a basket was lowered into the water.

Duncan was heaved into the basket and hoisted to the deck of the vessel. Because the winds were mighty and strong, the basket was swaying in every direction and spinning, making it difficult to take hold of.

Once the medics finally grabbed the basket and pulled Duncan on board. The medics were there waiting to take over and secure Duncan to the stretcher. They strapped him down and moved him inside, out of the wind and rain. The medics immediately started working on him.

One of the men started to take his ocean soaked clothes and gear off, putting warming blankets on him.

"Does he have a pulse?" asked one of the medics.

"Yes, he has a pulse. Pulse and respiration slow. I'm hooking him up to the cardiac monitor. Assessing O2 now," said another medic, quickly working under the stress of the storm and panic of saving Duncan.

"He's going into shock!" yelled the other medic and started reaching for two IV lines.

"Administering two lines . . . 2000 ml of Saline and 8mcg of Dopamine."

The medics were working on Duncan quickly and efficiently knowing they had a small window to stabilize him, if they could.

"Call for an airlift. I want it ready and waiting on shore, now!" shouted the lead medic on board.

The Coast Guard crew was maneuvering the waves and storm safely and quickly as possible trying to steer towards land. They knew Duncan was high risk and wanted to get him into acute care.

The lead medic addressed the team, "I don't know if he's going to make it. His pulse is slowing and he has severe hypothermia. Keep him warm. When the blankets cool put new ones on him."

"Can't we move any faster, let's go!!" shouted the lead medic.

Back at the office, Marlo and Sandra were discussing how intense the storm was.

"I can't believe this weather. It doesn't look like the storm is going to let up anytime soon," said Marlo worrying about Duncan.

She started thinking back to when they first met on the dock down at the marina, *Duncan was incredibly handsome standing in front of me with that raggedy white T-shirt, cargo shorts and his shoes untied, probably wondering what the heck I was doing and thinking, who is this kid? I didn't want anything to do with him. I wasn't even remotely thinking of having a relationship with a man and now look, I'm filled with anguish and worry for the man I love; who is up to no good on that damn boat!*

"I know, but this isn't the first storm we've had. Sometimes we have two or three storms like this a winter. This is actually early for a storm to hit," said Sandra doubting Clay has heard anything further from the weather station.

"Hey guys, I figured you would all be here," announced Brady, walking in the door along with the wind and snow from outside.

Papers on the desk were blown to the floor when Brady opened the door.

"Sorry about that, Sandra."

Brady bent down to pick them up.

"It's not the first time it's happened today," said Sandra smiling.

He stood on the rug brushing snow from his coat and hat and hung them up on the peg by the door.

"Hey Brady, would you like a cup of coffee to warm up?" asked Sandra.

"I would love a cup."

Scanning the office he said, "So, I've been a little worried about Duncan. I brought my Marine Band Radio so we could listen to the Coast Guard dispatches."

Marlo started to worry, but then thought listening to the Coast Guard might give her peace-of-mind because she would know what's going on.

Brady went to the back room in the office to set it up but noticed Clay already had one working. Clay told Brady to shut the door behind him. Staring at Clay, Brady had a concerned look on his face and slowly shut the door behind him.

"What's going on, Clay?"

"I've got bad news and I just found out when you were walking in the door. I didn't want the girls to hear. I don't know how to put this to you any . . ."

Brady cut him off in mid sentence, "Just say it, Clay." Clay shook his head not wanting to disappoint Brady.

"Duncan's boat went down 289 kilometers east of Resurrection Bay. He was rescued by the Coast Guard but is being airlifted to Anchorage."

Brady looked at Clay, reached for the door knob and said, "I'm going right now."

"Wait, the weather is too dangerous to travel in. You can't even see out there. You're going to get yourself killed," shouted Clay in a panic.

"My brother is in the hospital and could be dying or dead; I'm going!" yelled Brady not thinking of Marlo.

Marlo stormed in the office and frantically asked, "What happened to Duncan, is he alright? Where is he?" She looked at Brady, "Talk to me Brady."

"His boat sunk east of Resurrection Bay. He called it in before he lost contact with the radio and the Coast Guard picked him up. They airlifted him into Anchorage; I'm going to see him."

Marlo had tears in her eyes, "I'm going too."

"Marlo, you can't, it's too dangerous," said Clay nervously looking at Brady.

Marlo looked at Brady, "I'm going. Let's go Brady."

Both of them whipped their winter gear on and ran out the door.

Sandra looked at Clay and said, "They'll be okay. What happened to Duncan?" asked Sandra with a scared expression on her face. She's known Duncan a long time and feared something went awfully wrong.

Brady and Marlo were a half hour from Anchorage, driving as fast as they could without getting into an accident. The roads have been closed due to the heavy wet snow, but Brady ignored the warnings. They were almost there. Brady began kicking himself for letting Duncan try to get ahead of the storm.

He began speaking with anger, "I told him not to go, but he wouldn't listen to me. He convinced me that it would be okay."

Tears were falling from Brady's cheeks and Marlo was feeling emotional herself, it was hard to comfort Brady.

"Brady, your brother will be okay. He's a strong man."

"Marlo, the Gulf of Alaska is unforgiving and tremendously cold. You can't survive the frigid sea," Brady said firmly, trying to keep himself from taking his fury out on Marlo. Marlo sat in the passenger seat unsure of what to say to Brady and thinking how she wished to be in Duncan's arms.

Merging off the highway onto their exit, the road was covered with snow and drifts. Brady felt the truck starting to swerve, but managed to keep the truck from going into the ditch. Marlo was gripping the safety handle on the door, thinking, *we're going to die!* The lights from the hospital were in view and in a few short minutes, they would be there. After parking the truck and running through the emergency entrance, they saw the front desk.

Out of breath, Brady was panting and said, "My name is Brady James," taking a breath, "I'm looking for my brother, Duncan James. He was airlifted in from Seward. The Coast Guard rescued him."

Brady was still panting.

The nurse calmly responded and said, "Yes, he is here, but he's in intensive care right now. Let me get the doctor and he can discuss the matter with you."

Waiting as patiently as they could, Brady, pacing back and forth and Marlo, biting her lip with her arms crossed over her chest, were questioning with their eyes, *where the hell is the damn doctor!* A few minutes went by.

"Are you Brady James?" the doctor asked, being a little apprehensive, wondering if he had the right person.

Brady quickly said, "Yes, and this is Marlo Hart." Brady gestured to Marlo.

"I'm Dr. Meethe. I'm the doctor who is presiding over Duncan and his treatment. Can you take a walk with me please?"

They started walking to the I.C.U. and Dr. Meethe was filling them in. Brady and Marlo followed Dr. Meethe until they were standing outside the doors of the I.C.U.

"This is hard for me to say, but Duncan is fighting for his life right now. When the Coast Guard reached him, he was unconscious and went into shock. He suffered severe hypothermia and, at this point, we're just patiently waiting."

Brady and Marlo lost it, holding each other in the hallway. Looking up slowly, Brady asked, "Can we see him?"

"Unfortunately, not tonight; the risk is too high. Tonight is crucial; anything could hinder his attempt to survive. He has to remain in I.C.U. over night and then, if tomorrow he is transferred to a private room, under strict supervision, I will take you both to see him. Right now, the risk is too high. We have to wait and hope his strength pulls him out of this. He's a fighter. Anyone who can last more than fifteen minutes in the Gulf of Alaska is a survivor."

Brady and Marlo just stood there.

"I'll show you the waiting area and have the nurse bring you some blankets a couple of pillows and coffee."

Following the doctor down the hall where the cleaning crew was starting their shift, they trudged into the waiting area. Brady and Marlo were all alone.

The room was dimly lit with two brass table lamps with pull switches dangling, three leather couches and a few mahogany end tables. There was a TV, a radio and the distinct scent of disinfectant filled the room. The carpet was plush and pictures of landscapes were centered on the wall.

Showing Brady and Marlo the waiting area, Dr. Meethe said, "This is where you can wait. You can stay the night and I will come get you in the morning, after I check on Duncan."

"Thank you, Dr. Meethe. Please tell us anything you find out," said Brady, keeping Marlo from collapsing to the hospital floor.

"I will. Please, get some rest."

When the doctor was gone, Marlo tried to say something, but couldn't get her thoughts organized.

"Omigod, I don't know what . . . what happened how could this what do we do now?" Marlo asked in confusion and sadness, her eyes puffy from crying.

"We wait. That's all we can do," said Brady walking Marlo to the couch in the corner of the waiting room.

Brady sat next to her with his elbows on his knees resting his forehead in his hands.

"I can't believe this is happening. I knew the boat was old, but I didn't think he would get caught in the storm. Maybe something happened and the engine quit and he was adrift or the storm was moving faster than he anticipated. I don't know."

Brady heard someone approaching them and looked up.

"Are you Brady and Marlo?" a woman asked, approaching them with blankets and coffee.

"Yes," replied Brady.

"I'm the nurse that will be on the floor tonight. If you need anything you can go to the desk of the I.C.U. and ask for me. My name is Katie Burke. Is there anything else I can do to make you more comfortable?" she asked with empathy in her eyes.

"This is fine, thank you, Katie," Brady said taking the blankets and coffee from her.

"Alright then, please try to get some rest. I know it's easier said than done."

"We'll try. Thank you again," said Brady.

Brady and Marlo sat on the couch staring into the void, not saying a word. Marlo was feeling a draft and pulled the blanket over her, covering her shoulders with the heated blanket and Brady sat next to her. She leaned into him putting her head on his shoulder, crying. He wrapped his arm around her and held Marlo to comfort her and himself.

"Everything is going to be okay, Marlo. Duncan is strong. He's going to make it."

Brady held onto Marlo and stared at the wall. From the drive to Anchorage, to the trauma at the hospital, and the stress of worrying about Duncan, Marlo and Brady fell asleep on the couch in the waiting area.

The next morning, Brady could feel something softly pushing on his arm and hearing someone say, "Brady . . . Brady, wake up, it's Dr. Meethe."

Coming to, Brady bolted to his feet and recognized Dr. Meethe.

Everything came rushing back.

"Where is he? Is he okay? Did he make it through the night? Can we see him? Marlo, wake up. Dr. Meethe is here."

Marlo woke up and saw Dr. Meethe. She was instantly in tune with what was going on.

"Good morning, I hope you managed to get some sleep considering the circumstances. I want you to know that Duncan made it through the night, but when we were relocating him to his room, he went into a coma. Now, I want you to know this does happen sometimes. The duration of the coma is up to him. We can not predict how long he will be in a comatose state. However, he will be watched over and you are aloud to see him."

Hearing what Dr. Meethe said, Brady quickly asked, "How long could he be in this *coma*?"

"It really is up to him, Brady. He could be in for a day or three months," said Dr. Meethe wishing he had a better answer.

Brady looked over at Marlo, "Are you ready?"

"I am Brady, let's go see Duncan."

Marlo took Brady's hand and they walked together with the doctor to his room. Before the doctor let them in the room, he wanted to talk to them quickly.

Stopping in front of them he said, "Before you go in, I want you to know that he is in a critical state. You must keep your voices down and remember that he endured severe trauma. You can hold his hand and talk to him. Let him know you're here."

Slowly opening the door, Brady let Marlo go in first and followed closely behind. The light in the room had a soft and soothing glow. He was in a private room which had an ample amount of space for visitors. He was hooked up to IV's and beeping monitors that echoed in the room. Duncan looked peaceful, lying in the hospital bed with his arms down by his side. Marlo carefully reached for his hand and held it, caressing the top of his hand with her thumb.

She whispered to him, "Duncan, its Marlo. Brady and I are here with you. You're going to be okay. Duncan, can you hear me? It's Marlo."

Brady stood behind Marlo with tears of joy seeing his brother alive, but sad knowing he may never come out of the coma. Brady went to the other side of Duncan and sat beside him in a blue pleather chair, also reaching for his hand. He held it and said,

"Hey buddy, it's your pain in the butt brother. What were you thinking, going out there? You should have said, "The hell with the boat, I'm staying with my girl."

Hearing Brady, Marlo tried to smile, but couldn't. She couldn't help, but tear up. Looking at Duncan in the hospital bed connected to IV's and electrodes, Brady and Marlo were beside themselves. They didn't know how to deal with this. They had questions that couldn't be answered. They looked at each other and new one thing for sure, their love for Duncan.

Duncan was laying in a hospital bed fighting for his life and there was nothing Brady or Marlo could do, except wait.

"We should call Sandra and Clay and let them know what's going on," said Marlo.

"That's a good idea. They're probably worried about Duncan's condition and us arriving at the hospital, safely," said Brady.

"I'll do it Brady, you stay with Duncan."

Marlo got up and left the room and walked to the nurse's station, needing a moment alone.

"Could I please use your phone to make a call to Seward?" Marlo asked the nurse sitting behind the desk, who was working on some charts.

She looked up and said, "Sure, just dial the area code and the number."

"Thank you."

Dialing the number, Marlo was not thrilled to break the news to Sandra and Clay.

"Sandra, its Marlo."

"Marlo, is Duncan okay? What's going on? Thank God you both made it to the hospital safely."

"They kept him in I.C.U. last night and moved him to a private room, this morning. But, when they moved him, he went into a coma. Brady is in the room with him now," said Marlo trying to choke down tears.

"What do you mean 'coma'? Is he going to be okay?"

"The doctors are watching him closely. I don't know. We have to wait and see. I think one of us will come back and get a change of clothes and some personal items, then return to the hospital."

"No, don't do that, listen," said Sandra. "Clay and I are coming up to the hospital and we can bring you what you need. Clay can go to Brady's and get his stuff. We'll be up there later today. Let Brady know," offered Sandra with sincerity.

"I will Sandra and thank you."

"Not a problem, we'll be there as soon as we can."

Sandra hung up the phone and informed Clay what was going on.

Marlo headed back to Duncan's room to tell Brady the details. "That sounds good," said Brady, staring at Duncan.

The day went on. It was long and there were no signs of Duncan waking up. Sandra and Clay arrived a couple hours after Marlo had spoken to Sandra. After seeing Duncan and staying for a while, they went to the waiting room to leave Brady and Marlo with him. Night was soon approaching and Sandra and Clay had to get back.

They went in Duncan's room and Sandra whispered to Brady and Marlo, "Hey, we need to go, but he's going to make it. We just know it. Duncan is a survivor. He's not going to leave just yet."

Just before Sandra and Clay were going to leave, Sandra remembered, "By the way, I put your bags behind the curtain."

Then, with a sympathetic smile, she shut the door. Sandra and Clay had to get back, but weren't looking forward to driving in the storm. The plows couldn't even keep up with the roads.

Three days went by and Marlo and Brady were by Duncan's side hoping and praying everyday for him to wake up. He didn't move a finger or twitch an eyelash. He just laid there, quiet and peaceful.

"Marlo, listen. We have to get back to civilization. If Duncan isn't going to wake up anytime soon, we can't just be sitting here everyday, waiting and hoping, when there are things that have to be done at home, too. I have to run the pub. Duncan would kill me if he knew I just sat here and let our pub crumble to nothing. We worked night and day to get that pub up and running. He loves that place."

Marlo tried to interject, but he wouldn't let her.

"And, you have responsibilities running the office. Sandra needs you. Duncan will be fine here at the hospital. You can do this, Marlo. We'll come up everyday to see him, but we have to get on with our lives. We can do both . . . we can."

Marlo did not want to leave Duncan's side in case he woke up. "Brady, I'm staying. If you want to go, that's fine. I'm not leaving him."

Marlo looked at Brady with the expression of, *who are you to tell me to leave the man I love in a coma, laying in a hospital bed fighting for his life, who could wake up at any moment, to work in the office for Sandra?*

"Marlo, please come. He'll be fine with the hospital staff and we can come back."

"No! I'm staying, Brady—just go. I'll be fine here with Duncan," said Marlo with a stern voice, protecting her rights to stay with Duncan. She knew by leaving him, she wasn't leaving him for good, but she needed to be by his side.

"That's fine, Marlo. I understand," replied Brady giving Marlo a loving embrace, goodbye.

He looked back at Duncan and walked out of the room.

Pulling into Birch Cabins, the sides of the drive were eight feet high after it was plowed. Seward took a pounding and it still hasn't let up. There was already a new four inches on the drive and continuing to come down in buckets. Brady pulled up to the cabin, sliding because he forgot it was slippery. He jumped out of the truck and walked into the office. He saw Sandra sitting at the front desk, tapping her pen and gazing off into space, like she always does.

"Hey, Sandra . . . I wanted to tell you that Marlo is going to be staying at the hospital with Duncan. I tried to get her to come back with me, but she wasn't having it. She was adamant about staying by Duncan's side."

"I know your heart was in the right place, Brady, but you can't separate a woman who's in love. I'm happy she found her one and only," said Sandra.

"But, I know you have an office to run and Marlo is in charge of the afternoons."

"Brady, I'll be fine here. I've done it for years by myself."

Sandra was looking at Brady, worried about him, "Are you okay, honey?"

"I'm fine. I'm just concerned about Marlo. I can see she's being strong, but she needs a break. She hasn't been sleeping or eating; I'm worried about her, Sandra."

"It's nice to know you care about her, too, Brady."

"Is it that obvious?"

Laughing, Sandra said, "Yes, is that such a bad thing?"

"No, I guess not."

Sandra thought, *how cute of Brady to love Marlo like a sister, a sister he never had.*

"That woman is all heart and stubborn, too. She's Duncan's match. I don't see her going anywhere Brady, unless Duncan is by her side."

"You're probably right, Sandra. You've always been good with this match-making sense you have."

"No, I'm just good at reading people, is all." Sandra looked at Brady and said, "I know you want to protect her because Duncan can't and that's okay. But, she'll be okay with Duncan at the hospital. You're a good man, Brady James and I know you love Duncan more than anything. He's going to pull through this. I know it."

He looked at Sandra and couldn't hold back the tears any longer. He wept into her shoulder while she held him and rocked him, comforting him with her warm embrace and affection.

Brady finally looked up at Sandra, "Sandra, I need to call Marlo. Can I use your cell phone?"

"Sure, just dial like your calling long distance."

Brady called the hospital and asked for Duncan's room and Marlo answered, "Hello?"

"Marlo, its Brady. I wanted you to know I made it back safely. The roads are horrible. How's Duncan?"

"No change. I'm sitting here with him. I'm glad you made it back, Brady. I know the weather is frightening out there."

"Marlo?"

"Yes, Brady."

"I'm sorry for trying to get you to come back with me."

"That's okay, Brady. I understood what you were saying, but I just couldn't leave him."

"I know Marlo, and . . . thank you for your support. I know you love Duncan and I know his love for you will pull him through this. And, I love you too, Marlo. I'll take you for my sister-in-law any day of the week."

Marlo paused and said to Brady, "Thank you, Brady. And, I love you, too."

Marlo hung up and Brady pushed the off button on Sandra's cell phone.

"Everything good, Brady?" asked Sandra with a comforting smile on her face.

"Yeah, everything is good."

"Why don't you head home and get some sleep. You haven't been home since the accident."

"Alright, and thanks Sandra . . . for everything."

"You're welcome, Brady."

Brady got in his truck and drove down the road to take care of things that have been put off, temporarily. He knew in his heart, Marlo was the woman for Duncan. He was a lucky man to have a woman like Marlo, love him with so much passion.

When Brady returned home and feeling somewhat relaxed, he opened a can of beer, took a long drink and stood by the patio doors, gazing at the moons' luminous glow, glistening over the lake. Later that night, he cried himself to sleep, wondering if he was ever going to hear his brother's voice again.

The next day, Marlo woke up in the blue pleather chair that was next to Duncan's bed, overhearing muddled conversation. Marlo sat up and rubbed her eyes, and thought, *that must be the staff starting their shift*. She looked at Duncan and held his hand.

"Good morning, Duncan, time to get up, love. Rise and shine." She stared at him. He didn't move or make a sound, but Marlo knew he was in there. "It's still snowing. When you're all better, we can have a snowball fight or go sledding."

Marlo scooted closer to Duncan and rested her elbow on his bed with her head cocked in her hand. She smoothed her fingertip over his eyebrows and started to cry. Marlo couldn't believe this was happening to her. How could this be happening to *her*? First, her parents, and now, the one man she finds and falls in love with, who loves her just the same, is lying in a hospital bed in a coma. Marlo sniffled and wiped her tears away, wondering whether or not he was going to hold her in his arms again. "No! I'm not going to think like that," she reminded herself. "You are going to make it Duncan, you are." Marlo smoothed

Duncan's covers, kissing him on the cheek. She thought, *come on baby, you can do it. Just open your eyes, please. Please open your eyes. I want you back. Come back to me, love.*

Marlo waited out the rest of the day doing a word search puzzle book. The nurses came in periodically to check on Duncan's vitals.

Marlo would have a brief conversation with some of the nursing staff. Then, they would leave and go back to doing whatever it is nurses do. It was a long day. She sat in her chair listening to the continuous beeping of the monitor and watching for any change. She adjusted herself in the chair and said, "I need to get up and walk around. I know what I'll do; I'll go to the cafeteria and get a Diet Coke. That sounds good right now." She was in need of something sweet.

Marlo walked through the halls slow and steady, running her fingers along the never ending wall and followed the smell, lingering from the cafeteria. She sensed a wave of sadness come over her and immediately began to feel overwhelmed. She noticed the intense lights in the hall were a florescent rectangular shape and spaced every five feet or so. They were bright and blinding to the eye. She strained to see and turned away.

Marlo entered the cafeteria and went to the cooler that held the soft drinks. Pulling a Diet Coke from the row of sodas, she heard someone come up behind her.

"Are you Marlo?" asked a voice.

Marlo turned and saw an elderly woman with a cane. She looked to be in her early eighties and was cute as a button. She had silvery white hair pulled up into a bun with some loose strands of hair falling around her face. She had big blue eyes, full of wisdom and wore oversized round framed glasses. She was wearing a soft looking light pink leisure outfit and white tennis shoes with wide soles.

"Yes, I am. Can I help you with something?" asked Marlo not realizing the woman knew her name.

"Are you the woman who is staying at the hospital every night, talking to your husband?"

"Yes, but how did you know my name?"

"Oh, I know things. I've been here with my husband. He has phenomena. I've seen you in your room talking to your husband. Is he going to be alright?" asked the little old lady.

"He's not my husband, but I hope he's going to be alright. I love him very much. He's in a coma and I know he's going to come out of it, it's just a matter of time."

Marlo looked down at her feet and felt tears surfacing.

"Oh, dear, I'm so sorry." The lady moved in really close and Marlo bent down to listen,

"I know he's going to make it because I can see the love between the two of you. That genuine love you have for each other will pull him out, you'll see."

Marlo smiled at the woman.

"Thank you. I hope you're right. Sometimes I fear he's not going to wake, but then I dismiss the thoughts, quickly."

"Oh, I'm right. I have a way with knowing these types of things, dear."

"May I ask what your name is?" inquired Marlo with a comforting smile.

"Oh, how silly of me; my name is Annabelle, but you can call me Annie. All my friends from my bridge club call me, Annie."

Marlo extended her hand and said, "It's a pleasure to meet you, Annie and thank you for making me feel better."

"Oh, you're most welcome, dear. I better be going now. I need to get back to George. He gets ornery when I'm not there. Good luck, Marlo. Everything will be just fine."

"Thank you, Annie."

Marlo thought, *that was nice of her to make me feel better.* Marlo purchased her Diet Coke and watched Annie hobble out of the cafeteria. "That was a sweet woman. I hope I get around that good when I'm in my eighties."

When Marlo was leisurely walking back to Duncan's room she could hear people talking and laughing with their families when she passed by their doors. She hoped that Duncan would talk and laugh with her about all the good times they had.

Approaching Duncan's room she opened the door and walked in, quietly. She sat next to Duncan in her chair and set her soda down on the night stand. She smoothed his blankets for the hundredth time and said, "Duncan, I love you. I want to stay here with you, but I have no more clean clothes and . . . I don't know. What should I do? I want to stay here with you, I do, but I know I need to get back to the cabin. The electricity went out and I don't know if it came back on. Also, I don't know if my food spoiled or if Sandra put it in coolers for me. I know the fire went out and it's probably freezing. Should I go back? What do you want me to do?"

Marlo sat there waiting for an answer even though she knew she wasn't going to hear one. She was exhausted and felt overwhelmed. She laid her head on his blanket releasing her sadness. She felt torn between leaving and staying. If she left, she felt she was leaving him. If she stayed, she would go crazy, watching and waiting for Duncan to open his eyes. She whispered, "Duncan, I'm going to go, but I'll be back. I will visit everyday, I promise. I have to go home, but know that I love you and I will be with you everyday in my heart and I will visit you. I love you, Duncan."

Marlo made a decision. She gave Duncan a tender kiss on the lips and looked down at him for a minute. She grabbed her things, slowly opening the door; she turned to Duncan and said, in a loving voice, "I love you, Duncan with all my heart," and walked out.

Marlo hesitantly walked over to the nurse's station.

"I'm going to go, but I'll be visiting everyday. I just can't stay here."

The nurse looked up and said, "I know, honey. It's hard, but we'll watch over him while you're gone. You be careful heading back."

"Thank you, I will."

Marlo walked down the hall and remembered that Brady drove them to the hospital. She didn't have her Jeep. She dialed Sandra on her cell because Brady was working at the pub.

"Hello, Marlo?"

"Hi Sandra, I need to come home. Is there anyway you could come get me from the hospital? Brady drove here and I stayed behind, forgetting I didn't have a way home. I'm sorry," said Marlo feeling awful for having Sandra come get her.

"I was just sitting here watching TV with Clay. I'm on my way."

"Thank you, Sandra. I'll be waiting at the entrance."

"I'll be there in about an hour."

"Okay, bye."

Marlo walked to the front entrance and waited on a wooden slatted bench. She wanted to wait with Duncan, but knew if she went back in there; it would be hard to leave him again. She stared outside and watched the snow fall in nickel size flakes. It was beautiful and it looked like she was staring into a gigantic snow globe. Marlo laid her head back against the wall and closed her eyes, waiting for Sandra.

She thought to herself, *I need to call Clare. I haven't told her anything that has happened.* Marlo reached in her pocket and pulled her cell phone out. When she was waiting for Clare to answer, she started to cry.

"Marlo, how are you? I was wondering when I was going to hear from you again."

Marlo tried to stifle her cry, "I'm not good. Duncan is in the hospital."

"Oh no, what happened, Marlo!?"

"He was taking out his fishing boat to avoid a storm that is still passing through. His boat took on water and he was in the ocean until the Coast Guard rescued him, but he's in really bad shape, Clare."

"Slow down, Marlo . . . what do you mean, in bad shape?" Marlo took a breath and let it out slowly.

"He's in a coma and the doctor doesn't know when or if he'll come out of it. He's fighting it, Clare. I know he is."

"Do you want me to come there and be with you? I can come. Jack and the kids would be fine."

"No, that's okay. Stay with your family. I have Brady, Duncan's brother and Sandra and her husband, Clay, to help me. Thank you though, it means a lot to me."

Clare was pacing in her kitchen and didn't know what to do. "Are you sure you don't want me there?"

"I'm sure. It's okay, I'll be fine, Clare."

"What happened to him, though . . . exactly?" asked Clare.

Clare wanted to know the specifics to get a better understanding of what Marlo was feeling.

"Well, when they finally got to him, he was unconscious. He suffered severe hypothermia and because of the hypothermia, his body went into shock. They stabilized him on the boat, but had him airlifted into Anchorage when they came ashore."

Marlo was rubbing her forehead. "Omigod, that's horrible," said Clare.

"Then he went into a coma," said Marlo. "They put him in I.C.U. for the first night and then, when they were transferring him to a private room, he went into a comatose state. He's been in a coma ever since."

"Marlo, honey, I'm so sorry. I wish there were something I could do. I can come up there to be with you."

"No. It will be okay, Clare. You should stay home with Jack, Dilly and Bentley. They need you at home. I'll be fine, really. I'll keep you posted on anything new. I'm hoping he wakes up soon. I've been here since he first was admitted. I have to get back to the cabin. There are a lot of things that need to be taken care of. I called Sandra to come pick me up. I'm waiting for her now."

"Okay, well, I'm happy that someone is there to help you. Thank Sandra and Brady for me when you see them. I'm worried about you, Marlo."

"Don't worry. I'm fine and Duncan will be fine, too," said Marlo, hoping her words would come true, "and Sandra is going to be here soon, too. I should go. I'll call you when something changes, Clare. I love you."

"I love you, too, Marlo. Be careful and we'll pray for Duncan, everyday."

"Thank you, Clare. I'll talk to you soon, bye."

Hanging up, Marlo felt a little better talking to Clare. She saw headlights pulling into the hospital. It was Sandra. Marlo stood up and grabbed her bag. She lifted the bag and hung the strap on her shoulder. The doors slid open and Marlo walked to the truck.

After a depressing drive home, Sandra dropped Marlo off at her cabin and told her good night. Marlo went in her cabin and flipped the light switch. *The power is back on.* She dropped her bag on the floor and sat in her worn leather chair, Duncan's favorite. She noticed the fire was burning in the woodstove. She stood up and walked to the fridge and saw everything was fine and cold. *Sandra and Clay must have taken care of everything. That was nice of them.* She sat back down and cried until she couldn't cry anymore. She felt her whole life flash before her. She didn't know who she was without Duncan. Marlo yelled, "You can't die, dammit! You can't die, I need you!" Marlo drifted to thoughts of her mother to comfort her and gave in.

Chapter 17

Two weeks later, after many sleepless nights, Marlo drove to Anchorage to have one of her regular visits with Duncan. The whole way there Marlo was wondering if Duncan was ever going to wake from his deep sleep. She isn't giving up hope, but the feeling of him not waking up is conquering her wanting him to.

Marlo quietly turned the nickel plated knob and opened the door to Duncan's room, laying her coat over the back of the chair against the wall and sat down beside him. "Hey Duncan, it's me, Marlo. Today was crazy. The town of Seward had dump trucks getting rid of all the snow and trucking it somewhere. I don't know where to, but I just can't believe the ridiculous amount of snow that fell during the storm." Marlo got up from the chair and walked over to the window. She pulled the curtains back and looked out into the courtyard. "You have a beautiful view. The courtyard has a water fountain in the middle with stone benches all around it. The water fountain isn't turned on, but it's still pretty."

Walking back to his side, Marlo sat down. Running her fingers over his hair and feeling his warmth, she said, "Clay and Sandra send their love and Brady said he is going to come up tonight. They all miss you very much and can't wait to see you, again." Marlo studied Duncan's features. She reached down and picked his hand up, slowly placing it on her cheek, "I'm sorry for whatever I did to make you angry with me. I miss your touch, sweetheart. I miss your gentle words. *Please*, come back to me, *please*. I can't live a life without you. I love you, I live you and I miss you."

Marlo lovingly held Duncan's hand to her face, looking at him in silence. She began thinking into the future. She started thinking how Duncan would be a wonderful husband and she would be a loving wife. They would live a happy and fulfilling life with each other and make a family. The two of them would build a house and make a home. Marlo couldn't believe this was happening to her. The man she was destined to be with is hanging on for his life. A moment later, she felt something. She felt something distinct. She felt Duncan's finger move. Marlo gently lowered Duncan's hand and ran to the door.

She opened it and yelled down the hallway, "Nurse, come quick, its Duncan . . . Hurry!"

Dr. Meethe and two nurses came running down the hall to Duncan's room. Marlo just started rambling.

"I . . . I had his hand on my face and then I felt something. He started moving his finger. He moved his finger!"

Dr. Meethe and the nurses looked at the monitors and checked the numbers. They didn't show any sign of improvement.

Dr. Meethe turned to Marlo and gently said, "Marlo, I know you want Duncan to wake up and I know you want him to move, but the monitors show no change. It was a reflex. I'm sorry."

Marlo had anger in her eyes, "No, his finger moved, it did. I felt it! Monitors can't tell you everything!"

"Marlo, this happens all the time. Sometimes they move and everyone jumps at the chance to see their loved one open their eyes, but they don't. We checked the monitors, Marlo. I'm sorry."

Leaving the room, the doctor and the nurses left Marlo with Duncan.

Marlo sat with Duncan, crying. "Duncan, I know you're in there. I know you can hear me. Please wake up, please. You just moved your finger and I know it wasn't a reflex, it was you. Wake up Duncan." Staring at Duncan's closed eyes, Marlo felt lost. She closed her eyes for a moment in despair and then opened them. She tilted her head and shook it side to side thinking, *I know you're in there, baby. It's Marlo, wake up Duncan. Please wake up. Don't leave me. I need you.*

Marlo kept staring and Duncan's eye lashes, willing them to move, but nothing happened. Just when she was starting to believe the doctor, they started to flicker and his eyes were rolling from side to side under his eyelids. "Duncan, Duncan, its Marlo. Wake up love, wake up. I know you can do it, open your eyes Duncan." Hoping Duncan could hear her, she waited, biting on her lip.

Duncan slowly opened his eyes and showed his beautiful greens to Marlo and softly said, "Hey you, where am I?"

Marlo burst into tears, holding him, hugging him and kissing him. "Don't you ever leave me again, do you hear me!?! Don't you ever leave me, again! Omigod, you're really awake. I love you sweetheart. I love you."

Duncan looked at Marlo and said, "Why do I feel like I've been hit by a truck?"

When Duncan saw Marlo, it all started coming back. *The boat, the water, the Coast Guard, the one thing he holds dear. The boat sank and I . . . I'm in the hospital.*

"How long have I been in the hospital?"

Marlo looked at him, "Two weeks and four days. Hold on baby, I have to get the doctor."

Calling down the hall again, the doctor and nurses came running.

Standing over Duncan, watching the doctor and nurses check his vitals, Marlo said, "I told you he moved."

After all the commotion and checking Duncan's vitals, Dr. Meethe said, "Welcome back Duncan. Marlo hasn't left your side. Your brother has been with you, too. It's so good to see you again, awake and smiling. You're a fighter."

"I'm starving," said Duncan, looking at Marlo and Dr. Meethe.

Dr. Meethe and Marlo started laughing, "I bet you are. Let me get someone in here to help you with that."

Marlo sat on his bed next to him and leaned in, "I was so worried about you. I'm so happy you're awake. Duncan, I'm sorry for making you angry, can you please forgive me?"

She leaned in and he slowly reached up trying to make his muscles do what he told them to do and put his hand around her neck, pulling her to him and kissed her with passion.

"I love you, Marlo and I will never leave you again, I promise."

Marlo couldn't help but cry and put her head on his chest.

Holding each other for another moment, Duncan said, "Marlo, the day I was on the boat working, I went to the café to get some lunch and I saw you with him."

"Luke?"

"Yes. I thought you and Luke were starting to see each other because he was in the office the day before. I felt something awkward when I walked in the office and then, when I saw you in the coffee shop, I just couldn't handle it."

"Duncan, that's what this was all about? I wish you would have talked to me about it. I saw him one day when I was walking and I asked him what brought him to Birch Cabins. He said his parents died in a car accident four years ago. Duncan, his parent's car was the other car that was in the same accident as my parents. I didn't have all the information yet, so I wanted to meet him for coffee to discuss things further. Then I was going to tell you about it. When you came to the café and saw us talking, that's what we were doing . . . discussing the accident. He came up to Alaska searching for answers. After talking to me, he felt he had closure and decided to go back home. Oh, Duncan. I wish you would have talked to me," said Marlo.

Duncan sat there and then realized, "Luke's parents were in the other car in the accident? Wow, I can't believe it. That's so weird. You never realize how small the world is, until something like this happens."

Duncan looked into Marlo's eyes and said, "I'm sorry, baby. I should have trusted you. I'll always trust you from now on, I promise. Please forgive me."

Marlo leaned in and kissed him with more passion than she's ever felt for any other man.

"Duncan, I love you."

". . . And, I love you, Marlo."

They lay in each others arms for a tender moment and then Marlo said, "Let's call Brady and get him up here. He's been lost without you."

"Omigod . . . Brady! Let's do it, you dial and I'll talk," said Duncan.

"Okay, it's a plan."

Marlo dialed the number and Duncan waited for Brady to answer. "James' Bros. Pub, Brady speaking."

"Are you going to come up here and see your pain in the ass brother, or are you going to serve drinks to lushes?"

Total silence and then tears.

Barely able to speak, Brady managed to say, "Duncan, you ass, I'm on my way. I love you."

"Hurry up. I hear I've been in this bed for too long."

"I'm on my way, don't close your eyes. I'm coming. I love you."

Hanging up the phone, Brady didn't even turn off the lights; he locked and left.

Driving up to Anchorage, Brady managed to call Sandra and Clay. "He's up! Duncan's awake! Hurry, I'm driving up there now." He hung up and yelled, "He's awake! My brothers' awake!"

When Brady arrived at the hospital, he sprinted to the hospital entrance and immediately headed to the elevators. He pushed the No. 3 button. When the elevator doors opened, Brady raced down the hall to Duncan's room. Everyone knew Marlo and Brady, so of course they didn't say anything to him.

By the time Brady reached Duncan's room he was out of breath. He walked in and there was Duncan smiling at him. Marlo was sitting by his side. Brady looked at Duncan, bent down and hugged him, not letting go.

He whispered in his ear, "Don't ever leave me, again; you practically killed me. I love you. I love you, Duncan. I knew you'd come back. I just knew it."

Duncan and Brady held each other for a moment and then when Brady pulled back, he said, "What did the doctor say? Are you going to fall back into a coma? What's going on? Talk to me."

Marlo let Duncan relax and she brought Brady back up to speed. "Duncan is not going to fall back into a coma. He has atrophy in his muscles and is going to need therapy. His stay in the hospital is going to be at least another week, week and a half. They want to keep an eye on him and monitor his recovery. They also want to begin therapy before he leaves the hospital. They're going to keep the I.V. in until they know he's clear of any other mishaps." Marlo took a breath. "They also said, the good thing about a coma is, his body has been healing this whole time."

Brady took in everything Marlo said and was so thankful his brother survived.

"How do you feel, Duncan?"

"Other than a truck running me over, I feel pretty damn good. I feel like I just had the best sleep of a lifetime."

Marlo and Brady stayed with Duncan the rest of the day. They caught him up on what's been happening. The nurse brought Duncan a bowl of chicken broth and chocolate pudding.

He looked at it and said, "I've heard hospital food isn't the greatest, but if this tastes half as good as it looks, I'm in heaven."

Brady and Marlo started laughing and couldn't believe that Duncan was finally awake.

A moment later there was a soft knock at the door. Sandra and Clay walked in. They couldn't believe their eyes. They were relieved to see Duncan awake and well.

"Hey guys, I'm glad you're here," said Marlo.

"Hi Sandra, Clay, it's so great to see you," said Duncan.

Sandra walked over to Duncan and said, "I'm so happy to hear your voice again, Duncan."

Tears filled her eyes when she bent to give him a loving hug. "Welcome back, Duncan. I knew you wouldn't leave us; you're too stubborn," said Clay, hugging him.

"How are you feeling?" asked Sandra. "I feel great. I feel alive."

"I bet you do," said Clay.

Just then, Dr. Meethe walked in, "Hello everyone. You have a lot of people that love you, Duncan."

"I know. I know," Duncan said, looking at everyone and resting his eyes on Marlo.

Dr. Meethe checked Duncan's heart rate and made sure his vital signs were good and he was comfortable.

He looked around and said, "It appears everything is going well with you. Keep up your strength. I'll be back shortly to check on you."

"Thank you, Dr. Meethe."

Everyone was pleased to hear the excellent news. They all were thrilled Duncan was a live and well.

An hour later, Dr. Meethe told everyone they had to go because Duncan needed his rest. Sandra and Clay said their goodbyes and told Duncan they would see him soon. Marlo and Brady were going to soon follow.

Giving Duncan time alone with Marlo, Brady said, "I'll wait for you in the hall."

"Thank you, Brady. I'll be right out."

Duncan gestured Marlo to sit next to him on the bed.

"Marlo, I love you with all my heart and I'm sorry I went out on the boat thinking I could get ahead of the storm. It was stupid and I wasn't thinking. I should have stayed with you."

"Duncan, don't apologize. You're here now and that's all that matters. I love you and I'm never going to leave you. You only did what you thought you needed to do. You're alive and you're on your way back to getting healthy," Marlo reassured him.

"What did I ever do to deserve you?" asked Duncan. "The same thing I did to deserve you."

The halls were quiet and dark. Duncan listened to a filtered humming noise that came from the light above his bed. He laid there staring at the ceiling and thinking, he was one lucky man. Suddenly his eyes were wide and panic set in. Wondering where the one thing that kept him safe all these years could be, he quickly hit the button for the nurse. The nurse entered the room.

"Yes Duncan, is everything okay?" the nurse asked.

"I had something on me when the Coast Guard picked me up. It was in my jean pocket. Can you please check my pockets?"

The nurse went to his closet and took his jeans out. She reached in his front left pocket and didn't feel anything. Duncan had a worried expression on his face. She reached in his right pocket and pulled it out.

"Is this it?"

"Yes, oh God, yes . . . that's it!" he said, with a feeling of desperate relief.

Walking it over to Duncan, she put it in his hand. "Is there anything else you need while I'm here?"

"No, thank you. This is all, thank you."

"Okay, good night Duncan, get some rest."

Smiling at Duncan, she quietly closed the door on her way out. Duncan held it in his hands and kissed it. He knew what was in his hands is what saved him.

He whispered, "Thank you for saving my life and bringing me back to Marlo."

Looking at it, Duncan began thinking back to that day.

The accident he witnessed four years ago. That was an awful day, seeing the death of a couple who were very close to him. He never has been able to erase it from his mind; the blood, the broken glass covering the highway, police cars, the fire truck and crew, the ambulance, and the crash were crystal clear in his mind. It was like being there all over again. He saw Marie crying for John, looking for him, calling for him.

He remembered the Paramedics trying their best to save her. The way she was fighting for her life, hanging onto Duncan like he was going to leave her. Giving him that one special thing that she kept on her; tears filled Duncan's eyes. The helicopter ride to the hospital, when he heard her take her last breath, whispering, *"Keep this safe for me, I know it will get in the right hands,"* was all coming back to him. The feeling of being in the ocean, helpless and scared of death, Duncan felt the fear Marie felt that same day, four years ago. And, it hit him, he finally figured out why Marlo looked so familiar. He opened it and looked at the pictures inside. He stared at them, looking at every detail. It held two pictures of two little girls. He couldn't believe it. He couldn't believe what he was seeing. Crying softly, Duncan didn't know what to do. How did Marie know that this special thing he was holding would get into the right hands?

Duncan was remembering all the times he'd taken Marie and John out on the fishing boat and how she loved watching John catch *'The Big One.'* He remembered all the good times they had together on the water. He remembered Marie's laughter and John's handshakes. He remembered John's expression and excitement when he had a rewarding day of fishing. He remembered Marie always so full of life. She loved coming up to Alaska; it was the one place she felt carefree and was always smiling. *Actually,* Duncan thought to himself . . . then drifted away from the thought.

Duncan began feeling tired and weak. He leaned over and put his special belonging in the drawer next to his bedside. Laying back down and adjusting his pillow under his head, he thought, *I have to explain this to Marlo. How is she going to react when I tell her about this?* Then, Duncan's eyes drifted closed.

The next morning Marlo came to the hospital to visit Duncan, bringing flowers in all different colors to brighten his room and to give him something pretty to look at.

"Good morning Duncan, how are you feeling?" Marlo asked, bringing the flowers to him.

"I feel pretty good. Are those for me?" Duncan inquired. "They are. Do you like them?"

"I don't *like* them," said Duncan and Marlo looked as if she was going to cry. "I *love* them! They're beautiful. Thank you. Bring them closer so I can smell them."

Moving them aside after he smelled them he leaned up and wanted a kiss.

After tasting her sweet lips, he said, "Mmm, just what I needed. The flowers are beautiful, thank you Marlo. Do you want to put them by the window for me?"

Smiling at him, she said, "I thought you really didn't like them."

"Of course I like them. I love flowers, especially ones from you."

Marlo smiled, shook her head, and thought, *you're lucky I don't beat you over the head with these flowers, mister.* Glancing over her shoulder and peering at Duncan, *I could never beat him with a bouquet of flowers. I love him too much,* and walked over to the window to set the beautiful arrangement on the sill.

"How did you sleep? What did you have for breakfast? Did you miss me? Tell me everything," said Marlo, leaning down to give him another good morning kiss.

"Good, hot cereal with brown sugar and yes."

Duncan has always had a playful way with Marlo. That was one of the reasons she loved him so much. He was always a spitfire she couldn't control.

Duncan motioned for Marlo to sit next to him, and said, "Marlo, we need to talk. There's something I need to tell you and it's not going to be easy."

Already worried, alarms going off in her head, wondering what happened between yesterday and this morning; Marlo started to freak.

"What's wrong? You're scaring me, Duncan."

"I'm not trying to scare you Marlo, promise. However, I need to talk to you about something extremely delicate and I need you to understand that I didn't realize this until last night after you left. Please know that I'm telling you the truth and I would *never* lie to you, you know that," said Duncan, trying to reassure Marlo of his love and hoping he connected with her.

"I understand."

Marlo was nervous and scared.

"Marlo, after I tell you this, I need you to remember that I told you I didn't realize this until *after* you left last night," Duncan repeated.

"I understand what you are saying. What is going on?" Marlo asked again with aches in her gut.

"I have something I want to show you."

Marlo didn't know what to think, but she was on the verge of going crazy with worry. Duncan opened his hand and revealed the locket. Marlo's eyes were fixated on it and the beauty it held.

Softly speaking, she said, "That looks like my Mother's locket. She wore it everyday and never took it off. She always kept it around her neck."

"It *is* your mother's locket."

Marlo slowly looked at Duncan. He opened it and revealed the pictures of Marlo and Clare. Reaching for the locket Duncan held in his hand, Marlo held it and didn't say a word. She didn't make a sound. She sat there, holding it and staring at it and he saw a tear sliding down her cheek. And he started to explain.

Chapter 18

"Four years ago, I was a volunteer firefighter for Seward. I was on call that night and we had to rush to the scene of an accident, a car accident. When I got to the scene, I saw Marie laying there on the asphalt fighting for her life calling for John, her husband. I held her and I stayed with her until she could barely speak anymore. The Paramedics called an airlift into Anchorage Hospital.

While I was with her trying to keep her alive and talking to her, she handed me the locket, and said, "Please, take this and keep it safe. I know you'll get it in the right hands."

I didn't know what she was talking about or what she meant, but I do now. Marlo, somehow your mother knew I was going to find you or you were going to find me and you were going to see this locket again," said Duncan softly, placing his hand on her lap.

Marlo just sat motionless, with her face wet and her eyes red staring at the locket and listening to Duncan. "Marlo, I've known your parents for years. I used to take them on fishing trips. That's how I first met them. Your parents were very close to me. I think your mother knew that we would one day cross paths and she knew I would get the locket to you. Remember when you said to me at the Kenai Fjords National Park on the blanket, *'my Mother used to tell me all the time, you'll find the man you're supposed to be with when you least expect it'*? Marlo, your mother used to tell me the same thing.

Every time she saw me she'd ask, 'So, Duncan, have you met the right woman, yet?' And, I'd look at her with a bright smile and say, 'Nope, not yet.' Then Marie would come back with, "You'll find the right woman when you least expect it." Marlo, she knew."

Marlo slowly looked up from the locket to Duncan and said, "My Mother, your Marie, brought us together. It was fate, Duncan. She never mentioned either of us to the other because it had to happen on its own, whether it would have happened or not." Then, Marlo said, barely being able to speak, "She never told me about you, not once."

"She never told me about you, either," replied Duncan, looking into Marlo's eyes, holding her hand. "It was your mothers' love for the both of us that brought us together. She somehow knew that we were going to meet one day and that's why she gave me the locket to hold onto," said Duncan.

"Maybe that's why I had this urge to come to Alaska to be with her, but it was *her* telling me to come to be with you, Duncan," said Marlo wishing she could hold her parents once more.

"Her locket is what binds us for life, Marlo."

She looked at him and said, "Duncan, I want you to keep this. My Mother told you to keep it safe."

"Marlo, I don't need it now. I have you. You are what will keep me safe," answered Duncan staring into Marlo's eyes.

"Where did you have this? How did you get it in the hospital?"

"I always kept it hanging from the mirror on my boat and when I returned from a fishing trip or just a routine run, I would thank your mother for my safe voyage. Before my boat went down, I grabbed it and tucked it in my pocket," replied Duncan, wondering what that puzzled look on Marlo's face, was for.

"What's wrong, Marlo?"

Holding the locket in her hands, she said, "This is what was sparkling from your boat the day I first met you. I was wondering what caught my eye when I turned to leave. Now, I know; it was my Mother."

Duncan stared at Marlo with a look of promise filling his eyes. He held his hand out to her waiting for her to rest her hand in his. He gently closed his hand, covering hers and gazed into her eyes and asked, "Marlo, will you be my wife?"

Marlo stared at Duncan, not realizing what just happened. She felt her whole world coming to a halt. The memories of her mother and the words that she said flooded her and she felt her mother there, with her. *Mom, thank you. I love you with all my heart.*

Marlo looked into Duncan's eyes and repeated, "Your wife?"

"Yes, love. Will you marry me?"

She was still for a moment and then he saw it, tears of joy.

"Yes, yes, a million times, yes!" Wrapping her arms around Duncan and kissing him passionately, she said, "Yes Duncan, I would be honored to be your wife."

With tears in his eyes, he said, "Come here, Marlo." He raised his hands and she leaned in. Duncan fastened the locket to Marlo's neck. "I love you, Marlo. I love you more than life itself."

A week and a half later and after extensive therapy, Duncan was sitting in his room, waiting to be discharged. He had his bags packed and his paperwork filled out.

"Wow, I can't believe I'm finally going to be going home. It almost feels surreal, this whole thing."

"I know love, but everyone is so excited to see you. I'm thrilled to have you home, again."

"Speaking of home, what are we going to do with my little cabin, which holds so many memories?" inquired Marlo with a raised eyebrow and a smile.

"Good question. We'll figure something out," said Duncan. Just then, Katie Burke came walking in the room.

"Well Duncan, you're all set to go home. Are you and your fiancé, all ready?" the nurse asked looking at Marlo and smiling.

"We are. It's about time I get home and start fishing again," answered Duncan and then glanced at Marlo.

"Well, we'll work up to that part."

Letting out a quiet chuckle, Duncan took Marlo by the hand and together they left the hospital.

Chapter 19

One Year Later...

It was Thanksgiving Day and Duncan and Marlo were hosting Thanksgiving dinner for Brady and Mandi, Sandra and Clay, and Clare, Jack, Dilly and Bentley. It was going to be their first holiday dinner with the whole family. The afternoon was cold and snow blanketed the frozen ground. It was a perfect day to have a warm fire crackling in the wood stove in the living room, while everyone enjoyed dinner.

"Duncan, did you bring wood in for the fire?" Marlo asked Duncan when he was coming in from the garage.

When Duncan shut the door, he walked over to Marlo and with a playful kiss, he said, "I did, love. How is the dinner coming? What do you need me to do?" asked Duncan, smelling the traditional holiday aroma of Thanksgiving fixings.

"I'm good. Everything is taken care of. Everyone is going to be here soon. I want this holiday to be a memorable one, spending it with our family. We have a lot to be thankful for, especially the memories that we hold dear and the new memories we are going to make."

Marlo stood there smoothing over the shirt on her belly.

"What's wrong, Marlo? Is everything okay with the baby?" asked Duncan with a concerned look on his face.

"Everything is just fine. I am the happiest wife in all Alaska. If you asked me a year and a half ago if I was going to be your wife one day, I would have laughed at you and said you were barking up the wrong tree."

Laughing at Marlo, Duncan said, "This is going to be the most perfect holiday ever."

Marlo walked over to the window looking out to the back of their property.

Duncan came up behind her, wrapping her in his arms, resting his hands on her stomach and asked, "What are you thinking about, love?" whispering into her ear.

"I'm thinking, thank goodness we paid an arm and a leg to buy the cabin off of Sandra and Clay and had it relocated on the back of our property, otherwise we wouldn't of had a place for Clare, Jack and the kids to stay."

Looking back over her shoulder at Duncan, Marlo looked up into Duncan's eyes and said, "Happy Thanksgiving, love."

She reached up and kissed him.

www.ingramcontent.com/pod-product-compliance
Lightning Source LLC
LaVergne TN
LVHW041703060526
838201LV00043B/550